continued . . .

"A delightful heroine, cherry-filled plot twists, and cream-filled pastries. Could murder be any sweeter?"

—Connie Archer, national bestselling author of
the Soup Lover's Mysteries

"A mouth-watering debut with a plucky protagonist. Clever, original, and appealing, with gluten-free recipes to die for."

—Carolyn Hart, *New York Times* bestselling author

"A lively, sassy heroine and a perceptive and humorous look at small-town Kansas (the Wheat State)!"

—JoAnna Carl, national bestselling author of
the Chocoholic Mysteries

"This baker's treat rises to the occasion. Whether you need to eat allergy-free or not, you'll devour every morsel."

—Avery Aames, Agatha Award–winning author of
the Cheese Shop Mysteries

"Parra takes the cake with this cozy romantic suspense title. While formulaically sound, a very clever twist makes small-town Kansas positively sinister." —*Library Journal*

"Lively characters enhance Parra's story, and the explosive ending . . . packs a real punch for this cozy. This series promises to be a real treat for readers." —*RT Book Reviews*

"*Gluten for Punishment* is a dynamite mystery that I have a feeling is going to be very popular with mystery readers. Whether you have a gluten-sensitive diet or you're wanting to sink your teeth into a fantastic new series, *Gluten for Punishment* is definitely worth a read!" —*Cozy Mystery Book Reviews*

"As a delicious cozy mystery, it is filled with quirky characters, handsome romantic interests, and at least a baker's dozen of unusual happenings, capped with a twist at the end . . . [A] witty and wily read that will appeal to both gluten-intolerant and gluten-tolerant readers alike!" —*Fresh Fiction*

Flourless to Stop Him

NANCY J. PARRA

BERKLEY PRIME CRIME, NEW YORK

THE BERKLEY PUBLISHING GROUP
Published by the Penguin Group
Penguin Group (USA) LLC
375 Hudson Street, New York, New York 10014

USA • Canada • UK • Ireland • Australia • New Zealand • India • South Africa • China

penguin.com

A Penguin Random House Company

FLOURLESS TO STOP HIM

A Berkley Prime Crime Book / published by arrangement with the author

Berkley Prime Crime Books are published by The Berkley Publishing Group.
BERKLEY® PRIME CRIME and the PRIME CRIME logo are trademarks of
Penguin Group (USA) LLC.

For information, address: The Berkley Publishing Group,
a division of Penguin Group (USA) LLC,
375 Hudson Street, New York, New York 10014.

ISBN: 978-0-425-25260-4

PUBLISHING HISTORY
Berkley Prime Crime mass-market edition / May 2015

PRINTED IN THE UNITED STATES OF AMERICA

10 9 8 7 6 5 4 3 2 1

Interior text design by Laura K. Corless.

*To my grandma Mary, who could bake
the most incredible bread. I can only try to be as good
in the kitchen as you were. Love you always.*

ACKNOWLEDGMENTS

I can't emphasize enough that it takes a village to make a book. I'd like to thank all my friends and family who support me in my endeavors and keep me sane when things get a little nuts. Special thanks to the good people of Berkley Prime Crime, without whom there would be only a story. And to my agent, Paige, who keeps me on track and in bookstores. Cheers!

CHAPTER 1

I love my family. I do. But there are times when I sincerely wish they would take a day off. *Rest* is not part of my grandma's vocabulary. We won't talk about the stir my brother Tim likes to cause. Or the nosey phone calls my sister Joan makes every day, letting me know that someone in the neighborhood watch just called her about something going on at the homestead.

The homestead is the large Victorian house I inherited when my mother died. The house is beautiful with three full floors of bedrooms rising above the wraparound porch. In fact, my best friend, Tasha, suggested it was the perfect size for a bed-and-breakfast.

What it really was, was the perfect size for my enormous family, which included fifty-two cousins. Mom had insisted in her will that I be given the house with the codicil that any member of my family could stay there when they needed to. Which meant that, while I might have been a newly single girl, I was rarely alone.

Lately my brother Tim, the last family member to live in the house, finally moved out.

That left only me and my best friend, Tasha; her son, Kip; and Kip's rescue puppy, Aubrey. With Tasha and Kip staying in the attic suite, I had the second floor to myself—at least for now. Christmas was coming and along with the holiday was the massive influx of family looking for a reason to visit Grandma Ruth.

Grandma Ruth had brilliantly moved into a seniors-only high-rise apartment with only one bedroom. With the way my Grandma drove her indoor/outdoor scooter nobody dared sleep on her couch, or worse, her floor, lest they—intentionally or unintentionally—get run over. At least not when there was a five-bedroom house open for their use only a few blocks away.

My family—all five siblings plus seven aunts and uncles plus fifty-two cousins—knew I was a soft touch. As long as they respected my gluten-free kitchen they could come and go as they pleased and always find a soft bed and clean linen welcoming them.

When it came to my gluten-free bakery, Baker's Treat, I was even more of a pushover. At first I took only Sundays off. I was nervous about being closed at all for fear I would lose customers. I mean, being a gluten-free bakery in the heart of wheat country was difficult enough without being closed when someone needed a cake. But my Grandma Ruth had told me a secret when I set up shop in my hometown of Oiltop, Kansas.

"Toni," she said in her cigarette raspy voice, "people want what they can't have. If you're always available, they'll take you for granted. I learned that the hard way." Her blue eyes glittered. "Always limit what you offer. It keeps them coming back."

Grandma Ruth was a genius—literally. She was a life-time member of Mensa, an international club for people who score in the top 2 percent of the population on a standard IQ test. I learned early on that it paid to listen to Grandma's advice—even if it seemed counterintuitive.

So it was that I closed the bakery on Sundays and Mondays. This Monday, I sat in the lobby of the Red Tile Inn, where Tasha Wilkes, my best friend and current roommate, was the manager. You see, the problem with having Mondays off was that everyone else didn't. Luckily I knew that I could always come over to the inn and visit with Tasha while she worked.

"How's Aubrey? Did he give you any trouble?" Tasha walked in carrying a box nearly as big as her.

Aubrey was the puppy Kip had rescued. "No, he's great. I put him out in the yard. There isn't a lot he can get into while I'm gone." I curled up in a wingback chair in the lobby and used the Wi-Fi to Christmas shop from my tablet. The inn had a comfortable lobby with a gas fireplace, two overstuffed couches, three wingback chairs placed strategically around the fireplace, and a bookshelf that offered novels for anyone not attached to the Internet.

"I'm glad we got him a doghouse for days like today," Tasha said and put the box down next to the front window.

Outside was gray and bitter cold, in keeping with a normal Kansas December. The ground was frozen and brown. The trees were bare and bleak against the eternally gray sky. It was the time of year when there may or may not be snow. Mostly there wasn't snow, only bitter cold wind and dreary clouds.

"His doghouse is stuffed with straw, and he has a heated water bowl." I flipped through pictures of gifts on my tablet. "I think he actually prefers the cold."

"I have to agree," Tasha said as she cut through the box tape to expose the contents. "It's all that Pyrenees fur. Two coats and I've been vacuuming daily. Who knew a dog would shed so much?"

"I hear him walking around upstairs at night."

"I know." Tasha pulled out the first of many artificial tree limbs covered in fake green needles and fiber-optic wires. "It turns out they're nocturnal. Which is fine. Trust me, after the incident in October I'm glad someone is on guard duty while we sleep. I'm sorry if he keeps you up."

"Oh, no," I said. "Don't worry, I like him. He's sweet and I think Kip has really blossomed since Aubrey has been with us."

"He has." Tasha studied me. "If I had known that a dog would bring out the best in Kip, I would have gotten one sooner."

"Don't think like that," I said. "Things happen when they do for a reason. Right?"

"I suppose."

A fire crackled on fake logs in the fireplace across from my chair. It put out heat that reached my knees. The lobby smelled of cinnamon and pine-scented candles. Christmas music played softly as Tasha assembled the artificial Christmas tree.

"I can't believe you're done with your Christmas shopping," I said. "I haven't even started."

Tasha shook her blonde curls. "I start my list in February and ensure I'm done by November first. The holidays are too hectic to think about shopping."

"I'm not that organized." I paged through the overstock website on the tablet. "Besides, no one knows what they want for Christmas until December, so buying in advance is worthless."

Tasha pulled a crocheted penguin out of a box of ornaments. "You're looking at it all wrong."

"How so?" I drew my eyebrows together. Of course no one could tell since my red hair meant they were so light they were nearly nonexistent.

"I never worry about what they want in the moment.

That's too hard. Instead I keep an eye on the sales throughout the year and if I see something that reminds me of a person I buy it. Nine times out of ten I have a winner. Seriously, it's about the people, not what's popular at the time."

"Nine times out of ten?" I teased.

"Well"—she stopped and put her right hand on her chin—"there was this time in high school. I was dating Lance Webb."

"He was in Richard's class, wasn't he?" I could usually place people's age by which of my siblings went through school with them. Richard was older than me, which made every boy in his class cool at the time.

"Yes," Tasha said and sighed. "He was tall and athletic and had the prettiest blue eyes."

"I remember him," I said. "He was on the football team, right?"

"Yes, he wanted to be a quarterback, but Tim had a lock on that position even though he was two years younger, so he ended up a running back. I was so in love with him. I heard him tell someone he wanted to get a CD player for his car."

"It wasn't built-in?"

"Not back then—all he had was a tape player."

"Oh my gosh, I remember tape players. . . ." I laughed. "How far we've come. I bet my nieces have no idea what a tape player is."

"Kip does." Tasha hung another ornament. "He's been researching the history of recording from Alexander Graham Bell to today."

"Let me guess, you bought Lance a CD player. . . ."

"Yes, I saved and saved and bought him a custom car player. I was so excited. I had it wrapped and stored in my closet for two months."

"What happened?"

"Lance dumped me for Suzy Olds two weeks before Christmas."

"Oh." I sat up straight. "I remember that. She wore that gold dress with fishnet stockings to the Christmas dance."

"He took one look at her and I no longer existed." Tasha picked up a red-and-gold glass ball ornament.

"Did they ever get married?"

"No." Tasha's eyes sparkled with mischief. "Suzy met a guy in college who had a pedigree and a trust fund."

"Ha! Serves Lance right." I leaned back into the chair. "What did you do with the CD player?"

"I sold it to Orland Metzger. It turns out it was a hot gift that year and all the stores were sold out. So I made a tidy profit."

"See? You have the best Christmas luck. If I buy something early it goes on sale—deep discount—two weeks later. Or worse, for instance, I bought my niece Kelly a china tea set."

"Oh, pretty."

"It was the year she decided she was a feminist. She gave me a lecture about gender toys and how sexist tea sets were. Then she promptly put it in the Goodwill bag."

"Ouch."

"Right? Meanwhile her brother, my nephew Kent, wanted a toy he'd seen the week before Christmas. Nothing else would do." I rolled my eyes. "Isn't Kip influenced by all the Christmas toy commercials and the giant toy catalogs?"

"Kip is easier than most kids. He obsesses over one thing and doesn't even see the need for anything other than what interests him at the time."

"I wish my nieces and nephews were that easy." I sighed. I came from a big family. When I said big, I meant big— unfashionably big. Grandma Ruth had eight children and most of them had eight or more children. I was lucky in that my mom and dad had only six kids. But of us six, my younger brother, Tim, and I were the only two left without kids. This meant we were expected to be the cool auntie and uncle who bought the good stuff at Christmas.

"Just get the kids board games. They have some really nice ones out these days, and it's something different that they can do when the family gets together." Tasha studied the tree and added another penguin to an empty spot.

"That's Tim's fallback gift." I pursed my lips and eyed the latest techno gadget. "Do you think Grandma Ruth would want a mini tablet, or is her current tablet good enough?"

"Ha! It's hard to tell with your grandma. I mean, it's cool that she's an early adopter, but it also means that she has everything the day it comes out."

"Right?" I muttered. "What do you get someone who has everything?"

"Again, I don't wait until three weeks before Christmas to start looking."

"Yes, well, that's good advice for next year, but doesn't help me now." I uncurled my jean-clad legs and stood to stretch. My green sweater hiked up as I raised my arms, exposing my pudgy white tummy. I yanked it down as I looked out the window. "Is Maria working the housekeeping shift today?"

"Yes, why?"

"She's coming this way and she looks very pale. I hope she's not getting sick." I watched as the tiny Hispanic woman hurried across the parking lot. Her normally rich brown skin was ashen, and her happy chocolate eyes were wide with terror.

Tasha put down the ornament and went to the door, yanking it open. "Maria, what is it? Are you okay?"

"No, no, I am not okay," Maria said as she puffed through the door. Her hands fluttered on her stomach. She wore a light gray housekeeping uniform and a thick cream sweater over it. Her legs were encased in white tights and her feet wore sturdy dark athletic shoes. "You have to call the police, Miss Wilkes."

"Okay." Tasha put her arm around Maria's shoulders. "Why? Did someone hurt you?"

"Here, sit. You look like you might collapse." I pulled a chair toward her as Tasha put her hand on Maria's elbow and drew her to sit.

"Room two-oh-two," Maria said breathlessly as she sat. "You must call the police. There is a very dead man in the bathtub."

I looked at Tasha and she looked at me. "A dead man?"

"Yes, yes! Call the police."

I pulled my phone out of my pocket and hit the speed dial number that went straight to the police. "911, how can I help you?"

"Sarah? This is Toni Holmes. I'm out at the Red Tile Inn and Maria Gomez says there's a dead man in the bathtub of room two-oh-two."

"Seriously?" Sarah Hogginboom worked the dispatch desk at the police station. She liked my pastries and had her boyfriend pick her up a gluten-free Danish whenever I was open.

"Seriously," I said as Maria sat back and closed her eyes. Tasha went over to the watercooler and poured Maria a cup of cold water.

"Did you see the body?" Sarah asked.

"No." I left Maria to Tasha's care and walked out into the icy-cold air. "I'm heading over to the room now."

"Don't touch anything. The guys are on their way over."

"I won't touch anything. I learned my lesson." I climbed the concrete steps to the second floor. The Inn was an older model motel where all the doors opened to the outside. Room 202 faced west, toward the clubhouse lobby, in the center of the U-shaped hotel.

The door to room 202 stood open. Maria had pushed her housekeeping cart just inside. There was a large canvas bag on the end of the cart to hold trash. There was a drawer for cleaning sprays and mops and rags and brushes, while the shelves held fresh sheets, towels, tissues, and toilet paper.

The Red Tile was a no-frills motel a half mile from the turnpike entrance. It usually drew weary travelers, truckers, and, on rare occasion, people with family in town.

"I don't see any obvious signs of struggle," I said to Sarah and I stepped farther into the room. "The beds are made so whoever it is hadn't slept yet. There's a duffel filled with clothes and such on the floor by one of the beds."

"Be careful," Sarah said.

I pulled my key chain out of my pocket. I had a palm-sized can of pepper spray attached to it and put my finger on the trigger. "I am." The bathroom was at the back of the room. The door stood open and I peered inside. The light was on. The white vinyl shower curtain was torn from the rod and tangled around the fully clothed body of a man who appeared to be in his thirties. He had on jeans and a dark tee shirt with the words ARE WE HAVING FUN YET? scrawled across in white. The man's arms showed signs of needle marks. His mouth hung open, and blood pooled under his head. His blue eyes stared at the ceiling. White foam caked his mouth. His hair was thin with a few long strands of blond pasted down over a shiny dome where it wasn't coated in brownish-red blood.

"Toni?" Sarah's voice pulled me back to reality.

"Yeah, I'm fine. He looks pretty dead. Do I need to check for a pulse?"

"No, the guys should be there any second. Can you hear the sirens?"

I paused, trying to sort the sound of my pounding heart from the rest of the room. Somewhere music played. The announcer said it was radio station 102.9. I carefully walked out, one foot in front of the other, following the same path I had walked in. The television was off. The clock radio on the night stand blinked, revealing the source of the music.

When I got to the doorway I heard the sirens. "I can hear them," I said.

"Good. Stay on the line with me until they get there."

"Okay." I watched as a police car pulled into the parking lot followed by an ambulance. I waved my arms to let them know where I was. It wasn't hard to see since it was after noon and most of the hotel was cleared out for the day. Checkout time was 11:00 A.M. and check-in time was at 3:00 P.M., so we were at the odd housekeeping time between occupants.

Not too many people spent more than one night at the Red Tile. It was more of a stopover hotel than a destination.

Officer Calvin Bright climbed out of the police car. He nodded toward me and headed up the stairs.

"I'm going to hang up now," I said to Sarah. "Thanks."

"Okay," Sarah's voice said. "Toni?"

"Yes?"

"Take care of you."

I could detect the concern in her voice. "I will," I said. "I'm pretty sure this one isn't linked to me. Not this time."

"I certainly hope so. I'm starting to dread hearing your voice on the line."

"I know," I said. "I know." I hung up as Officer Bright came around the corner. Calvin was a good-looking guy with brown hair and thoughtful brown eyes. There was a calmness about him that came from years of knowing he was able to take down any bad guy. He was also dating Tasha. Which made him a real hero in my eyes as she had gone out with so many losers before him. Officer Bright treated my best friend like a princess. I had to give the guy props for that.

"Toni." He nodded his welcome like most guys do.

"Hi, in here." I waved toward the open door. "Maria found him."

Officer Bright stopped inches from me and the door. His dark gaze studied me. "Did you go inside?"

"Yes, I had Sarah on the line when I did," I said and

clutched my phone in one hand and the pepper spray in the other. "I didn't touch anything."

"Okay. Stay here." He held out his hand palm-up and then pulled out his gun and stepped inside.

I could have told him it was clear, but I thought he needed to figure that out on his own. So I hugged myself against the bitter cold and leaned on the warm brick wall outside the door.

An ambulance crew had arrived right behind Calvin. They made their way up the steps.

"Hey, Toni." Pat Sheridan dragged a stretcher behind him in one hand and his medical bag in the other. Kathy Neal lifted the back end of the stretcher and helped him maneuver it around the corner.

"Hey, Pat. Hey, Kathy." I acknowledged the EMTs. "He's in there." I jerked my thumb toward the open door.

"Are you okay? Did *you* find him?" Kathy asked.

"I'm fine, and no, I didn't find him. Maria did." I sent her a small smile. "Tasha's taking care of Maria, and I'm here waiting for you."

"Does Maria need us to check on her?" Pat asked as he stepped over the threshold.

"No, I think she's fine. Just a bit of a shock is all."

"We'll check her out before we leave." Pat disappeared into the room, dragging the stretcher. Kathy followed behind.

A second squad car pulled up beneath me. The lights flashed opposite Officer Bright's car, creating a frenzy of flashing blue and red. Officer Joe Emry stepped out of the car. He hitched his gun belt up on his skinny hips and looked around.

"Up here," I called from the railing.

"I knew that." Officer Emry cleared his throat. "I'm checking for anything suspicious." He wandered around the lower deck of rooms for a while.

I rolled my eyes. Officer Emry meant well, but he had

the brains of a gnat. My family called him Barney Fife. He was a skinny guy on a power trip that came with wearing a badge in a small town like Oiltop. At least Officer Bright was first on scene. As I said, Calvin was a large bear of a man with a killer square jaw. A big difference from the giant Adam's apple on toothpicks that was coming up the steps. A third car pulled up and Officer Phil Strickland stepped out.

Officer Strickland was a twenty-year veteran of the police force. He rarely came out from behind the desk, so I was surprised to see him here. Then I remembered that Grandma Ruth said Strickland had started campaigning for Hank Blaylock's job as chief of police. As far as Grandma was concerned Hank wasn't going anywhere. But it did answer the question as to why Strickland was there. I watched him walk over to Officer Emry and speak to him before turning and heading toward the stairs.

The odd part was that Officer Strickland never even looked up. He must have been familiar enough with the Red Tile to know where room 202 was without needing any direction. I rubbed my arms and shivered in the cold. Officer Strickland came around the corner and stopped next to me. He was about six feet tall, with gray hair and brown eyes. He wore dark dress pants, a white shirt, and a black tie under his leather coat. His feet were encased in black leather cowboy boots, and he wore a Stetson hat.

"What happened?" His voice was as smooth as his expression.

"Maria opened the room to clean and found him. I called 911."

He narrowed his eyes. "Did you touch anything?"

"No."

"Good." He went inside, leaving me to blow on my blue fingers.

Next to arrive was my friend—most of the time—and local reporter Candy Cole. Candy's dark blue Toyota whipped into the parking lot at a speed that should have gotten her a ticket. Except that most of the Oiltop police force was busy with the dead guy. Not that it mattered what the police were doing. Candy always drove like a bat out of hell. She never got a ticket. I suspected it was because she bribed the police force with regular breakfast donuts, bagels, and assorted pastries. I knew this because she bought them from me.

That, too, had a purpose. You see, neither Candy nor any of the officers needed to eat gluten-free. Candy could have gotten her sweets anywhere and probably had in the past. But recently she had decided that I was a magnet for news and she was going to stop by every day and ensure I didn't discover something she needed to know about.

She stepped out of her car, her cell phone camera rolling. "Hey, Toni." She waved up at me. "Did you find the body?"

I waved. "No, Maria did. She's with Tasha in the lobby."

"Thanks!" Candy headed toward the clubhouse. Her champagne blonde bob was camera perfect. She was my height—around five foot seven—in four-inch killer heels. Today she wore a trench coat against the bitter cold wind. All she needed was a fedora to look like a 1940s Hollywood star.

I shivered and turned back to the room. "I'm going to the clubhouse," I called in to the busy crime scene. The contrast to the inside and the outside struck me as huge. Inside was warm, dim, and stinky. Outside was bright sunshine, ice-edged wind, and the fresh scent of snow. How it could smell of snow on a bright cloudless day had always baffled me, but it did.

"Don't talk to anyone until you're interviewed," Officer Emry said behind me.

"Candy's here," I said as I stepped back out into the cold.

"I saw her," he said and sniffed. "Don't tell her anything until we get your statement."

"Okay." I shrugged. "You know Grandma Ruth would

kill me if I talked to Candy first." Grandma had been the county's top reporter in the day. She was officially retired but still wrote a daily blog. A blog that was meant to scoop the press—especially Candy. It was a competition between the two to see who could do a better job of reporting quickly and accurately.

"Don't talk to your grandma, either." Officer Emry narrowed his eyes and swallowed hard. His Adam's apple bobbed in his skinny neck.

"Emry?" Officer Bright stepped out of the tiny bathroom. "Did you bring a camera?"

"Yes." He raised his hand and a digital camera dangled by its string. "I'm ready to record the crime scene."

"Better get started," Officer Strickland said, his tone at once dismissive and authoritarian. "The EMTs want to take the body to the morgue."

"I'll be in the lobby when you need me," I said and pointed toward the other building.

"I'll be over there in a few minutes to take statements." Officer Bright nodded. "Do me a favor while you're down there."

"Sure, what?"

"Find out who the room was registered to," he said. "See if Tasha has a camera on the parking lot. If we can find footage of whoever else was in the room it would be very helpful."

"Sure, no problem," I said. The trip down the stairs and across to the lobby was short and quick. Spurred on by my nearly frozen feet, I rushed into the lobby and went straight for the fireplace to warm my hands.

"Where's your coat?" Candy asked. "It's twenty degrees out there."

"I left it hanging." I pointed to the wrought iron coat tree next to the door. "I wasn't thinking about the cold when I left."

"I bet you weren't." Candy made a note in her notebook. Her bright pink planner had notepaper and a pen always handy. "Can you tell me what happened? What'd you see when you got to the room?"

"You know I can't say anything." I rubbed my hands together and held them out to the heat.

"She has to ask," Tasha said as she came out from the office next to the reception desk. "I told her we couldn't tell her anything until the police took our statements."

"A girl has to try," Candy said. She raised her hand and snapped a cell phone photo of me warming my hands.

"Hey," I protested and grabbed a tissue. The difference between hot and cold had left me with a runny nose. The Christmas tree twinkled in silent disapproval. "No pictures."

"We're in a public place." Candy snapped a second picture.

Tasha stepped in between her camera and me. "Oh, stop it. Toni didn't do anything but call the police. I know. She was with me all morning."

"Fine, let me talk to Maria." Candy headed toward the office.

"No." Tasha put her hands on her hips and stopped the overzealous reporter. "The office is private property and off-limits."

"Oh, come on, you know I'll be talking to Maria whether it's now or later," Candy said.

"I'm opting for later," Tasha said and pointed toward the lobby door. "Why don't you go bug the cops?"

"It looks like they're bringing out the body," I said and pointed with my chin. The lobby windows revealed a flurry of activity.

Candy hurried out to capture pictures.

"That was convenient timing." Tasha sent me a look.

"Calvin needs to know who the room was registered to and if you have any security footage."

"Yeah, I figured." Tasha's baby blue gaze grew concerned. "It's not good news, Toni."

"No?" I drew my eyebrows together. "I didn't recognize the dead guy. . . ."

"Good," Tasha said. "That's what I thought when I saw your face. I was worried, but when you didn't look stricken I figured whoever had died in that room was not who was registered."

A bad feeling crept down my spine. "Who's the room registered to?"

"Your brother, Tim."

CHAPTER 2

"Oh no." I sat down hard on the couch closest to the fireplace.

"I know." Tasha took my hands in hers and rubbed them. "With your brother's juvenile record, this doesn't look good."

"I don't understand." I cocked my head. "Tim signed a lease on a new place. He moved out of the homestead a month ago. He had his life together."

"I wasn't working last night so I really don't know what happened, but there's a signature on the registration," Tasha said. She pulled out the credit card stub. It had Tim's name and a bold scrawl across the top.

"I'm going to call him." I pulled my cell phone out of my pocket and scrolled through my contacts until I came to Tim's, then I hit CALL.

"If I were you, I'd call Brad, too. Tim's going to need a lawyer." Tasha tucked the receipt back into the register drawer. "I can't hide this from the police—or Calvin. I respect him too much, plus I'd lose my job. It's bad enough that I told you to call Brad. Calvin's going to be pretty mad when he finds out."

"Don't tell him."

"I think I'm in love with him," Tasha said, her big eyes filled with trepidation.

"Oh," I said and gave her a big hug. "That's great."

"I love you more," she said. "It's why I told you to call Brad. Now go make that call."

"Okay," I said and stepped away from my friend.

"Hello?" Tim's voice sounded tired on the other end of the phone. I turned from Tasha and walked to the farthest corner of the lobby.

"Tim, it's me, Toni. Are you okay?"

"Sure." He yawned. "Why? You know I work third shift. This is the middle of my night."

"Did you pay for a room at the Red Tile Inn?" I asked.

"What? No . . . Why would I do that? I just moved into my new place."

"Where were you last night?" I watched as Officer Bright instructed Officer Emry to stand guard over the room.

"Geeze, Toni." Tim yawned again. "You're not Mom, you know."

"I know." I switched ears as I followed Officer Bright's progress down the steps and across the parking lot. "This is important. Do you have an alibi for last night?"

"An alibi—what are you talking about? I was at work."

"Are there witnesses?"

"Toni—"

"Listen carefully." I spoke fast, doing my best to get it all out before Officer Bright entered the lobby. "There's been a murder at the Red Tile Inn."

"What? When? Who?"

"I think last night," I said. "Maria found the body about

an hour ago. I called you because the room was registered in your name."

"What?"

"Officer Bright is going to find out that the room was registered to you and then they'll be calling you in for questioning. So please, whatever you do, have an alibi. I'm going to call Brad right now."

"Toni, this is a bad joke to play on a man who's gotten only four hours of sleep."

"I'm not joking. I've got to go. Don't talk to anyone until Brad gets there." I hung up on my brother as Officer Bright stepped into the lobby. I smiled at him. He nodded and headed to where Tasha worked at the counter.

I turned my back on him and hit Brad's number on my cell phone.

"Ridgeway and Harrington Attorneys at Law," Brad's receptionist, Amy Jones, said. "How can I help you?"

"Hi, Amy," I said. "This is Toni Holmes. I need to speak to Brad. It's a matter of life and death."

"Um, okay, hold on. Let me see if I can find him."

She put me on hold and the Muzak played in my ear. I glanced over and saw Tasha handing Officer Bright the room receipt. My heartbeat picked up. "Come on, Brad," I whispered. I turned my back on the officer and Tasha. If he wanted to catch my attention he'd have to call out or come get me.

"Brad Ridgeway." Brad's voice was a deep rumble and a comfort. Back in the day, Brad was a high school jock. The tall, handsome, deadly blond kind with electric blue eyes and a killer body. He'd played everything from football to baseball but had excelled at basketball and gone to KU on a basketball scholarship before earning his law degree.

Brad had been crush-worthy in high school and continued to be crush-worthy as a grown-up lawyer with his own practice. There were simply two things wrong with that thought:

1) I wasn't ready to date after my divorce from hell and 2) Brad was my lawyer. You should never get involved with your lawyer. Even if he smells divine.

"Hi, Brad, it's Toni."

"Hey, Toni, what's up? Amy said your call was life-or-death."

"Maria found a dead man in room two-oh-two of the Red Tile Inn," I said. "I'm here with Tasha."

"Please tell me you're not a suspect again."

"I'm not a suspect."

"Good."

"Tim is."

"Oh." He blew out a breath. "That's not good."

"Listen, can you go to Tim's place?" I stared out and up at the open door of room 202. "I think he may be in real trouble."

"Ms. Holmes, who are you talking to?" Officer Bright asked over my shoulder.

"Got to go." I hung up the phone before Brad could answer. I felt as guilty as a kid caught with their hand in the cookie jar. My face heated up. With my being a redhead, my porcelain skin would never let me get away with anything. "I'm sorry, what?"

"Who were you calling, Toni?" Officer Bright took in my heated face. "Was that your brother Tim?"

"Um, no." I shook my head. "Why would I call my brother?" I widened my eyes and tried to look innocent.

"According to the hotel registration, room two-oh-two was rented by your brother. Have you seen him?" Officer Bright tilted his head. His brown gaze studied me.

It made me very aware of each facial tic. I'm certain my skin was blotchy with guilt. "No, I haven't seen him today," I replied as honestly as possible. "He works third shift at FedEx and is usually sleeping at this time of day." I swallowed. "You say the room was registered to Tim?"

"That's what the record shows," Calvin said. "Does this look like his signature?" He held out the slip of paper.

"Well, now, I'm not sure." I studied the paper. "I suppose it could be . . . but I'm not a handwriting expert. Really I haven't seen Tim's signature in a while." I took a deep breath and tried to calm my nerves. "You don't think my brother was involved in this murder, do you?"

"Being as the room was registered in his name, he is a person of interest. Do you know where he is?"

"I suppose he's home sleeping." I shrugged. "I don't know for sure. He moved out of my house last month."

"Can I have his new address?"

"Sure. Listen, you can call him if you want. . . ." I pulled up Tim's number on my cell phone.

"No need. Give me the address and I'll send Emry over to ensure your brother's still alive."

I blinked rapidly. "Wait—you think Tim could be dead?"

"Most likely not," Officer Bright reassured me. "But we should check on his well-being, and if he's good, then we need to speak to him."

"I sincerely doubt Tim killed anyone," I said in defense of my baby brother.

"Maybe, maybe not," Officer Bright said. "Either way I need you to stay out of the investigation, Ms. Holmes. Can you do that?"

"It depends, Officer Bright."

"On what?" He put his hands on his hips.

"On how much trouble Tim's in. I know my brother. He wouldn't kill anyone."

"Let's hope you're right," Officer Bright said.

"Oh, I'm right," I said. "I'll bet my life on it."

"This time we'll hope you don't have to go that far."

CHAPTER 3

"What's the scuttlebutt?" Grandma Ruth drove her scooter up the ramp on the side porch and onto the gray-painted floorboards of the wide Victorian porch that wrapped around my house.

"Tim's at the police station being questioned," I said from my seat on the porch swing. The porch had a robin's-egg blue–painted ceiling. The siding on the house was clapboard and painted white, with the posts and eaves painted maroon and forest green in the tradition of the painted ladies of the time it was built.

Grandma Ruth frowned, her freckled skin bunched around her mouth. Grandma had been five foot eight, but time and bad joints had her hunched over to a little over five feet two inches. Today she wore her orange-red hair in a short cap of permed curls. Her black jacket was puffy from the feather filling. Her hands were covered by black knit gloves. She wore a bright printed skirt with little penguins dancing across a navy blue background. Her kneesocks were thick white wool and she wore white and navy athletic shoes.

A dark brown fedora perched atop her head. Her blue eyes sparkled. "Did you call Brad?"

"Yeah," I said. "He's with Tim."

"Well, it's freezing out here. We can either sit out here while I have a cigarette or we can go inside and warm up by the fireplace."

"I vote we go in," I said and got up slowly. "It's supposed to snow tonight."

"I heard, they're calling for six inches," Grandma said as she drove her scooter along the porch behind me.

I opened the front storm door and then the white panel door and let her go inside first. She darn near ran over my foot with her scooter. "Hey!"

"Sorry," Grandma said almost gaily as she waved her hand in the air. "You need to make the door bigger. Handicap accessible," Grandma said as she motored her way into the foyer.

My mother had died the previous spring of cancer complications. Like I said, it was just me and Tasha and Kip living here now. Tim had moved out. Grandma lived in the senior care apartments on Central. My other brother, Richard, and his family lived in Washington State. My sisters Joan and Rosa lived within fifty miles of Oiltop and had the habit of popping over whenever they needed something— like space from their own broods. Or a babysitter. Or a party caterer. At least Eleanor lived in California and rarely showed up unannounced.

"You usually park the scooter outside," I said and closed the door behind me. The floor bounced as Aubrey came running through the foyer to see who was coming in. The pup made a flying leap into Grandma's lap. She laughed until she coughed. I took off my mittens, hat, and coat and hung them up on the coat tree in the foyer.

The house was over a hundred years old, and while it had been remodeled almost every ten years, there were rooms still stuck in the seventies. Then again, when you had a house as big as this one, there were a lot of rooms to remodel. Generally by the time you finished updating the whole house it was time to start over.

This explained the 1970s take on vintage Victorian den that now resembled a bordello on crack. It screamed outdated, from the dark red and cream velvet wallpaper to the dark wood and green tile around the fireplace.

"Grandma, no scooters on the carpet!" I warned her as she started to turn into the den.

"Geeze you're fussy." Grandma hit the brakes, leaving skid marks on the polished wood floors of the hallway. The house had a central foyer with the original wood floors. To the left was a formal parlor that opened into the den. To the right was the sweeping staircase. Behind the staircase and across from the den was the formal dining room. A tiny half bath was tucked in between the den and the eat-in kitchen at the back of the house.

"What? I'm not fussy. That carpet is close to a priceless antique," I joked. The carpet in the den was a deep green shag from the era before I was born. Over the years Mom had covered it with a variety of area rugs, so the center of the room was practically pristine flooring. Too nice to rip up and throw away just to update a room.

"Fine, I suppose a little walk won't kill me." Grandma pushed Aubrey off her lap and grunted as she climbed off her Scootaround senior scooter. The scooter took up most of the room in the hallway and would not have fit through the door to the den anyway. If she really wanted to scoot into the den she would have to go around and enter through the front room, where the pocket doors were wider. I suspected that was Grandma's real reason for giving in and walking.

She ambled over to the brocade- and velvet-trimmed love seat. "What do you have to eat?" She sat down with a humph and I noted the dust that puffed out.

"I have gluten-free lasagna I can heat up. I take it you didn't eat dinner."

Grandma frowned at me and took off her fedora. "They were serving some kind of casserole at the senior center. It looked oddly gray."

"No worries, I'll heat something up. Do you want salad?"

"Have you ever known me to turn down food?" Grandma called after me. "Put it in front of me and I'll eat it."

Which she did on a regular basis, thus adding to her ample size. I loved Grandma, but she had never been a small woman. Once when I was very young she had lost over 150 pounds and even gone so far as to have a face-lift to get rid of the loose skin that comes with such a large loss of weight.

"They called it a face-lift." Grandma would tell the story with a twinkle in her eye. "But they lifted everything from the belly button up." Her orange eyebrows would wiggle. "I lost nearly thirty pounds of skin and got a boob lift in the process."

Grandma Ruth was an old flapper with a wicked sense of humor. Over the years she had gained back all the weight and more. She would tell you she was old, so what did size matter?

"Is Bill coming?" I popped my head into the den. Bill was Grandma's boyfriend. A taxidermist she had met in an art class.

"No, his granddaughter had a play thing in Augusta," Grandma said and settled into the couch. "My fingers are cold."

"I'll turn on the fire." I put the key in the floor and turned on the gas, lighting the fireplace. "Let me have your coat."

I took Grandma's outer garments as the pup settled in her lap. "Aubrey, get down," I commanded. The puppy looked from me to Grandma and back to me. "No dogs on the furniture."

"What kind of rule is that?" Grandma asked as she petted Aubrey.

"A good rule to enforce now, when he's little. Especially if he grows to be the hundred-and-ten-pound dog the vet thinks he'll be." I looked at Aubrey and snapped my fingers. "Down. Off."

Grandma pushed him and the pup reluctantly climbed down.

"Good boy," I said and turned on my heel. I hung Grandma's coat and hat in the hall. Then I popped the lasagna into the oven to reheat. If it were just me I would have heated it in the microwave, but Grandma liked it reheated the old-fashioned way—in the oven.

I don't blame her. There was something about the microwave that dried out food. I fixed us both bowls of salad and poured Grandma a cup of coffee, placed it all on a tray, and took it into the den.

Funny, but I swear Aubrey had heard me coming and climbed out of Grandma's lap again. I narrowed my eyes at him. He did a turn and lay down at Grandma's feet.

"I can't believe you gave Candy the scoop on the murder," Grandma chided me when I reentered the den.

"I didn't give her the scoop." I set the tray down and picked up a bowl of salad, sat down in a flowered wingback chair. "She listens to the police scanner."

"I saw her article on the front page of the afternoon *Oiltop Times*." Grandma pouted. "She says you called the police when Maria found the body."

"I did."

"You could have called me right after." Grandma gave me the narrowed eye of guilt.

"There was no time." I settled back into my chair and took a nice forkful of salad. "I was lucky to call Brad before

Officer Bright could stop me." I shoved salad in my mouth so I had an excuse not to talk.

"We need some kind of text signal," Grandma muttered and smothered her coffee in artificial sweetener and a dash of cream. Then she picked up her own bowl of salad. "Like 411 or something, so I know to come hunt you down."

I chewed and swallowed. "I was at the Red Tile Inn. How would you have known where to find me?"

"There's such a thing as the senior network in this small town." Grandma's blue eyes twinkled. "I'm telling you that if you sent me a simple 411 text I'd be able to find you any-where, anytime, within five minutes. Then you wouldn't have to worry about the cops. It would simply be your old grandma, showing up as planned."

"Snapping pictures and writing in her notebook," I said and forked more salad in my mouth.

"Everyone in town knows I carry my notebook every-where. Once a newswoman, always a newswoman." Unlike me, Grandma had no qualms about talking with her mouth full of salad.

"Are you telling me that when Candy is in her nineties, she'll be running around with her computer tablet in hand, taking notes?"

"That's right." Grandma nodded and waved her fork, sending lettuce flying around the room, much to the pup's delight. "Once a newswoman, always a newswoman."

"Then how come you don't have a police scanner?"

"I had one a few years back, but Bill said it kept waking him up."

I winced and put my salad down on the table. "Grandma, I don't want to know that Bill spends the night with you."

"Oh, he doesn't. The police scanner kept disturbing his afternoon nap."

Not that the image of chubby Bill, with his shock of white hair and round jelly belly, napping at Grandma's was much better. "You're getting soft if you choose Bill over the news," I pointed out as I rose to check on the lasagna.

"If you dated, you would do things for your man, too." Grandma huffed.

"I'm still working through the trauma of my divorce," I said as I stepped out of the room. Mom's death had come on the heels of my divorce from Eric. I had come home from work early to find him naked in my bed with his best friend's wife. I was less disturbed by his behavior than I was by the idea that I had let him dupe me. It had been less than a year since I signed the divorce papers. I still didn't trust myself to make smart choices when it came to men.

I plated the lasagna and took it into the den. "Brad tells me the police grilled Tim for three hours." I snapped my fingers to catch the dog's attention and then pointed at the living room. The rule was no dogs in the area of food. I'd been lenient with the salad, but I wasn't going to tempt him with the casserole.

"Your brother had nothing to do with that murder," Grandma said and slurped her coffee.

"Well, I know that and you know that, but Chief Blaylock has no other leads at this time."

"That's because it takes six months to get evidence back from the county lab. Real life is nothing like those crime shows on television," Grandma said around a forkful of lasagna.

"I know," I said. "The county lab is understaffed, over-worked, and underbudgeted. You wrote a blog on it last month."

"And I got great feedback." Grandma waved her fork. "Paula Ashford is on the ballot for the county board. She needs to know that people expect more from the justice system."

"I'm sure Paula reads your blog." I took a bite of the lasagna. I had discovered gluten-free rice noodles at the grocery store. It was simply a matter of practice before I perfected my gluten-free lasagna recipe. Thankfully I wasn't lactose intolerant as well as celiac. I could indulge in ricotta cheese and mozzarella. I had added spinach and mushrooms to jazz up the meat sauce and ricotta filling. Not bad if I say so myself.

"Too bad you don't have any bread to go with this," Grandma said around her bites of dinner. "Garlic bread and butter would be perfect with this meal."

"I have gluten-free breadsticks in the freezer."

"Well, why didn't you heat them up?"

"I'm on a diet," I said. "You want me to start dating, then I need to get into fighting shape." Things had gone a little soft since I returned to Oiltop and started my bakery. I hadn't had a lot of time to devote to my health. It didn't help that I had been working on developing new recipes for the holidays.

"You might be on a diet, but I'm not." Grandma scooped up another forkful of lasagna.

"I'm not heating the breadsticks, Grandma," I stated. "Neither one of us needs them."

Grandma frowned at me. "Fine. I prefer real bread anyway."

It was my turn to give Grandma the evil eye. She was better at ignoring me than I was at ignoring her. "What are we going to do about this murder?"

"That's the question," Grandma said. "You have to investigate. We can't trust Officer Emry to investigate his way out of his squad car."

"Officer Bright is good at his job."

"Officer Bright was in Tim's class in school. Those two were huge rivals, if you don't remember."

Okay, so I didn't remember. High school was a blur of angst and drama. The last thing I paid attention to were the boys in Tim's class. "I don't remember, but even so, they're both adults now."

Grandma frowned at me. "Apparently you're not a good observer of men."

I cringed. "Guilty as charged." I raised my hands in the air. "It's why I shouldn't date."

"Dating is a whole different story." Grandma shrugged. "A woman your age should be out having fun. Not stuck in an old house with an old woman, discussing old rivalries."

I got up and gathered up the empty dishes. "So you came to eat my food and give me a hard time about my life?"

"I came to see you." Grandma was not bothered in the least by my words. "You were involved in another murder. I wanted to ensure you're okay."

"I'm okay, Grandma." I picked up the tray of empty dishes. "I'm sorry Candy beat you to the scoop on the death of a man at the Red Tile."

"I'm not worried about a little competition from that young woman." Grandma stood as well and waddled out to the hall with me. "I've got something better than the police radio."

"What's that?" I narrowed my eyes.

"I've got the senior grapevine. Nothing better than a gaggle of retirees to keep you up-to-date on the comings and goings in a small town."

"Then you don't need me to investigate." I walked into the kitchen. The floor of the kitchen was patterned with black and white tiles. The cabinets were original to the house. Mom had painted them white at some point. The countertops were recycled glass in a soft mixture of colors that ended up blending to mostly gray. The backsplash was made up of black and white subway tiles. The pattern mirrored the floor.

My bright pink stand mixer stood in its place of honor on the counter by the window. I remember doing dishes as a kid and spending an hour looking out that window to our fenced-in backyard.

"I don't need you to get a decent story." Grandma leaned her considerable girth against my cream-painted wall. "But that doesn't mean your brother Tim doesn't need your help."

"If Tim needs my help, he'll ask for it." I rinsed out the dishes and put them in the dishwasher. "So far only Joan has called me." I waved toward the phone and the currently blinking light letting me know I had voicemail.

"Joan wants you to investigate?" Grandma frowned.

"Joan wants me to bring cookies to Emma's classroom for her birthday celebration at school." I added soap to the dishwasher and started it.

Aubrey trotted through the kitchen and scratched at the back door. I opened it and let him out into the cold, fenced yard.

"She didn't know about Tim being implicated in a murder. You need to call her and tell her."

"Why? So she can talk me into investigating? Or so she comes to Oiltop with her brood to ensure we're all behaving ourselves here."

Grandma grinned. "She has always been like your father with that. Practical to a fault."

"What's the fault?"

"No imagination," Grandma huffed. She turned on her heels and waddled over to the scooter, which she had purchased when the county took away her driver's license. She drove the thing into any building with access ramps and some without. She also drove it down the middle of the street. My brother had put a tall orange triangle on the scooter so that people could see her coming and get out of the way. "Are you going to help your brother or not?"

I ran my hand over my face. "I tell you what. I'll help investigate if Tim asks me. That's it."

"Fine."

"Fine."

"Good."

I narrowed my eyes at the sneaky look in her eye. "Good."

"Got to run, kiddo." Grandma reversed her scooter until I had to yet again jump out of the way to keep from losing my toes. "Give an old woman a kiss."

I stepped up and kissed her on her grizzled cheek. "Love you, Grandma."

"Love you, too, kiddo," she said and waved as she scooted out the door. She paused the scooter half in and half out of the front door. "Oh yes, I almost forgot. Mindy is coming for a visit and I told her there was an open room in your house."

"Mindy?" I asked and winced inside. Mindy was not my favorite cousin. She acted as if she was too good for the family. "When is she coming?" I mentally did a quick inventory of bedrooms and clean sheets.

"Soon," Grandma said. "Don't forget, you promised to investigate this terrible murder."

"If Tim asks, then I'll investigate," I said again. "In the meantime I have to get a room ready for Mindy, and I have peanut butter cookies to bake tonight for an online order."

"Love the peanut butter cookies. Save me some!" And just like that, Grandma Ruth was gone out the door and down the ramp before I could so much as thank her for thinking of me—even if it wasn't for the best.

CHAPTER 4

"I need a place to hide," Tim said as he stood in the lamp-light behind the bakery.

"It's four in the morning," I said as I unlocked the back door. "There's no one to hide from."

"Come on, Toni, this isn't funny." Tim followed me inside. He'd never settled down. My oldest brother Richard's responsible streak had sent Tim in the opposite direction. While Richard worked hard, Tim glided through life. His tall, lanky body and scruffy dirty-blond hair made him a favorite with the ladies. "The cops have someone cruising through my neighborhood once an hour."

"Oh, come on," I said as I flipped on the lights. "It's not that bad." The kitchen of the bakery blazed into full view. The scent of natural cleaner filled the air. It was a delicate balance between the health inspector's standards and the health of my customers. I tended to clean with all-natural products like vinegar, lemon juice, and baking soda. People with gluten allergies are often sensitive to the environment. Any kind of chemical, even cleaners, could cause a reaction.

This meant that my kitchen usually smelled like salad dressing until I got the proofer warmed up. Then the scent of yeast rising and cinnamon filled the air.

"I'm telling you, Toni. The cops are out to get me." Tim pulled out one of the chairs at the table I had snugged up against the wall opposite the countertops. He flipped the chrome chair with red vinyl cushion around and swung his legs over it. He put his forearms on the back of the chair and rested his forehead on his arms.

I put my purse on the counter by the coat tree next to the door. Hung my keys up on the hooks near the door and took off my puffy jacket. December meant I came to work in darkness and went home in darkness. It also meant that bitter windchills danced around the buildings downtown. Puffy down coats were my favorite thing to ward off freezing to death.

"Are you talking about Officer Emry? Because everyone knows he's not exactly the brightest bulb in the box." I hung my coat on the tree and pulled an apron off the hook.

"It's Bright." Tim spoke to the floor. "He wants me to come back for more interrogation. Thank goodness you sent Ridgeway over. Brad kept me from hours of questions, and who knows what would have happened."

"Nothing," I reassured him. "You're innocent." I pulled the large white apron over my head and wrapped the ties around my waist, pulling them tight.

"Innocent guys go to jail all the time." Tim blew out a long breath and ran his hand over his face. "Don't you listen to the news? They just released some guy after twelve years in prison. DNA finally proved he didn't do it."

I put my hands on my hips and frowned at my brother. "That's not going to happen to you."

"Then there was the guy whose daughter was murdered

and after twelve hours of interrogation and grief he confessed." Tim's blue eyes grew wide. "No one believed him when he withdrew his coerced confession. Six months later they found the actual guy who killed his kid."

"Seriously, stop it," I said. He was worrying me. "You won't confess unless you did it."

"That's what everyone thinks."

"I'm making coffee. It's too early for me to deal with all this negativity."

"We have to find the real killer," Tim said. "Grandma Ruth says you can do it."

I put a filter in the hopper and opened the canister with the coffee inside. The sharp scent of roasted beans filled the air. "Grandma likes the idea that I can do it," I said and measured the grounds. "I'm a baker, not an investigator."

"You solved the last two murders," Tim pointed out.

"I thought you didn't pay attention to me." I hit the BREW button and turned toward my brother.

Unlike my puffy coat, Tim wore a denim coat with shearling interior. It hung open, exposing a black sweatshirt and the edge of a red tee sticking out underneath. His jeans were clean but well worn. His feet were encased in brown steel-toed work boots. Tim was ruggedly handsome and wore it well.

"How can I not pay attention to you? You're my sister," he groused. "So are you going to help me or not?"

"Well, of course I'll help you," I said. "You are my brother. Besides Oiltop is a small town. What happens to you affects the entire family."

"So you're saying you'll investigate, but only because it would save your business." He straightened away from the back of the chair.

"Okay, sure." I shrugged then looked at him with the expression a sister gives a brother when she thinks he's acting stupid.

"Great." Tim put his hands on his thighs. "What do we do first?"

"*We* don't do anything," I said. "You go home and go to bed. You have to work."

"How am I supposed to sleep? Someone used my name to rent a room and kill a man."

"Did they tell you who the victim was?" I pulled big ceramic bowls of yeasty dough out of the refrigerator and put them on the countertop. "When I went to bed last night they were still saying it was an unidentified man."

"Yeah, you know people should die with ID on them." Tim leaned forward onto the back of the chair.

"So they still don't know? How can they connect some random guy to you?"

"That's it," Tim said. "They tried to get me to ID the dude."

"They showed you pictures?"

"Yeah, nice, right?"

I sprinkled sticky rice flour on the cold marble slab on my countertop. "Did you recognize him?" I dumped the large bowls of dough into piles to warm. The scent of yeast and dough wafted through the air.

"Naw, his face was too messed up. I don't think I know him."

"So then what? Did someone steal your identity?" I grabbed two thick white ceramic mugs off the shelf and poured us both cups of hot coffee. I handed Tim his cup. I grabbed half-and-half from the refrigerator and poured some into mine. I used to like my coffee black but had read that coffee could leach the calcium out of your bones. If you drink it with a splash of milk you slow down that process.

Grandma Ruth had shrunk nearly four inches with osteoporosis. I hoped to not repeat her mistakes. I mean, what do we have grandparents for if not to learn from them? Of course, we were both divorced, so I suppose there are some things a girl has to learn for herself.

I handed Tim the creamer. He poured some into his coffee and then dumped in half a cup of sugar. I shook my head and sipped my warm, rich, creamy, bitter brew. "How can you drink it so sweet?"

"How can you drink it so bitter?" he countered with a raised eyebrow. "I don't think I had my identity stolen," he said and tasted his coffee. "But that's a good point."

"Don't you check?" I asked. "They have these companies now that will keep an eye out for identity theft."

"Who has the time?" He leaned on the chair back, the warm mug held between his hands. "Besides, this is Oiltop. Who would steal my identity here?"

"Someone did." I lowered my chin and gave him the *duh* look. "Unless that was you at the Red Tile Inn."

"It was not me." He narrowed his eyes at me. "I'm getting myself together. Isn't that what your forties are for?"

"I thought that was what your thirties were for," I teased. "Twenties are to figure out who you are. Thirties to get your stuff together and forties to be a grown-up."

"Being a grown-up stinks," Tim said.

"Sometimes." I nodded my agreement. "I'll have Grandma do a credit check on you and see if anything is out of the ordinary. If we can prove your identity was stolen, then they have to dismiss you as a person of interest."

"Fine."

"In the meantime you can crash back at the house if you think the cops will keep you from getting sleep."

"Thanks." Tim rose and finished off his coffee in one single gulp. "Are Tasha and Kip still there?"

"Yes," I said. "Also, Grandma said something about Mindy coming for a visit. So take the back bedroom. There are sheets and blankets in the cupboard."

"Mindy? I haven't seen her in like five years."

"I know, right? Grandma tells me Mindy is serious about this new guy she's seeing."

"Is she bringing him?"

"Maybe, I don't know. Grandma didn't say." I shrugged. "She might want Grandma's approval."

"Cool, now I *have* to stay at the house." Tim grinned, stood, and kissed me on the cheek. "Consider me moved back for a bit, okay, sis?"

"Okay." I patted him on the arm. "Just pay attention to your credit, okay? I mean, if someone stole your identity, you could have bills you don't even know about."

"Yeah, yeah." He buttoned up his coat. "Solve this thing for me, okay?"

"I'm not making any promises. It's Christmas and do-or-die time at the bakery. Plus I think I'm really bad at investigating. I don't want to muck it up for you, either."

"Yeah, I get it," he said. His tone sounded defeated.

"Calvin's a good guy, really. I think you can trust him."

"I hope you're right." He popped a NASCAR cap on his head. "Lock the door behind me."

I stuck my tongue out at him, but did as he said and turned the dead bolt behind him. Oiltop might not be Chicago, but that didn't mean we didn't have our fair share of crime. I learned that after George Meister's murder just outside the bakery's front door a few months ago.

Turning on the radio, I let the soft sounds of twenty-four hours of Christmas music waft through the kitchen. I know listening to the radio is old-fashioned these days, but I like the homey feel of Christmas music and the sound of the local news.

At least they weren't giving the farm report on this station. While I didn't need it, quite a few of my customers still got up and listened to the report. It was part of living in the country, surrounded by farms and ranches.

I took out the dough that I prepped the night before and made donuts and rolled pastries. There was a nice rhythm to baking. It was almost like a dance. Most of the dough was made ahead so that all I had to do in the early morning hours was bake, cool, and frost to fill my counter. While those batches baked, I made a couple dozen big muffins. More batches came out of the oven and went on cooling racks while fresh batches went into the oven.

I had three batches of gluten-free rolls and breads to make. A couple of customers came in for bread on Tuesday and I had a daily order of ten sub rolls for the deli down the street. That order had been a coup for me. With the help of handsome rancher Sam Greenbaum, I had managed to convince the deli owner to add gluten-free choices to his menu.

So far he'd been happy with the rise in demand. I bit my bottom lip and kneaded the first bowl of dough. Sure, the demand might simply be from people's curiosity and experimentation with eating gluten-free, but for those of us who *had* to eat gluten-free, it was nice to have options. Since he'd already had gluten-free versions of deli meats and cheeses, the bread was the only missing ingredient for fast lunches.

My thoughts turned to the impending visit of my cousin Mindy McCree. I was one of fifty-two of Grandma Ruth's grandkids and even more great-grandkids. The members of my family tended to identify themselves by their birth number. I'm number two of six. Mindy was number seven of twelve. My uncle Alfred had twelve children. Six with his first wife, Betty, who had died in a car accident caused by a drunk driver. Then he had married my aunt Helen, who gave him six more children. Mindy was the oldest of Helen's girls and about ten years younger than me.

She lived in New York City and had spent her twenties traveling Europe on scholarships. Last I heard she was in law school and had been hired by some quasi-famous law firm. Grandma was proudest of her grandkids who took up the family cause of higher education. Not that she wasn't proud of me and my bakery. She simply liked to point out that I could be a lifetime Mensa member, too, if I only put my mind to it and took the test.

I had enough to do keeping my bakery going; the last thing I needed was to prove my intelligence level. Besides, baking gluten-free was a creative challenge that kept me busy. Let my cousins be Mensa members and college professors. There was nothing wrong with my keeping the homestead as a base for the family. Was there?

After I had baked the morning dough, I started in on the daily breads. Today I created tiny sub rolls and placed them on a greased cookie sheet, then placed them in the proofer to rise. Next I made four loaves of white sandwich bread and three loaves of potato bread. Once I completed the usual morning baked goods, I concentrated on cookies. Christmastime was the season for cookie exchanges at schools and churches and clubs. Most women worked full-time and didn't have time to bake cookies—especially gluten-free cookies, so they relied on me to have a wide assortment available for their exchange offerings.

Today's cookies were pistachio thumbprints with cream filling and chocolate drizzle. Then there were usual chocolate chip and oatmeal raisin along with spumoni cookies with layers of pistachio, cherry, and vanilla. Next were pinwheels—a favorite of my father's father, a robust man with Popeye's strong forearms and a wicked mutter. If you listened carefully, Grandpa would say the most hilarious things. Most people today didn't take the time to listen.

Grandpa Henry had been kept alive decades past his shelf life by the pure stubbornness of Grandma Mary before they both passed away the same night. They had been married sixty-five years, and it seemed that Grandpa had stayed alive until Grandma died and then simply gone with her. I suppose that was a romantic view, but then I liked the romantic view.

Grandpa and Grandma had been gone five years now,

but every Christmas I made pinwheel cookies and remembered the other side of my family. The side with slightly fewer members, who worked the oil fields and factories.

The pounding at the back door startled me out of my thoughts and the fast dance of baking, filling, and frosting. I looked out of the peephole I had drilled. There was a bright orange triangle flapping in the wind. The loud banging again. *Wham, wham, wham.* "Toni? Let me in—it's cold out here."

I unlocked the door and hadn't quite opened it when Grandma pushed through on her Scootaround. "Grandma? It's five thirty in the morning."

"I know. I need coffee." She pushed her scooter up to the table, displacing the chair that Tim had tucked back under. "I take it the coffee's ready."

"Good morning to you, too," I said and dragged a third ceramic mug from the shelf. I poured thick hot brew into it and took it over to Grandma. She liked it as sweet as Tim did but instead of sugar, she used the pink packets. Not the blue ones; it had to be the pink ones. Grandma was also a lifelong member of Weight Watchers. It worked when she followed it—following it was the key. These days she didn't care about her size, but the pink packets were a habit from those days that stuck.

"I've been awake for hours," Grandma said. "Trying to figure out who the victim was and why the killer would frame your brother."

Grandma took her brown fedora off. Today she wore a multicolored knit scarf that my cousin Desiree had knitted her. It was longer than Grandma was tall, but she wore it proudly wrapped around and around her neck. Under the scarf, she wore a thick puffy coat that had been blue at one point but now had coffee and cigarette stains on it until it was nearly brown. Under the coat I saw a white Peter Pan collar with a bright blue butterfly print on it.

Grandma Ruth's sense of style always amazed me. Her

legs were covered in brown corduroy men's pants, her feet encased in thick boots. I handed her the coffee mug.

"No gloves, Grandma? It's less than twenty degrees outside." I frowned at her.

"Gloves are in my pockets," she said and took the mug. Her fingertips were a telltale blue.

"You can't type if you don't have fingers."

"I had them on, but I took them off when you didn't answer my first knock. I figured they were muffling the sound."

As if her gloveless hands were my fault.

She pulled five pink packets out of the holder and shook them deftly before tearing the tops off and dumping the contents into her cup. "Spoon?"

"Right here." I handed her a spoon from the side drawer. "Tim is going to stay at the homestead for a while," I said. "I told him Mindy was coming, so he's crashing in the back bedroom."

"Good." Grandma nodded and stirred her coffee. She reached for the small pitcher of creamer that I kept on the table and poured a good dollop into her drink. "Do you have any leftover donuts?"

"No leftovers, I made cranberry walnut today," I said. "They're in the front counter but if you wait a few minutes there are some cinnamon spice donuts in the oven. You can get them super fresh."

"I don't see why you can't fry your donuts like everyone else." Grandma wrapped both hands around her mug and sipped her coffee. Her heavily freckled skin had a lovely tan hue to it that made her look nearly as orange as her hair. Her fingernails were strong and clipped short. A reporter needs to type more than she needs to have long nails, Grandma had always said.

I liked her plain nails. I kept mine plain. There was something clean and honest about hardworking hands. Besides,

I always chipped my polish and with my hands in dough every day it really wasn't the best to cover my fingers with polish. "Baked donuts are healthier," I said. "Besides, I don't have a fryer."

"You should invest in one." Grandma nodded. "You could fry everything from donuts to fruit to candy bars. I bet they would sell better, too."

"Maybe," I acknowledged. "But I think there's enough sugar and fat in gluten-free food without frying. Besides, I read somewhere that a fried diet was responsible for an increase in stroke risk."

"A person has to die sometime," Grandma said. "At least I'd die happy."

I raised my right eyebrow and put my hands on my hips. "You don't have to eat my pastries."

"I didn't say there was anything wrong with your baked goods. They're good . . . and they're baked. Just saying you should get a fryer, too."

"Grandma, why are you here?" I returned to mixing cookie dough.

"They identified the body," Grandma declared. "It was Harold Petry."

CHAPTER 5

"How do you know it was Harold Petry?" I asked. Harold was Tim's best friend. I think I would have recognized him. Of course, I hadn't seen him in four years, but that didn't mean I wouldn't know him when I saw him. Did it?

Besides, Tim would have definitely known him. Hadn't they shown Tim pictures of the dead guy?

"I can't reveal my sources," Grandma said and slurped her coffee. "Tim's going to be a wreck when he finds out."

I bit my bottom lip. "It can't be Harold. Both Tim and I would have known it was him."

"They showed Tim pictures of the body?" Grandma asked with a scowl. She shook her head. "It's going to kill Tim. It was definitely Harold," Grandma stated. "Dental records and fingerprints ID'd him."

"But Harold was a heavy guy with dirty-blond hair. . . ."

"The kid lost a lot of weight lately. He claimed that he found a miracle weight-loss drug." Grandma drummed her long square fingers on the red Formica top of the table. "The kid tried to sell me some, but I refused to fall for that a second time."

"Fall for what?"

"The weight-loss thing," Grandma said. "Back in the day my doctor told me cigarettes would keep me slender. We all know how that turned out. Besides I think whatever he was selling made his hair fall out. He tried to cover it up with a bad comb-over but he wasn't fooling anyone."

"Do you think Harold was dealing drugs?" I finished making the pistachio cookies and put the dough in the fridge to chill. Then I grabbed a chilled bowl of oatmeal raisin dough and scooped the dough out of the bowl and onto oversized aluminum cookie sheets. Oatmeal raisin cookies were a staple in the bakery. I baked mine soft so that they were chewy and large enough that the little kids had to use two hands to hold them.

"I have no idea," Grandma said. "Are those donuts done yet? Or do I have to go snitch a couple from the counter?"

I put the cookie sheet in the top oven and checked the donut pan in the bottom. "These look done." As I pulled them out, the scent of cinnamon and nutmeg wafted through the air. "They're hot," I said. "When they cool, I'll throw a couple in frosting for you."

The fastest way to frost donuts was to literally toss them into a tub of frosting, twist, and set them on a wire rack long enough for the frosting to set. I had made a batch of cream cheese frosting for the donuts and the carrot cake cupcakes I planned to make before noon.

"I'm just saying the kid lost something like eighty pounds and claimed it was a miracle pill he took." Grandma watched as I popped the donuts out of the pan to cool. "You don't have to frost the first one. I'll sacrifice and eat it plain."

"Well, he didn't die of an overdose," I said. "There was blood everywhere. I'm certain he was mortally wounded."

"Knife wounds," Grandma surmised as I plated her donut and handed it to her.

"Hard to tell," I said. "The body was in the bathtub, wrapped in the shower curtain, and there was blood pretty much everywhere. Not that this is decent conversation for breakfast."

"I lived through the Great Depression," Grandma said and bit into her donut. "I can eat just about anything at any time." She patted her stomach. "Got the weight to prove it."

I popped a second pan of donuts into the oven. It was nearly six and my assistant would be here by six thirty, when I opened the front door. So far I had donuts and muffins and Danish already in the glass containers. Cookies would be next along with two cakes that I had baked last night and frosted this morning.

Variety is the spice of life, or so I've been told.

"Unless you know how was he killed," I said as I scooped more cookie dough onto a cooled sheet.

"I do. My sources tell me he was stabbed."

"Hmm." I frowned. "I didn't see any knives."

"You didn't really look for them, either," Grandma said and picked up her plate. "I'll try the frosting now. Let you know what I think."

I dropped the small scoop into the dough bowl, wiped my hands on a towel, and took her plate. "True, I didn't look for a weapon." I plucked a donut off the wire rack, threw it into the vat of frosting, twisted, and pulled it off, letting the frosting ooze over the donut and onto her plate.

"Two would be nice."

"I thought you needed to watch your sugar intake," I scolded and put the plate with one donut down in front of her.

Grandma cackled her booming scratchy laugh until she coughed. "I'm always watching my sugar, kiddo. It doesn't mean I don't like an extra donut now and then. Especially if they're good-for-you baked and not fried." She wiggled her eyebrows and bit into the donut. "Mmmm, mmmm."

I shook my head. "So what we have is a dead best friend in a hotel room rented in my brother's name. The only thing saving Tim is the fact that he works at night."

"That's the thing," Grandma said around a second bite. "The estimated time of death is from four until six in the evening."

"Wow." I pulled out the chair and sat down hard. "Whoever framed Tim knew his schedule."

"Yes." Grandma nodded sagely. "Tim usually sleeps until four or five. He's not likely to have an alibi during that time."

"Why kill Harold?" I wondered. "Clearly this is more than identity theft."

"Identity theft?"

"Tim came by this morning to ask if he could stay with me. I said yes, then I told Tim that whoever rented the room could have simply stolen his identity." I shrugged. "It's plausible."

"Not if they did it and then killed Tim's best friend." Grandma frowned and handed me her empty coffee mug.

I got up and refilled her mug, handed it to her, and went back to my cookie dough. "You're right. There are too many coincidences."

"I'm glad Tim is staying with you," Grandma said. "With Mindy coming into town he'll have an alibi from now on."

"If it's not too late."

"We'll have to see how it plays out," Grandma said. "I'll do a background check on Tim to make sure everything is okay there. I'll head over to the courthouse to do some digging into Harold's background later today. There has to be a motive for murder. Which means Harold was more than a victim at the wrong place at the wrong time."

"Tim's social security number is in the family Bible," I said. Truthfully, everyone's social security number was listed in the Bible. It was Mom's way of keeping track of us. The social security number went down beside our name, birthdate, baptismal date, first communion, and confirmation. There was even a line for our wedding dates—although mine was crossed out.

"I've got it," Grandma said and tapped her temple. Then she twisted the colored scarf around her neck six or eight times, grabbed her gloves out of her pockets, put them on, and moved her scooter to the back door. "First I've got a water aerobics class at the Y. After that the library will be open. I'll get on the Internet and do some digging."

"Is Bill driving you?" I asked as I opened the door for her.

"Not today." Grandma drove her scooter out the door. The tip of the orange caution triangle bent as she went through the door then bounced back in a wild wave as she motored into the parking lot. "Bill's got a taxidermy seminar in Great Bend."

"It's too cold to drive your scooter," I said as I checked out the size and density of the flurry of snow that fell from the sky. "Why don't you wait? Meghan will be here shortly. I'll have her drive you."

"Nonsense," Grandma said and moved down the back parking lot. "It's only a mile or so. Toodles, kiddo. Lock the door behind you."

How come I had to lock a door in a perfectly strong building but Grandma could scooter away into the darkness? With that orange flag flying above her, I think she was a bigger target than I was.

CHAPTER 6

Being gluten-free is not a bed of roses. I am careful, seriously careful, and yet there are still days when I got "glutened." How do I know? I get sick—and not itchy, rashy sick, but tummy-bug sick.

"Meghan, are you sure you're okay with covering the bakery this morning?" I asked as my stomach rumbled.

My assistant was young and beautiful. Just nineteen, she looked more like a tattoo artist than a baker, but I loved her anyway. Today her hair was dyed jet-black with a hot pink streak in the front. Black cat-eye liner streaked along the edge of her lids. She had wide, dark brown eyes and pierced eyebrows dyed to match her hair. Her skin looked like porcelain and her mouth was painted in a bright red cupid's bow.

She had been more Goth when I hired her two months ago, but had recently segued into vintage pinup-girl makeup. She wore a white tee shirt and black pants. On her feet were the proper shoes for standing all day. She had rings tattooed on her right fingers. She had told me the tattoo was better than real because she could bake with her bare hands and not worry about cleaning under the rings.

I insisted that she be meticulous in my kitchen, and she was.

"Hey, no worries." Meghan tied the apron around her waist. "You have the morning rush ready. With the cookie dough prepped as well, all I have to do is bake." She waved her hand elegantly from the square blocks of frozen cookie dough I had made and frozen the night before toward the double oven. "Go home. Get some rest."

"Thank you," I said sincerely and grabbed my coat from the coatrack next to the door.

"Any idea how you got glutened?" Meghan asked. "People will want to know."

"Not here," I said and waved my hand around the kitchen. "I cheated last night and grabbed French fries from the fast-food place on the corner. I know better. . . ." I sighed.

"It just means you're human." Meghan smiled. "Who can resist the siren call of hot greasy potatoes? Besides, like you said, they should be gluten-free. They're just sliced potatoes deep fried with salt. Right?"

"In theory," I said. "In reality there are a million ways for the fries to come in contact with gluten. They probably fried something coated in flour in the same grease. It's as crazy as putting the gluten-free mixes next to the flour on the grocery store shelves. At least I'm not so sensitive I can't walk down the flour aisle without getting sick."

"Thank goodness for that," Meghan agreed.

"I'm going to go take some medicine and rest. I'll be back in time to close up," I promised. "Thanks!"

"Hey, no sweat. This is the kind of stuff I signed up for." Meghan smiled, stretching out the bright red into a perfect pouty grin. Oh, to be nineteen again.

"Great." I pulled on my hat and gloves. "You have my cell phone number if you need to get ahold of me."

"I do and I won't," she said with a laugh. "Don't worry, your baby will be safe with me."

"I'm counting on it," I said and stepped out into the cold. Since the sun had come up, the temperature had actually dropped. The sunlight was weak against a gray overcast sky. It smelled of snow and I wrapped my scarf around my face as I trudged across the parking lot. The bakery van was white, utilitarian, and, with only 75,000 miles on it, a great bargain. Thank goodness my brothers were good with mechanical things. I depended on my delivery van. I had a sneaking suspicion that without Tim, the vehicle would have kicked the bucket last year.

I rattled in an empty van down Main Street to Central. Turning left onto Central I headed west. My bed called me from the distance. My stomach rumbled and threatened me with terrible things.

Altogether it was stupid of me to think I could cheat—especially with the holidays just around the corner.

I arrived home to find Tim's car parked in the street in front of the house. The driveway was blocked by a black Audi. I parked beside it, squeezing the van into the small space between the sleek black car and the house.

"Mindy must be here," I muttered to myself and headed into the kitchen. Inside was warm and well lit. My cousin Mindy stood at the stove, cooking something in a frying pan that smelled like an omelet. Yum, if my stomach weren't a big mess.

"Hi, Mindy. That smells good." I hugged my cousin.

"Thanks, I got in when Tim did this morning. I'm hungry, but all you have is frozen bread. I don't like it frozen, so I stopped at the store and picked up some fresh." Mindy pointed at the toaster and a pile of toast on a plate. "I hope you like whole wheat."

"Oh." My shoulders dropped. "Um, I'm gluten-free."

"What? What's that?"

"I have celiac disease. It means that if I eat gluten it damages my insides. Like right now—I ate takeout French fries yesterday and I'm suffering today."

"Oh." She drew her perfectly groomed eyebrows together. "You're sick?"

"Yes, it's not pretty." I stepped over to the sink and grabbed a water glass from the cupboard on the right side of the sink. "The reason my bread is frozen is because it's gluten-free. It doesn't have wheat, barley, or rye in it; therefore it spoils quicker. Freezing it keeps it fresh."

"Really?" She picked up the frying pan. "So I contaminated your kitchen when I brought in fresh bread?"

"Sort of." I winced. "I'll need to get a new toaster and whatever dishes you used will have to be separated. You can't wash or sterilize gluten away. It has to be dedicated."

"I'm so sorry! I had no idea." Mindy slumped against the counter.

"It's not your fault." I put my hand on her arm. "People who don't have experience with celiac don't understand how crazy things can make you."

"What happens? Can I ask?" She slid a perfect omelet onto a plate. "Do you break out in a rash? Does your throat close up?"

"I get terrible stomach issues." I hugged my belly as it rumbled. "Like IBS symptoms."

"Oh, oh dear." She pursed her mouth and winced. "I'll take this out to the dining room."

"Okay, just please keep it separate."

"Sure, sure." Mindy walked with me to the dining room. "It must be really hard to worry about gluten. At least it doesn't make you so sick you die." She sat down at the table. "I read last week where a boy ate part of a cookie and it literally killed him."

"Peanuts," I said. "Or tree nuts, I bet."

"Yes, I think it was a peanut allergy. Is that why you're home?" She forked up some eggs. "Tim said you would be working until eight P.M."

"Yes, I'm not doing so well."

"Then go on up to bed. I know my way around the house. I'll be fine." Mindy's large brown eyes were a photographer's dream.

"Does Grandma Ruth know you're here?"

"Yes, I called her," Mindy said. "We're supposed to have dinner later and catch up."

"Cool." I kissed my cousin's cheek and headed out of the dining room.

"Toni?"

"Yes?" I looked back at her.

"I'm going to be here awhile, is that okay?"

"Sure." I gave her a half shrug. "There's plenty of room in the house. You know that Tasha and her son, Kip, are living on the third floor, right?"

"Yes, Grandma and Tim told me."

"And have you met Aubrey?"

As if on cue, the puppy came tearing down the stairs and flew into the dining room. He jumped up on the table, grabbed a piece of toast, and went to the far corner to sit and grin as if he'd accomplished the best trick ever.

"Aubrey, no!" I said and walked over to him. He tried to run into the kitchen, but I grabbed him and took the toast from his mouth. "Kennel." I took him by the collar and dragged him into his kennel on the enclosed mudroom near the door. I put him inside and shut the door. He turned quickly to face me and wagged his tail.

I struggled not to smile at his antics—at least until I got out of view.

The moment I crossed into the dining room, I grinned and Aubrey barked behind me.

"What was that?" Mindy looked horrified as I imagine anyone who unexpectedly came into contact with a large-breed puppy who stole the food off the table.

"Sorry, that's Aubrey—Kip's dog. He's just a puppy and still in the pushing boundaries mode."

"Nice." Mindy shook her head. "I didn't really want that toast anyway." She patted her perfectly flat stomach. "I'm watching my figure."

"Do you mind going in in a minute or two and letting him out of his kennel? He gets timed out but we don't want to make him wait too long. Besides, if you let him out he'll love you forever for rescuing him. That is, until he forgets and tries another one of his antics." My own stomach rumbled loudly as if to join in the conversation. "Did Tim tell you which bedroom I made up for you?"

"Yes, thanks. Go on. Go rest." She waved her hands as if to shoo me out of the room. "I've got the dog and the kitchen cleanup. Feel better."

"I hope to," I said and went upstairs. I didn't mind a full house. My bedroom was attached to a Jack-and-Jill bath that was shared with a room that was currently used as a guest room. I had put Mindy in Mom and Dad's master bedroom. Tim should be sleeping in the third-floor back bedroom that used to be a sunporch but Mom had enclosed for year-round sleeping.

The house really was large enough to be a bed-and-breakfast. I suppose with Tasha no longer working at the Welcome Inn she could now run the house as a B&B. Except I think she liked her work at the Red Tile Inn. Maybe with the discovery of a dead body, that had changed.

I made a mental note to ask Tasha about it. But first I was headed to bed where I hoped I could sleep off some of my problems.

CHAPTER 7

The sound of the doorbell jangling woke me from a fitful sleep. I glanced at the clock. It was 3:00 P.M. Whoever was at the door was insistent and now pounded as well as jangled. The puppy barked as if to warn us of an intruder.

"I'm coming, I'm coming," I grumbled and stumbled out into the hallway to meet Tim at the stairs. He looked like death warmed over. His hair stood up on one side and he had dark bags under his eyes.

"What the heck?" he asked as we hurried down the stairs. It sounded as if whoever was at the door was about ready to bust it down. It didn't help that Aubrey barked and leapt at the door as if begging them to come in.

I reached it first and saw Officer Emry's serious mug as he raised his hand to bang again. I yanked the door open leaving him to whoosh his hand through the air. "Yes?"

Aubrey rushed out to wind his way around Officer Emry's legs, his large tail smacking the police officer in a flurry of happiness.

"What's with all the knocking?" Tim grumbled behind me. "You know I sleep days."

"I have a warrant to search the premises." Officer Emry puffed up his chest and stuck out his chin. There were two junior officers standing behind him. I had no idea what their names were, but their faces looked familiar, which meant I knew their families.

"Aubrey, come here." I grabbed the puppy just seconds before he stuck his nose in the wrong place.

"You have to have just cause for a warrant," Tim said.

"You being here is cause in my book," Emry said.

For a moment I thought Tim was going to lunge at him. My brother always had a bit of a temper and when woken up abruptly tended to act before he thought. I stuck my hand out to halt him. Tim narrowed his eyes and leaned against my hand. Officer Emry leaned back a fraction. Aubrey barked for good measure.

"Stop! All of you." The dog went quiet and the two men relaxed. "Let me see the warrant." I held out my hand toward the officer.

He put the paper in my hand and then placed his hands on his gun belt. "Please step aside," he said and eyed Aubrey. "Put the dog away." I pushed Aubrey onto Tim and maneuvered both of them behind me as Officer Emry opened the door. "Is there anyone else in the house?"

"Yes, my cousin Mindy is staying with us. Tasha and Kip are both out." I glanced at the grandfather clock in the hallway. "But they will be home any moment."

"I'm calling Ridgeway," Tim groused and held Aubrey with one hand and took out his cell phone with the other.

"Call him all you want; we have a warrant." Emry swaggered into the house with the two junior officers.

"What are you looking for?" I asked as I skimmed over the legal document. "I could help you find it."

"We're looking for evidence of drugs and drug paraphernalia," one of the junior officers said. He was blond and blue-eyed, with the German good looks of a Kansas farm family. I noted his name tag said Warwick.

"Good luck finding that," I said with a laugh and waved them inside. "I've got some aspirin in the medicine cabinet, along with all kinds of stomach remedies."

"Dealers don't usually keep their stashes in the medicine cabinet," Officer Emry noted and narrowed one eye.

"There are no drug dealers in this house." I rolled my eyes.

"We have just cause to believe there are." Emry stared at Tim.

I frowned and looked at my brother. "Tim?"

"I have no idea what he's talking about." Tim shrugged. His green tee shirt moved with his broad shoulders. He had pulled on a pair of jeans that sat on his hips unbelted so that the top of his shorts showed.

"Start at the top and work your way down," Officer Emry ordered the two junior officers. Officer Warwick took the stairs two at a time.

"Let me warn my cousin." I went to take the stairs when Officer Emry stopped me with a hand on my arm.

"They'll knock before entering."

"I'm calling Ridgeway," Tim said again and this time dialed his phone. "This is harassment."

Aubrey let out a loud bark as if to agree.

Officer Emry jumped at the sound and put me between him and the pup. "Keep that dog restrained."

"He's only a puppy."

"A monster-sized puppy," Officer Emry said as he eyed him cautiously.

"He has a kennel on the back porch. Tim could crate him if he makes you uncomfortable."

"Keep the dog away from me and no one will get hurt," Emry said. "You two need to stay in the front parlor or I will have to arrest you for interfering."

"Ridiculous," I muttered. Emry ignored my remark, hitched his gun belt on his hips, and followed Tim back toward the kitchen. I noticed that I had left my purse and cell phone on the counter. I followed the officer back into the kitchen.

He opened cabinets and drawers, pushing aside my containers of flours and sugars and spices. "I doubt there are drugs behind my xanthum gum," I said.

"Just doing my job," he muttered. "I'm here to catch a killer and I won't let any part of the investigation go wrong."

I shoved my hands in the pockets of pink-and-white pajama pants. I had put on a long-sleeved tee shirt and discarded my bra as I'd been feeling bloated and hated anything tight on my body. Right then I wished I had grabbed my bathrobe when I'd come downstairs.

Emry ignored me and went through the drawers, searching the kitchen thoroughly from top to bottom. I casually snagged my purse and phone and went back to the front parlor, where Tim sat sprawled out in Mom's blue wingback chair. His hands were in his pockets. His legs were spread wide and his feet shoved out in front of him. His hair still stood on end on the left and his expression was one of disgust.

Aubrey sat at his feet, his head between his paws, looking for all the world as if we had let the bad guys in and wouldn't let him do his job.

"Are you okay?" I asked.

"Ridgeway said he'd be here soon to look at the warrant and ensure they don't go any further than the judge said they could."

I sat on the blue-and-white-striped settee and put my purse at my feet. "I'll call Tasha and give her a heads-up."

I hit her number on the phone and put her on speaker. I perused the warrant as the phone rang.

"Hi, Toni." Tasha's voice came through the speaker. "I'm at the school in the pickup line. Do you need something?"

"Hey, Tasha, you're on speaker. I'm at the house with Tim. Officer Emry showed up with two helpers and a warrant to search the premises."

"Oh dear, that's not good."

Aubrey raised his head and cocked it to the side at the sound of Tasha's voice.

"Are you a suspect?"

"No," I said.

Aubrey sat up as if he wanted in on the conversation.

"It's Tim, isn't it?" Tasha sounded worried.

"I haven't done anything, Tasha," Tim said loudly.

"I didn't think you did," Tasha agreed.

"I thought you should know that they may be going through your things." I glanced out the window to see Brad's Cadillac pull up behind the police cars. "Brad's here."

"I'll take Kip to the deli for a snack," Tasha said. "Seeing the police go through the house will upset him."

"I agree. We'll keep you posted."

"Thanks, Toni," Tasha said. "I'm pulling for you, Tim!"

"Thanks, Tash, but there's nothing you have to pull for." Tim flung his right leg over the arm of the chair. His posture was that of a surly teenager.

"What is going on?" Mindy walked into the parlor. "I was online when they knocked on the bedroom door, said, 'Police,' and entered before I could say anything. It's a good thing I was dressed." She wore a comfy-looking pair of black yoga pants and a tee shirt. Of the three of us, Mindy seemed the most pulled together. Her light brown hair curled perfectly around her face.

"According to this warrant, they have reason to believe there is the possibility of drugs and/or drug paraphernalia in our house."

"It's a dictatorial regime." Tim sneered.

Mindy laughed at my brother's obvious frustration. "The whole thing is ridiculous. They seriously got a judge to issue a warrant to search the homestead for drugs?" She held out her hand and I handed her the warrant.

"Tim's under investigation for a homicide," I said.

"Even more ridiculous," Tim grumbled. "I came over here to get some sleep. Can I sue for work missed brought on by sickness from lack of sleep?"

"Only if you can prove the correlation," Mindy said as she looked over the warrant. "This warrant is iffy at best."

"How do you know?" I stood and held out my hand to get the document back.

"I'm a paralegal." She shrugged. "Law is kind of my thing. I work at Shubert and Engle."

"Shubert and Engle?"

"One of the most prestigious litigation firms in New York City," Brad said as he stepped into the parlor. "I hope you don't mind, but the door was literally wide-open."

"Oh, hello." Mindy raised her shoulders and dipped her head to look up at Brad with wide eyes. I knew that look. Mindy could get any man she wanted. It was second nature to her. I really wished I had at least combed my hair and that my stomach weren't making that obvious grumble sound.

"Thanks for coming so quickly." Tim stood and the men shook hands. "This is crazy. Emry's power hungry."

"Mindy says this warrant is weak." I handed Brad the papers.

"Are you going to introduce us?" Mindy asked, her eyebrows raised.

"Oh, right, sorry," I said. "Mindy McCree, this is Brad Ridgeway, our family attorney. Brad, this is my cousin Mindy."

"So nice to meet you," Mindy said and flashed her perfect teeth. "You've heard of my employers?"

"Sure." Brad gave a short nod and turned his attention to the warrant. "My law school had a class on their win/loss rate and some of your more well-known cases."

"Well, not my cases, exactly." Mindy touched her chest with her fingers. "I'm only a paralegal, but the firm has been in business for nearly a hundred years and has brought in some of the finest legal minds in the nation."

"You must be very busy at work," I said. "Plus, didn't Grandma say you had a serious new boyfriend? How did you find time to take off for this visit?"

Mindy flinched. "We broke up last week. I'd banked quite a bit of vacation. I had to use it or lose it." She shrugged. "That's what happens when you work in a busy environment for nearly ten years."

"Wow, ten years," I said. "Has it really been that long?"

Mindy nodded.

"You're right about this warrant being weak," Brad interrupted and glanced at Tim and I. "This was signed by Judge Loblow. He golfs with the county prosecutor. They're both up for reelection next fall."

"What does that have to do with the warrant?"

"Capturing a murderer would go a long way toward winning votes."

"Politics stinks," Tim grumbled, shoving his hands in his pockets and hunching his shoulders. "I wouldn't have even come to crash here if the cops hadn't hounded me out of my own apartment."

"The warrant restricts their search to only the open areas," Brad said. "Unless you gave them permission to look through drawers, etc."

I frowned. "I didn't exactly give them permission."

A crash came from the dining room.

"I'll take care of this." Brad hustled toward the sound. Today he had on a pair of dark blue jeans, a white dress shirt, and a dark brown suit coat. His feet were encased in leather cowboy boots. His blond hair was combed back and curled by his ears.

"Wow, cuz, you didn't tell me you had a hottie for a

lawyer." Mindy stuck her head out of the parlor to watch Brad walk away. "Is he married?"

"No," I said. "But he did mention something about a New Year's Eve date."

"We have a couple of weeks until then." Mindy rubbed her hands together. "All's fair in love and war."

"Exactly," said Tim. "This thing with Emry is war as far as I'm concerned. Officer Bright, too. Come to think of it, Dan Kelly the prosecutor, is helping harass me. I call an all-out war on them all."

"Come on, it's not that bad," I said. Another crash came from the dining room. "Okay, is that Grandma's china? Because a warrant does not give them permission to break things."

I took off like a shot and hit the dining room with a full head of steam. "For goodness' sake, what are you doing? Breaking all the plates?" I asked as I rounded onto the picture of Officer Emry digging around the glass china cabinet my great grandmother had left to my father who had left it to my mother who had left it to me.

"He claims the door was left open." Brad had crossed his arms over his chest, leaned his bum against the table, and calmly lifted his phone and took pictures of Officer Emry, head and elbows in the cabinet, pushing things around.

"That door was not left open." I pushed the door closed, basically shutting Officer Emry out of the cabinet. "I'm sorry, but my attorney tells me that your warrant does not allow for searches or seizure of goods behind closed doors."

"Unless I have suspicion of drug paraphernalia," Officer Emry said, his giant Adam's apple bobbing as he spoke. "I thought I saw a bong in there."

"A what?"

"A glass apparatus for smoking," Brad said as calmly as he could, but I noticed the corner of his eye twitched. "More commonly used to smoke illegal substances."

"There aren't any illegal substances in this house, nor are there any glass pipes to smoke them with." I crossed my arms over my chest. I could feel the heat in my cheeks. "I know what a bong is," I stage-whispered to Brad.

"As your lawyer, it's my duty to clarify." Brad chuckled at my discomfort.

"The only things in the cupboard are Grandma Ruth's collection of hand-blown art glass." I put my hands on my hips. "You had better not have broken any. They are all one-of-a-kind pieces."

"I only rattled them." Emry lifted his chin. "I'm tasked with doing a thorough investigation."

"Open search only," Brad pointed out. "My clients do not authorize you to go any further than the warrant allows."

"Well, now, I opened kitchen cupboards in front of her and Toni didn't have a problem with that."

"I didn't know you weren't allowed that kind of search," I said. "I take back any implied permission to go through my things."

"Fine," Officer Emry said. "It doesn't mean we can't go through your brother's things."

"What are you looking for . . . exactly?"

"Any evidence of drugs," he said.

"That's what the warrant says," Brad agreed. "Why?"

"Telling you that would obstruct the investigation."

I rolled my eyes at his explanation. "Does this have anything to do with Harold's death?"

"I can't answer that." Officer Emry continued to walk through the room, lifting things that were in plain sight and looking under them as if I might have hidden a stash of drugs under my mother's ceramic poodle.

"So Harold died in a drug deal gone wrong," I surmised.

"I did not say that." Officer Emry narrowed his eyes. "But the killer would know for sure. You were at the hotel yesterday, weren't you? Why?"

"I was visiting Tasha," I said and raised my own chin. "You don't have to be a killer to put two and two together on the drug search and the murder."

"Wait—you identified the dead guy?" Tim asked.

I bit my lip. I'd forgotten that Tim had been sleeping and didn't know about Harold.

"Yes," Brad said with concern in his gaze. "The victim was positively identified as Harold Petry."

"What?" Tim ran his hand through his hair, tugging at it. "No, no, I would have recognized Harold. That was not Harold."

"Dental records and fingerprints tell us it was Harold Petry," Officer Emry said. "I understand you two had a falling-out a year or more ago. Gives you motive."

"What? No, that's crazy. I have nothing to do with drugs or Harold's murder. He was my best friend." Tim pushed against the doorjamb. "He was my freakin' best friend."

"Your name was on the room registry," Emry stated. "A good investigator looks at the obvious first."

"It's obvious I had nothing to do with it. I would not kill my best friend." Tim closed his eyes in disbelief. "Someone is framing me, and when I find out, I'll—"

"You'll what?" Emry narrowed his eyes and hitched his gun belt.

"Let his lawyer know and cooperate with the police to bring the killer to justice." Brad filled in the awkward silence. "Come on, Tim, let's go make sure those two newbies aren't tearing your room apart."

I watched Brad expertly corral my brother and push him up the stairs. Then I frowned at Officer Emry. "Tim didn't know it was Harold. How could you be such a jerk?"

"Oh, he knew," Officer Emry said. "He and Harold were drug dealing together and I'm going to find proof."

"There aren't any drugs in this house."

"Then you have nothing to worry about, do you?" he asked. "It would be best if you leave this investigation to the professionals."

"Oh, I'm not going to investigate. I have dozens of cookies on order and I'm not feeling well. The last thing I have time for is to follow up ridiculous clues some idiot is falsifying to frame my brother."

"Good," Emry said and sniffed. "See that you stay out of this investigation."

"Quit coming into my home and I'll be happy to stay out of it."

"Keep your brother out of your house and I will have no need." His blue eyes glittered.

"He's my brother, and this is his home." I gazed at him defiantly and scrunched my eyebrows. "What is it that you have against Tim anyway?"

"Hey, I'm going to go pick Grandma Ruth up for an early senior dinner," Mindy said. She had pulled on a camel-colored wool trench coat and brown gloves. "Want to come?"

"I can't," I said as Officer Emry moved on to the den. "I've got to get back to the bakery."

Mindy shook her head. "It takes a lot of dedication to be a baker if you're going when you're not feeling well. Wait—can you do that? Can you cook when you're sick?"

I let out a long breath. "First of all, I have celiac disease. It's a chronic condition that is not contagious. You can't give it to anyone . . . except maybe your children, as it tends to run in families."

"Wait, we're family."

"Yes, and you should be tested. Sometimes the symptoms can be masked or show up in arthritis or other autoimmune problems," I answered. "Not that a blood test is conclusive. Second of all, I'm devoted to my work because it's my dream job. I'm living my dream life." I waved my hand.

"Your dream life includes caring for your mother's house and being invaded by policemen at random?" Mindy's eyes were hard. She snorted. "Some dream."

"Okay, so it's not a perfect dream." I shrugged. "But it's my dream. What's yours?"

"My dream?" Mindy pursed her red-painted mouth. "To live in New York and to have money and sophistication."

"How's that working for you?" I put my hands on my hips.

Mindy's mouth went flat and she wrung her hands. "I'm fine. I have a great apartment in Manhattan and that is far better than some old house in Oiltop, Kansas."

I took a deep breath. Mindy had never been my favorite cousin. She always hated to acknowledge that we were her family. As a kid she'd told everyone she was an orphan. As soon as she'd graduated high school, she had left Kansas for New York and never looked back. That is, until she showed up at my door this morning.

"Look I don't want to fight." I put up my hands. "I'm a little cranky is all. Go have dinner with Grandma. Tell her I said hi."

Mindy's shoulders relaxed. "Okay. I will." She gave me a quick hug. "Keep an eye on that gorgeous lawyer for me, okay?"

"I'm sure you're better at that than I am," I said and patted her back.

"I know." She grinned and winked.

A glance at the clock in the foyer told me it was nearly four. I needed to find Brad and see if he would stay until the cops left so that I could get back to the bakery.

My biggest hope was that this time, they didn't confiscate anything of value, like my computer. During my last investigation they took my computer, which was bad. A lot of my online business information was on that computer. Which reminded me, I should probably get a backup for my hard drive. I added that item to my mental to-do list. I sighed. I did not have time to investigate anything. How was I going to get out of helping Tim when he and Grandma Ruth were so insistent that I do?

CHAPTER 8

"I can't believe you're not investigating." Tasha and her son, Kip, sat at the small table in the bakery kitchen and watched me make cookies.

"I promised myself I'd stay out of this one," I said. "I have to trust Officer Bright."

"You know how I feel about Calvin," Tasha said. "I am very close to thinking he's the one for me. But according to Tim, the police searched our home with no real compelling reason other than the prosecutor plays golf with the judge. Calvin can't be everywhere to ensure this is done right."

"My teacher says it takes a lot of proof to get the paper to search your property," Kip said.

I looked at him with curiosity. "She does? Why were you talking about that?"

"They're learning about the constitution in class," Tasha said.

"They can't search your stuff without a lot of suspicion." Kip played with the little colored packets of sweeteners.

"The police got an anonymous tip that Tim had brought drugs to the house." I layered my second batch of triple-layer cookie dough with white chocolate cookie dough and dark chocolate cookie dough with the pistachio dough. Both kinds of triple cookie used three types of dough that were rolled out into a rectangle. They were then stacked one on top of the other and refrigerated for two hours. Once they were cold enough you could slice the dough into layered bars and bake them into the classic triple cookie. I liked to make the Neapolitan with pistachio and cherry and the dark and white chocolate with pistachio for the holidays. They looked really pretty on a cookie tray.

"That's ridiculous," Tasha said.

"That's what I said. Then Brad called. It seems Officer Warwick discovered cocaine in the garage." I rolled out dough, putting my anger into my rolling pin. "I couldn't believe it. There is no way there were drugs in or near my home. I explained that anyone could have had access to the garage. Tim is being framed."

"They found drugs in our garage?" Tasha's eyes were wide with horror.

"Cocaine's real name is benzoylmethylecgonine," Kip said as he ran a toy car around the edges of the table and down the sweetener packet roads. "It comes from the leaves of the coca plant."

"Really?" I raised an eyebrow and gave Tasha a look. Tasha shrugged.

"Yes," Kip said without looking up. "It can be used as a stimulant, an appetite suppressant, and a topical anesthetic. It's illegal to possess, produce, or distribute cocaine for non-medical purposes in almost every country."

Tasha and I stared at Kip in stunned amazement.

"Where did you learn that?" Tasha asked.

Kip shrugged, his attention on the toy car. "I read it on a website."

"I thought your computer access was restricted," I said.

"I was working on a research project for school."

"What kind of research project?" I pressed. Seriously, what were they teaching in schools if a fifth grader could tell us what benzoylmethylecgonine was?

"We're studying Peru," Kip said.

"Huh." I turned back to my cookies.

"Surely Officer Warwick could tell it was planted." Tasha wrapped her hands around a thick white ceramic mug filled with coffee.

"Brad was there," I said, embarrassed that my lawyer had witnessed the discovery of drugs in my garage. "He argued that the garage door was broken and anyone could get inside, which is true. But Officer Emry threatened to press charges against me for possession."

"Wow." Tasha shook her head. "How do you avoid that?"

"I'm not certain I can; I mean, it was found on my property. The only argument we have is that they can't prove why it was there or who put it there. Still, it builds the case against Tim or even me."

"What about me or Kip or Mindy? What about Grandma Ruth or any one of the members in your giant family. For all you know, that could have been there for decades."

"Officer Emry is sending it away to the state lab. There's some kind of test they can run on the drug that gives an approximate date of manufacture."

"Wow, what can't they figure out?"

"They'll also look for fingerprints," I said. "But with the lab backed up, it might be a month or more before we know anything."

"What are you going to do in the meantime?" Tasha wondered.

"I had Tim install a lock on the garage. Then I'm going to make gluten-free cookies for the cookie exchange, and

I'm going to run my business. I refuse to live my life around policemen and their silly theories."

"But Tim is clearly being framed."

I frowned. "I know. Grandma thinks I should investigate. I want to help. I really do, but I have Christmas baked goods to get out. This is my make-or-break season for the bakery. I could lose everything I've been working for if I don't get these baked goods out and shipped on time. We won't even talk about the cards I need to write and send and presents to purchase for my friends and family. Investigating crimes takes time and timing. Half the discovery is being at the right place and at the right time to uncover clues. I simply don't have that kind of time."

"Did you ask Grandma Ruth?"

"I'm certain she's doing her own investigation for her blog." I shrugged. "I'm hoping with Grandma on the loose I don't need to investigate." It sounded lame to my own ears, but things were desperate at the bakery. I was working fourteen-hour days, sick or not.

"Grandma Ruth is in her nineties. I'm not at all certain that she can stay awake long enough to solve a murder."

"That's silly. As Grandma often told me, who better to investigate than a retired person?"

Tasha frowned. "I don't like it. Tim is a great guy. There's no way he did this."

For a brief moment I wondered what would happen if Tim had done it. Then I shook my head and went back to baking cookies. There's no way Tim would kill anyone let alone his best friend. Plus, Tim was smart. He'd never put a room in his name and then kill someone. It didn't add up. It was common sense not to leave your name at the scene of the crime.

"I'm leaving it to the professionals," I said under my breath. "I have to or I'll lose my livelihood. I have to trust that Officer Bright is smart enough to arrest the right man."

"Are you making chocolate chip cookies?" Kip asked. "I like chocolate chip."

"I made the dough earlier when I found out you were coming," I reassured him. "Do you want to help me bake them?"

"Sure." He jumped up. "What's first?"

"First you need to get the dough out of the fridge." When he rushed to the refrigerator I continued. "The chocolate chip cookie dough is in the yellow ceramic bowl on the second shelf, to the back."

"I found it!" He pulled out the big bowl.

I had him put the bowl on the table, then wash his hands and put on an apron while I dug up a small scoop.

"You scoop them like this," I said, careful to show him the proper amount on the scoop. "Then place them on the cookie sheets in rows of four across. You should get six rows down."

"Four times six is twenty-four," Kip said.

"Yes, it is." I patted him on the shoulder. "Did you do that math in your head?"

"I'm good at that," he said and scooped dough.

"Yes," I said. "Yes, you are."

"I don't like it." Tasha stood.

"I'm sorry? You don't like math or you don't like Kip making cookies?" I glanced over and noted Kip had a stricken look on his face as he stood frozen with a scoop full of dough in his hand.

"No, no," Tasha reassured her son. "I like math and it's okay for Kip to make cookies."

The boy smiled and continued to plop dough on the cookie sheet.

"I don't like that you're trusting our small-town police force to keep your brother from being framed."

"How can I fit in an investigation? Do you have time to help me bake or investigate? I don't think so. Besides, Tim might think he wants me to investigate but he doesn't really want me in his business."

"Are you certain of that?"

"I know my brother." I remained firm. "It nearly killed him to come over and ask if he could crash at the house. He's an individualist. Can you imagine him letting me go through his life with a fine-tooth comb? Seriously I wouldn't want Richard in my business. Tim doesn't really want me in his. He's just tired and feeling abused."

"The way things are going, he may be a bit more than abused if someone doesn't help him." Tasha's words echoed through the kitchen ominously.

I hoped with all my heart that she was wrong.

CHAPTER 9

They say that numbers don't lie. But they certainly kept me from sleeping. I'd sat down earlier in the evening and done my weekly accounting for Baker's Treat. The only way I would make it through the next six months was if I delivered on all the potential business over the holidays.

It never failed that orders fell off dramatically in January when everyone made resolutions to eat less. I had to be prepared for the expected slump in sales.

Getting through diet season without losing money meant that baking and shipping would become my life until New Year's Day. I would have no spare time for anything but sleep.

Grandma's insistence that I take days off every week was fine in theory. But if I didn't work all day in the bakery and all evening at home filling orders, I would not have enough cash stashed to keep Baker's Treat open until tourist season in the spring. Luckily I'd had the foresight to run a special on a social living network to buy two dozen, get one dozen gluten-free cookies free. It had increased my orders to the point that I would reach my goal of funding the bakery through diet season if I stayed on task, focusing solely on baking.

I barely had time to get enough sleep, which was why it was so frustrating to toss and turn during the precious few hours I had allotted.

Forget about time for Christmas. I swore that next year I was going to start Christmas shopping in February like Tasha. For now I had to accept that this year was a wash. At least the family's traditional great reveal—where we uncovered Christmas decorations from the 1970s that hung in the basement year-round—meant that decorating was done. The fact that they were up year-round was suddenly a good thing. I had no time to even do my own tree in the parlor like I had hoped.

Grandma Ruth had volunteered my house for the family Christmas Eve dinner before church. At least that was potluck.

My assistant, Meghan, was a dream stepping up and handling the counter business while I took orders and kept the mixer busy with cookie dough.

Don't get me wrong. I love to bake. But I hated to be so dependent on income that I had to say yes to every order. Times like this I wished I had stayed a mail-order business. Or turned the house into a bed-and-breakfast like Tasha had suggested a few months ago. But knowing that someone had been hiding drugs in my garage for the police to find showed me that opening my property to the public might not be a good idea.

Thank goodness Tim and Mindy entertained each other, because I was a terrible hostess. I'd come home at nine and baked another ten dozen peanut butter cookies before I'd climbed into bed.

Knowing how sensitive some people were to allergens, I always made my peanut butter treats at the house and not

the shop. It was difficult because Kip was sensitive to peanuts. I had to ensure he was safely upstairs when I baked.

I liked to use almond flour in my recipes, so I wasn't tree
nut free, but peanuts are a legume and so I reasoned that
they were best baked separately so that there was no cross-
contamination for those with allergies.

The Baker's Treat website spoke of my attention to detail
for allergies. Having experienced the bad effects of eating
even the tiniest bit of gluten, I was diligent in my work.

Faced with financial ruin or heroic baking, I chose heroic
baking. I was relatively young and could get by with a minimum amount of sleep for thirty days if it meant keeping
Baker's Treat alive. Or so I thought.

It would help, though, if I actually slept in the five hours
I had. I glanced at the clock. It was 2:50 A.M. I had to get up
to go to work in ten minutes. Sleep had been fitful for me
as Tasha's words about leaving my brother's fate in the hands
of Officer Emry kept running through my brain.

I decided to take pastries to the police department when
Meghan got in in the morning. A talk with Officer Bright
might really help ease my mind. I might be able to choose
hard work to keep Baker's Treat afloat, but I couldn't choose
my bakery over my brother's life. I simply had to squeeze
in time to keep ensuring that Calvin was doing his job or I
wouldn't sleep at all, and lack of sleep made for bad baking.

I got out of bed, turned off my alarm before it could
sound, and hit the shower. Dressing in my uniform of black
slacks and white Baker's Treat tee shirt with a big pink
cupcake logo, I contemplated the combined fates of my bakery, my brother, and the odd jealousy I felt when Mindy
batted her eyelashes at Brad. What was wrong with me? I
had promised myself not to date for a full twelve months
after my divorce. When I made the promise I was considering my divorced friends and how quickly they jumped from

one bad relationship to another. The last thing I wanted or needed was to make the same mistakes I had with Eric.

My ex-husband was gorgeous and had made me feel like a goddess. That was until I realized he was making a lot of women feel that way. It seemed marriage vows only worked for me. Eric had kept on playing the entire span of our three-year marriage. But, you see, I have this thing where I believe in my vows. When I said "I do" it meant that all others were forsaken. It was part of the deal that he forsake all others for me, too.

Eric hadn't seen the problem with his transgression. He couldn't understand only sleeping with one person the rest of his life. I shook my head at my own naïveté. I picked up the brush from my dresser and brushed my fine yet crazy curly red-blonde hair into a low ponytail.

The lack of sleep had me looking even more washed-out than usual. I put on some BB cream, pinched my cheeks, and dabbed mascara on my nonexistent eyelashes. A glance at my reflection caused me to sigh. There was no way I could compete with Mindy. Brad might have thought he was interested last month, but now that tiredness put deep shades of purple under my eyes, I wouldn't blame anyone who backed away slowly.

I had a bakery to save from financial ruin. Why, oh, why was I fixating on my visiting cousin's flirtations? Disgusted with myself, I turned from the mirror and nearly tripped over Kip's puppy. "Whoa, hello, Aubrey, try not to sneak up on me like that. Someone's bound to get hurt." I patted him on the head. The vet said he was nine months old and already he was so big I didn't need to bend down to pet him.

Aubrey just looked at me with playful eyes. I went downstairs to the kitchen and the dog followed behind me. Usually Kip had the puppy sleep with him. So either Kip was up at 3:00 A.M. or the puppy had begged to be let out. It sounded as if someone was in the kitchen. I stepped into the light from the stovetop fan. "Kip?"

"It's me," Grandma Ruth said from the dark recesses where the kitchen table sat.

"Grandma, what are you doing here? Did Bill bring you?"

"Naw, Bill's out of town for his aunt's funeral," Grandma said with a wave of her large square hand. "Are you going to make coffee or simply waste time staring at me?" Grandma wore a quilted plaid men's shirt and a long red butterfly skirt. Her black socks came up to her knees and stood out against the white of her athletic shoes. A brown fedora sat on top of the table. Her puffy down coat hung from the back of her chair.

"I'm making coffee," I replied and headed toward the machine. I suppose I should purchase one I could set with a timer so that the coffee turns itself on a few minutes before I get up. But really, how hard is it to push one button in the morning?

I let Aubrey out into the dark fenced yard to do his business and grabbed two pale blue thick ceramic mugs from the cupboard beside the sink. "You need cream with your sugar?"

"A splash will do just fine," Grandma said. I pulled out the tiny container of half-and-half from the fridge. By this time the coffee was finished, filling the air with its sharp fresh scent. I poured us each a cup and took them to the table, where I set one in front of Grandma and the other in front of the empty chair.

Grandma added an incredible amount of artificial sweetener to her coffee and then a splash of half-and-half until her glass was practically overflowing.

"Bill still had an aunt who was alive?" I had to ask. I assumed the man was close to Grandma's age.

"She was born after him." Grandma bent down and slurped the coffee from her cup until it was low enough for her to pick up without spilling. "Bill's grandmother had two families. She had two kids when she was in her teens and then two more when she was in her late thirties. Bill was ten when his aunt was born."

"Wow, then she died young."

Grandma grinned. "It's all relative, isn't it? You were surprised she was alive until you learned she was seventy-nine. Now she's young."

"I guess you're right." I ran my fingers along my coffee cup. "What's on your agenda for today?"

"Oh, the usual." Grandma slurped more coffee.

"What's the usual? You're here early. That's not usual. Did you find out anything yesterday about Harold or the possibility Tim's identity was stolen?"

"I'm checking on Tim. It's not usual that he's moved back in with you. As far as I can tell, Tim's identity is safe. Have you discovered anything more about the murdered kid and who might have put Tim's name on the registration?"

"I know I said I'd investigate if he asked me—and he asked me. But I can't this time, Grandma." I picked up my coffee cup and warmed my fingers. "I'm loaded down with orders for Baker's Treat. That's the business I want. I'm not a private investigator."

Grandma pouted. Her freckles ran together in the folds of her pout. "But you're so good at it."

"I nearly got killed both times," I said and shook my head. "I don't see how that translates to 'good at it.'"

"You saved me." Grandma put her hands on the table. "Who knows what would have happened if you hadn't investigated."

"I'm not good at investigating. I trust that Brad and Officer Bright and Chief Blaylock can do their jobs. Tim is clearly innocent. It will all work out."

"What about the drugs that they found in the garage?"

I winced. "Those had to be planted. Whoever is framing

Tim is doing a bad job at it. The garage was unlocked. The police have no evidence that those drugs belonged to me or Tim or anyone in the neighborhood."

"Your mother would have died of embarrassment if drugs had been found in the garage while she was alive."

"I know," I said wryly and sipped my beverage. "I was horrified until I saw Tim's face. It doesn't help that his best friend growing up was murdered, but then to be framed for it. It's awful. Whoever is doing this is really screwing with Tim. It makes me so angry." I hardened my expression. "When they discover who is behind this, I'm going to have a word or two to say to them."

"Tim riled someone, that's for sure. He tells me he hasn't gotten into trouble in years."

"Yes, he swore the same thing to me," I said. "It makes me wonder if someone didn't wait to frame him. Take my friend Todd. He waited years to get back at a bully. Not that Tim would ever bully anyone. But people carry resentment for a long time."

Grandma pursed her mouth. "That could be. But that takes a lot of patience. Men don't usually have that kind of self-discipline."

"That's true," I agreed, raised my eyebrows, and nodded. "In my experience patience is not a male virtue."

"Not much of a female virtue, either, if you ask me."

That made me smile. I pushed my chair away from the table and stood. "I've got cookies to make. Do you need a ride home?"

"No, I have my scooter," Grandma said.

"It's dark and"—I glanced out the window as I put my cup in the sink—"snowing." I opened the door and let Aubrey in. The puppy shook the snow off, flinging it all over the small mudroom. I grabbed a towel near the door and dried him off. "Really, Grandma, you can't drive your scooter down the street in the dark and snow. It is December."

The puppy got free and snagged the towel out of my hands, shook it hard, and ran off, towel dragging on the ground beside him. I straightened and washed my hands.

"When I was young, people walked in the dark and the cold all the time. Besides, I'm meeting Mindy for breakfast," Grandma said. "She's going to take me out. So she can take me home if the scooter can't. By the way, she's afraid to cook in your kitchen. She said you were weird about her using your toaster."

"She brought real bread and made toast." I crossed my arms over my chest. "You know that any exposure to gluten can make me sick. I can't afford another attack. I've got to meet my orders this month to stay in business for another year."

"Are things that tight?" Grandma's blue eyes filled with concern.

"They'll be fine, if I work," I reassured her.

"You don't have to work alone." Grandma crossed her arms to match me. "You have family who can help."

"I know," I said and shook my head. "But Baker's Treat is my dream, Grandma, not Lucy's or Tim's or Richard's or Rosa's or Joan's or Eleanor's."

"That doesn't matter," Grandma insisted with a wave of her hand. "We have family to help us out in a pinch. Don't get all proud and stuck-up, thinking you don't need our help."

"I'm not stuck-up or proud." I straightened and dropped my hands, taken aback by her comment.

"Yes, kiddo, you are." Grandma gave me a look. "You think you don't need your family. You do."

I swallowed a lump that formed in my throat. "Of course I need my family. Everyone needs family."

"Promise me if you need us, you'll ask. Don't let your business go under without asking for our help. Remember how furious you were with Tasha for not telling you about her troubles with the Welcome Inn?"

"Yes." I nodded.

"We feel the same about you."

Well, that was certainly something to think about. Here I was embarrassed by my big family. I thought it was such trouble that they always were asking me to host this party. Cater that holiday. Investigate random crimes. It never occurred to me that they expected me to do the same to them.

A wave of guilt flooded me. I pushed it aside. "Why is Mindy here, Grandma? She keeps telling me about her perfect life in New York. If things were so perfect, why is she staying here? And another thing, her boyfriend that you told me about is nonexistent."

"She's here to visit her Grandma before I die," Grandma Ruth said as she went back to her coffee. "Besides, she's your cousin and you have room to house her."

I grabbed my coat from the hooks by the back door and sat on the bench to put on my winter boots. The forecast was for four inches of snow today. "She thinks Brad's cute," I mentioned as I tied my laces.

Grandma raised her eyebrow and studied me. "What do you care? You're not dating the man, although I have no idea why."

"I don't care." I shrugged. "Except . . ."

"Except what?"

"I don't want to see Brad get hurt."

"Why would Mindy hurt him?"

"She's only visiting. She's made it very clear she's not staying."

"She works for a famous law firm." Grandma shrugged. "She might be able to get him a job in New York City."

"Oh . . ." I paused. "Do you think he'd leave Oiltop?"

"He's a smart man," Grandma said casually. "I would bet he would go for the right offer. What's keeping him here?" She gave me the sideways eyeball.

I shrugged. "Sure, I can see that. He deserves the prominence of a New York law firm if that's what he wants."

"Exactly. You can't expect anyone to put their life on hold just because you are."

"My life is not on hold."

"So you say. Have a good day." Grandma concentrated on her coffee.

"Bye." I walked out the door into the particular quiet of early morning snow. It was dark. The air was still. Snow fell straight down in big fat flakes.

I looked up to the sky and stuck my tongue out to try to catch a flake or two.

I didn't have time to date. Why, then, was I so mixed up inside over the possibility of Brad dating Mindy?

CHAPTER 10

"How long has your brother been dealing drugs?" Candy Cole walked into the bakery. She looked gorgeous with her slender figure, her cool porcelain skin, and her champagne-colored bobbed hair. Today she had on a thick wool coat cut in the "fit-and-flare" style and a dark fedora with a gold bow. She wore ridiculous high-heeled boots that made the girl in me think, *Cute!* While the grown-up in me thought, *Really? How do you walk in the snow in those?*

"Good morning, Candy," I said and glanced at my assistant, Meghan. "What can I get you this morning?"

"Coffee, please, and one of your fruitcake muffins," she answered. I didn't know how she ate like she did and still remained slender. Some people were blessed with the perfect metabolism.

I grabbed a thick white oversized cup and saucer and handed it to her to pour her own coffee. Then I placed a gluten-free fruitcake muffin on a small white plate.

"Seriously, Toni." Candy took the cup and saucer and

handed me her debit card. "How long has Tim been dealing? Was he able to keep it from you the entire time or did you suspect something?"

I made a face. "Tim has never dealt drugs. If he had, our mother would have whooped him and then sent him to Grandma Ruth for her to whoop."

Candy leaned in over the counter. "Off the record, how long have you known?"

"Two seconds," I whispered back. "Ever since you said so when you walked in." I straightened and handed her back her card. "Seriously, Tim has never dealt and never will deal in drugs. No one in my family would do that. It's not in our DNA."

"Are you sure?" Candy raised one golden eyebrow. "The police have unearthed hotel records going back a year or more. It seems your brother ran an active business out of a variety of hotels."

"What? That's crazy." I frowned at her. "Seriously, the only time I've ever seen Tim even the least bit high was when Chrissie Bale left him and he got drunk. The man hasn't been high ever."

"How do you know? You've only been back in town ten months. . . ." She stuck her chin out and picked up her dishes. "I have it from a good source that the police found a dealer's bag of drugs in your garage. How do you explain that?" She poured coffee in her mug. Any outsider would think she was simply having a conversation with me. But I knew that Candy was smart as a whip and just as sneaky. Her phone might be recording our entire conversation. In the state of Kansas it was legal to tape conversations as long as one person knew they were being taped. In this case, Candy knew.

"The garage hasn't been locked in years. Anyone could have put that bag there. Besides, it seems pretty convenient that no one has ever found drugs on our property until last night, when the police came on a 'leaked' suspicion." I put air quotes around *leaked*. "Someone is working very hard to frame Tim."

"If that's true—and I'm still of the belief that Tim is a drug dealer, but if he's not, it certainly seems like a lot of trouble for someone to go to in order to frame him. How do you explain that?" She set her dishes on the closest table, sat down, and tasted her coffee.

"Someone is out to get him." I put my hands on my hips.

"Most criminals are too lazy to frame someone." Candy took a bite out of her fruitcake muffin. "Wow, are these good," she said. "Not only are criminals lazy, but they tend to not be very smart. If—and I say 'if' in a very nonbelieving way—if someone is framing Tim, they are not only smart, but one step ahead of Hank and Calvin." She shook her head. "Frankly, I don't see how."

I tilted my head and studied her. "Perhaps the criminal is counting on you to be lazy and not pursue the reasons why anyone else would frame Tim."

Candy laughed. Her laughter was lovely and loud like ringing bells. "Well, now you have me there." Candy winked. She sipped her coffee and finished off her muffin. "I guess that means you aren't going to help me investigate this one."

"Not this time." I put my hands in the pockets of my wrap-around apron. "It would be awesome if you came up with something on your own, though. Keep me posted, okay?"

"I will. If you will."

"It's a deal." I stuck out my hand. She got up and put her slender, perfectly manicured fingers in mine and gave them one firm shake.

"Deal." She gathered up her things and waved good-bye. "Remember we shook on it. That means I get first exclusive when Tim confesses."

"You can't confess to something you didn't do. Think

outside the box, Candy," I shouted as she walked out the door into the whirling snow. I shivered and went back into the kitchen.

Meghan worked on cutting out sugar cookies in snowman and Christmas tree shapes. The ovens kept the kitchen warmer than the front with its big windows. It smelled of vanilla and spice and baking yeast breads.

Today Meghan had her black hair pulled up in a beehive bun. Her lips were painted candy-apple red. Her eyes were accented with black liner. Like me, she had short fingernails. Not only were they easier to keep, but they were more sanitary for a baker. We used spoons to taste test, etc., but we rolled out enough dough to know that clean hands free of decoration worked best in our environment.

The only time I missed having a perfect manicure was when Candy was in the room. Her nails were always camera ready.

"The snowmen give us more cookies per batch of dough," Meghan observed. "I would have thought the Christmas tree would have." She worked the metal cutters back and forth, cutting one cookie right side up and the other upside down.

I looked over her shoulder. She really was leaving very little scrap dough. I frowned. "Maybe I should get one of those rollers with the cookie cutters on it so that all you have to do is roll over the dough and it cuts with the edges so clean there aren't any scraps."

"You could." She shrugged her white polo-covered shoulders. "I like how organic the cookies feel when you do them like this. It really gives it a home-baked feel."

"True," I agreed. "It's why I originally used the metal cutters. I didn't want anyone to think they're getting factory cookies. Unfortunately, it takes more time per cookie."

"I think people appreciate it when you take time."

"Yes, I agree," I said. "But it means there is less time for sleeping."

"You know Grandma Ruth says there is plenty of time to sleep when you die."

We both chuckled.

I went to the freezer and pulled out a long roll of cookie dough. Then I sprinkled sugar on the cold marble slab and unwrapped the roll onto the sugar. After I pushed up my sleeves, I pulled a fresh silver knife out of the knife drawer, cut even half-inch strips from the roll, and put the cookies on a cookie sheet. These were pistachio cookies—green for the season. After they were baked I'd frost them with chocolate or red buttercream. "Are we on schedule?"

Meghan glanced at the sheet I had put up in front of her, detailing minute by minute what had to be done in order for us to meet all our Christmas requests.

"Barely," she said honestly and shot me a look. "You figured for some time to wait on customers, but I'm not as fast as you are when it comes to cutting cookies."

"You worry too much about perfection," I said and pointed with my chin. "Part of the homemade feel is an imperfect snowman or a wonky Christmas tree. The ladies who give our cookies to class parties or cookie exchanges don't want people to know they bought them."

"Huh, I hadn't thought of that," Meghan said. "I'll be sure and put in an imperfect one now and then."

"The colored icing will finish off any imperfections." I popped a full cookie sheet of pistachio cookies into the top oven.

"That reminds me, we're out of red icing," she said. "I washed the icing bucket and prepped the ingredients."

"Thanks!" I grabbed a bowl and wiped off the clean plastic bucket, then poured powdered sugar, water, vanilla, a pinch of salt, and red food coloring made from beets into a large bowl and put it on the mixer stand. I pushed the stand into the up and locked position and let the paddle wheel blend the ingredients into a lovely red Christmas icing with enough substance to hold its shape when piped.

The door bells jangled and I looked up at the clock. It was 11:00 A.M. This was usually our slow time, when most people had finished breakfast and were not yet ready to think about tonight's dessert or this afternoon's snack.

"I'll get it; you keep cutting." I wiped my hands on a towel and walked out into the shop. Standing in front of the pastry cabinet was a man who looked vaguely familiar. "Hello, can I help you?"

"Oh my gosh, it's Toni Keene. How are you? I haven't seen you in years." He was tall with dark hair and pretty blue eyes. He had the look of a local rancher, with his shearling jacket and dark denim jeans. "You don't know me, do you?" His grin widened. "It's Lance Webb. I was in your brother Richard's class. I thought you were in Chicago. What happened? Why are you working at this weird bakery?"

"Hi, Lance," I said and tried to smile. "You look good."

"You do, too," he said with a wink. "You've grown up well."

"Thanks," I said. "What can I get you?"

"Seriously, Toni Keene. What are the odds?"

"The odds are good," I said with a cheerful smile. "I own the place. Was there something special you wanted?"

"Oh, sure—wow, you own the place? Hmm, well, I was looking for donuts, and the donut shop was closed. Chris Walker said I should try this bakery." He looked over the baked goods in the counter. "Do you have any real stuff?"

"It's all real, Lance," I said. "It's just gluten-free."

"So, like, no wheat?"

"No wheat."

"What the heck is it made out of?" He took off his hat and scratched his balding head.

"Rice flour, corn flour, almond flour, to name a few

ingredients," I said and grabbed a bakery tissue. I reached in and pulled out a plate of petit fours. "Taste."

Lance made a face and took a step back. "Maybe next time," he said and put on his hat. "I really was only looking for donuts."

"I have those in the morning," I said. "But they're gluten-free, too."

"Well, maybe I'll come back in the morning," Lance said with a wink. "Toni Keene. Go figure."

"It's Holmes now," I said. "I was married."

"Was?" he asked, his blue eyes shining with interest.

"Yes, was," I said. "But not anymore. Anyway, Holmes is why the bakery is named Baker's Treat."

"I don't get it." He frowned.

"Sherlock Holmes . . . Baker's Treat?" I hinted. Surely he'd get it now.

"Still nothing," he said with a shake of his head.

"Sherlock Holmes and Baker Street . . ."

"Okay. . . ." He stepped back as if I had lost my mind.

"Never mind," I said with a shrug.

"Cool," he said and looked relieved. "You don't happen to know where there's a good donut shop that's open, do you?"

"No," I said.

"Okay, well, nice to see you again," he said and put on his Stetson as he headed toward the door.

"You, too," I said with a sigh as I watched him walk out. It was a shame to waste my time on people who came in and then refused to even taste the baked goods. I placed the tray with the tiny cakes back in the glass case as the door bells jingled. I looked up to see my favorite rancher step into the shop. Sam Greenbaum was tall, dark, and handsome in every sense of the word. He was older and it showed only in the crinkles at the corners of his eyes and the gray at his temples. He took his cowboy hat off the minute he walked in. His thick corduroy coat was covered in snowflakes and his dark lashes held melted drops.

He had the broadest shoulders I'd ever seen, and that was saying something because Brad's shoulders were pretty broad. He sent me a smile full of straight white teeth. It was a heart-melting smile that I swear he must practice in his mirror every morning. It certainly worked on me.

Not to mention his tight-fitting Levi's, his brown cowboy boots, and the workman's gloves sticking out of his back pocket. All in all he was one nice piece of eye candy in the standard cowboy uniform.

"Hi." I smiled and tried not to melt too much.

"Hey." He studied me until my knees threatened to go weak. "I forgot my gram's got a poker game this afternoon."

Sam's grandmother was a social butterfly and a mover and shaker in Oiltop society. She also loved impromptu poker games and it was her love of entertaining that had first sent Sam out seeking treats for her get-togethers. He had stumbled upon Baker's Treat by accident, but every time he'd come back it was purely on purpose. Like Brad, Sam had asked me out more than once. It wasn't that I didn't want to get closer to those broad shoulders and that flat abdomen. It was that I wasn't ready for any kind of relationship. Not even with a nice-looking cowboy who bought his gram treats.

Trust me. While not taking Brad or Sam up on their offers of coffee, dinner, and company was like passing up a triple-chocolate raspberry dessert with whipped cream and a cherry, it was as good for me as watching my gluten intake. For once in my life I had to consider my well-being first.

"What would Gram's poker players like? Savory or sweet?" I asked. "I have both."

"I think they're going to be drinking tea, so anything sweet will do." He shook his head. "Tea and crumpets at a poker game. Weird, right?"

I laughed. "Not as weird as my family unveiling our 1970s Christmas decorations every Thanksgiving."

"Okay," he said and played with the brim of his hat. "Your family wins the weird award."

"I know." I shook my head. "It's why I moved to Chicago in the first place. I wanted to go somewhere where my family reputation wouldn't matter."

"I, for one, am happy you moved back to Oiltop. I think that Meghan feels the same." His gaze was serious, his smile widened, and his eyes sparkled. "Even if your family is weird."

"You gotta love weird." I shrugged.

"Speaking of family, Gram tells me you found another dead guy."

"Actually, the housekeeper, Maria, found the dead guy. I called it in to 911."

"Do you know what happened?"

I took out a long bakery box and put together two dozen assorted cookies and petit fours that I knew Sam's grandma's crowd liked with tea. "No, not really." I stopped and looked at Sam. "That's a lie. The dead guy was Tim's best friend growing up. Someone murdered him, and that someone is framing my brother, Tim, for the deed."

"Really?"

I set the full box on the counter and folded the top down carefully. "Really. They used Tim's name when they signed into the hotel room. I don't know if the murder was premeditated or not, but for some reason they intended for my brother to be a suspect should anyone question what happened in that room."

"The Red Tile Inn seems an odd place to plan a murder and frame someone."

"Not really." I rang up his order. "It's only a quarter mile from the turnpike exit and is often frequented by truckers and other weary travelers looking for a few hours of sleep before they continue on to Kansas City or Oklahoma City."

"I can see that. It is kind of on the outskirts of town."

He pulled two twenty-dollar bills out of his wallet and handed them to me. I made his change and handed it to him.

"Are you going to investigate?"

"I think I'll stay out of this one," I said. "I've got a business to run, and at some point you have to trust Chief Blaylock and Officer Bright to do their jobs. Right?"

He put the bills in his wallet and the change in his pocket. Then stuffed the wallet in his back pocket and picked up the pink-and-white-striped box. "If you say so."

"I do say so." I leaned on the counter. "Tell your gram I said hi."

"You know she's going to ask why I'm not dating you yet." His eyes sparkled.

"Tell her it's me, not you," I said gently.

"I'm a patient man." He smiled at me.

"First things first," I said. "I need to get through this month. Once I'm done with the holiday orders, I'll have more time to work on other parts of my life."

"Then I'll be knocking on your door New Year's Eve at the stroke of midnight."

"Ha! That's still weeks away," I reminded him. "You never know what will happen between now and then. You could meet someone else. Someone who makes you say, Toni who?"

He laughed and showed his even white teeth. "I highly doubt that."

I tilted my head. "Have you been good this year? Santa might bring you someone smart and beautiful for under your tree."

"I've been very good," he said with a short serious nod. "I only have one redhead I want to see under my tree."

I blushed. The heat in my cheeks caused me to fan my face. "There is no time this month, I swear."

"Fine, what are you doing New Year's Eve?"

"I'm going to the Pantry Club with Grandma Ruth and Bill."

"The Pantry? Isn't that the old timer's dance club out in Augusta?"

"Maybe," I said. "It's tradition for Grandma to go. Bill buys a table of ten every year, so Grandma asked me to come. My cousin Lucy says that it'll be big fun. All the old-timers come out in their jewels and furs and dance the night away. I hear there's a conga line and balloons fall at midnight."

"It sounds like the place to be on New Year's." He winked at me, picked up his box, and went to the door.

"I think the venue is sold out," I called after him.

"It's a good thing I have connections in the country club set." He set his Stetson on his head at a jaunty angle. "Have a good day."

"Bye." I watched him walk out and down the snow-covered sidewalk to his big black pickup truck. He was a lovely man. He and Brad had this contest about who would go out with me first. I shook my head at the girl in me who loved the competition. With Mindy sniffing around Brad, and Sam's grandma's society matchmaking, I knew there was a chance I might end up with neither date in January.

I needed to be okay with that if it happened. Right now I wasn't so sure.

CHAPTER 11

"Let me guess, you've been here at the bakery over twenty-four hours straight."

I drew my eyebrows together. "Why do you say that?"

"There's a cot in your office." Tasha nodded toward my empty office as she hung her coat and gloves up on the hooks in the back kitchen of the bakery. It was late afternoon and she was between work and having to pick up Kip from his tutor.

"Why do you assume it's for me? Tim could've gotten fed up with bunking at the house."

"I saw Tim at home this morning," Tasha said, grabbing a mug and pouring herself some coffee from the ever-ready pot in the back kitchen. She stirred in three packets of artificial sweetener.

"Fine, you caught me." I shrugged. "I've got to push out nearly one hundred orders in the next three weeks if I hope to have enough money to pay the mortgage next quarter."

Tasha climbed up on a kitchen stool and hugged the mug

in her hands. She looked gorgeous in dark blue linen pants and a white shirt patterned with tiny red and blue flowers. She tossed her blonde hair and it fell into place in perfect curls. "Is business down?" she asked.

Tasha had recently had to make some serious business decisions when her bed-and-breakfast went under. I hoped I wasn't going to be following in her footsteps.

"Christmas is one of the few holidays where I can pad my revenue for the lean times . . . like January, when everyone starts dieting for the New Year. Or March, when they start to think about swimsuit weather and their figures."

"But your food is gluten-free." Tasha tilted her head.

"Gluten-free means no gluten. It does not mean low-calorie or diet food." I went to the freezer and pulled out a batch of oatmeal–butterscotch chip cookie dough.

"Can you get your assistant to help you?"

"I have." I sent her a wry smile. "But Meghan doesn't own the place. There are only so many hours I can work her."

"You need a third person." Tasha sipped her coffee.

"True," I said as I scooped out dough and plopped it into neat rows on prepared cookie sheets. "But I have to be able to afford to pay a third person. It's sort of a catch-twenty-two. What I really need are more customers." I paused. "You'll never guess who stopped by yesterday."

"Who? Was it Chief Blaylock? Do they have an idea of who killed Harold?"

"No," I said with a sigh. "It was Lance Webb."

"Wait, *the* Lance Webb? The one I bought that CD player for?"

"One and the same," I said with a shake of my head. "What a winner. He came in looking for donuts and when he found out the bakery was gluten-free he refused to even taste anything. This is what I'm up against."

Tasha drew her eyebrows together, pursed her lips.

"Lance always was a bit of an arrogant loser. You should think about getting a loan from the bank."

"Are you kidding me?" I stopped, dough-filled scoop in hand. "The banks are worse than Lance. The bankers won't even look at me at a Chamber of Commerce meeting. It's as if, if they don't acknowledge me, I don't exist." I turned back to my cookie sheets and quickly finished filling them. Picked one up and put it in the top oven. Then I checked the bread baking in the bottom oven.

"I think that's terrible." Tasha shook her head. "They're missing out on income and supporting local businesses."

"It's part of living in a small town." I shrugged and put the second sheet in the oven. "The bankers in town are used to wheat farmers and beef ranchers. They don't know what to do with a gluten-free bakery. I think they think Baker's Treat is too big of a risk."

"Go online." Tasha sipped her coffee. "Get a loan from one of those online banks."

"That's a good idea," I said with a sigh. "What I need to do is sit down and go over my business plan again. The problem with that is . . ."

"You don't have time," she finished for me.

"It's a vicious cycle, isn't it?"

"Have you talked to Tim? He is so quiet. It's not like him to shut himself into a room."

"I think he's trying to stay out of sight until they figure out who killed his best friend," I said. "Poor guy."

"I think he's grieving. I mean, Harold was his best friend for years. Were they in touch still?"

I paused and thought about it. "You know, I don't know. I've been away too long." I drew my eyebrows together. "Funny, but Tim hasn't mentioned Harold in years. I heard they had a falling-out."

"Sounds like something you should find out," Tasha said

pointedly. "Maybe Harold was into drugs and that's why they quit hanging out."

I worried my bottom lip. "I really don't know."

"Your brother needs you," Tasha said cautiously. "Did he ask you to investigate?"

I took a deep breath and blew it out slowly. "He did. But I'm not a private investigator," I pointed out. "I'm afraid I'll make things worse."

"For you or for Tim?" Tasha asked.

"For both," I said and went back to work doling out cookie dough and filling baking sheets. "I need to concentrate on making Baker's Treat a success, and that's taking my every waking hour." I paused and winced. "Am I being selfish?"

"It's not selfish," Tasha said. "It's practical."

I put the empty bowl in the sink and sprayed it with water to keep the bits of dough from hardening. "Thank you!" It was nice to have a friend who agreed with you. "Do you think that Tim understands?" I wiped my hands on the dish towel I had pinned to the waist of my apron.

"Tim doesn't need you to save him," Tasha said.

"Wow, tell Grandma Ruth that. She's upset with me for not investigating. For a minute I thought you were, too." I pulled out a clean bowl and checked my list. Next up were cherry, pistachio, vanilla refrigerator cookies.

"I'm not upset that you aren't investigating," Tasha said. "I'm upset that you are working so hard. You can ask for help, you know."

"I know," I said. "Grandma scolded me, too. I told her that we have to trust Chief Blaylock and Calvin to do their jobs. It's why we pay our taxes."

"Calvin's supersmart and dedicated," Tasha said. "He'll figure it out."

"How's that going, by the way?" I asked.

"What?"

"Seems to me that the last time we talked about Calvin, you told me you thought you were falling in love with him." I measured ingredients and added them to the bowl. "Have you told him?"

"Yeah."

"But I haven't seen a lot of him lately," I said. "Is he okay with the way you feel?"

"We're taking things slow." Tasha sat back.

"Whose idea is that?"

"Mine," she said. "I really am falling for Calvin, but I'm trying to slow things down for my own good. I realized that I keep jumping from one relationship to another fast and furiously trying to create a family with Kip and . . . well, we've seen where that's gotten me in the past." Tasha's last boyfriend had tried to kill us both. She wasn't exactly the best at picking a good man.

"I understand. It's why I promised myself that I would wait a year from my divorce to date again. If you keep doing what you've always done you tend to get the same results."

"Right?!" She got up and filled her cup a second time. Then she pinched a muffin out of my seconds pile. I would sort out my baked goods and any that came out too crisp or not perfectly shaped I'd set aside. The seconds were usually given to family or friends. It's not that they weren't as good or as tasty as the premium goodies. It was simply a matter of professional pride not to sell anything less than a perfect baked good.

"Mmmm, this is good!" Tasha said. "Is that cranberry?"

"Yes, those are cranberry walnut muffins," I said. "I was experimenting with a variety of spices to go with the fruit."

"Well, these are perfect, if you ask me." She saluted me with the muffin and sat back down.

"So you're taking it slow with Calvin?" I didn't give up on my train of thought. Calvin had access to our house whenever he spent time with Tasha. Not that I suspected a police officer, but it did seem odd that whoever framed Tim was always one step ahead of the investigation.

"As slow as I can," she said as she bit into the muffin. "The man is gorgeous and has that broad-chested-hero thing going on. It's hard to say no to that." She sighed. "I really am quite in love with him. It's scary how quickly I fell for him. That said, I'm not getting any younger. If I want to have another child I need to do it in the next five years."

I snapped my head around. "You want more kids?" This was the first time I'd heard her say that was even a possibility. After Kip presented with Asperger's syndrome, Tasha had blamed herself and sworn off bringing any more kids into the world. I tried to reassure her that it wasn't anything she had done. I'd spent years sending her research on the issue, but she'd always been adamant that it was something she'd done. The jerks she'd married hadn't helped her with her self-esteem. That's why it was so surprising that she'd mentioned having another child.

"Kip's been learning about family at school. He was asking me why he doesn't have brothers or sisters. He also mentioned that you have a lot of brothers and sisters and so do all your cousins."

"You're thinking about more kids because of Kip?" I knew that didn't sound right.

"No, that's not the only reason. My biological clock is ticking." She sat back, her fingers curled around her mug. "Isn't yours?"

I swallowed. "Yeah, sure. I mean, I think about it . . . but it might be too late for me." I shrugged. "I went through this period with Eric where I was crazy to have babies. I mean, why else do you get married? But he was never ready and then I discovered I had celiac—not that I couldn't get pregnant but it took a lot of time to diagnose and I was on all kinds of prescription drugs before they figured out what it was. I didn't want to chance being pregnant with so many different drugs in my system. Then after I got straightened out, it was too late. I walked in on Eric and Tessa and the rest is history."

"And now you have Baker's Treat."

"Yes." I nodded. "Now this is my baby. But that doesn't mean I don't want kids. I'm not getting any younger, either. But I've seen too many women jump from one bad relationship to another because they are afraid to be alone."

Tasha colored. "It's not so much fear of being alone. . . ."

"Oh, honey, I wasn't talking about you." I went over and gave her a hug. "I'm sorry. I was talking about our classmates Cindy Oxford and Joyce Menard. All they did was cry and complain about their first husbands. Then when they were finally free to choose better men, they were so obsessed with finding 'the one' that they dated a new guy every weekend and were suddenly remarried before the first anniversaries of their divorces."

"Oh, true." Tasha patted me back. "Now they complain worse about their second husbands than they did their firsts."

"If it helps, I think Calvin Bright's a really nice guy."

"I know." Tasha sighed. "But cops have this reputation of being unfaithful."

"Really?" I tilted my head.

"Have you never heard that? Supposedly women throw themselves at a man in uniform. Especially one who 'rescues' them." She used air quotes around *rescues*.

"Calvin doesn't really seem the type to be unfaithful. He goes to church every Sunday. I see him coming out of the service."

"My first husband went to church."

"Okay, I get it. You're worried that he's a cliché." I went back to making more dough for the triple-layer cookies. "It seems to me that there's a cop-and-donut cliché as well. I have yet to see Calvin at Daylight Donuts."

Tasha smiled. "He says you have better coffee."

That warmed my heart. "See? I told you he was a smart man."

"I don't think taking things slow is bad this time." Tasha got up and put her cup in the sink. "But it's hard to be patient when your clock is ticking."

"Truer words were never said," I said. She gave me a hug.

"I've got to get to work. Let me know if you need help with your cookies. It's what friends do."

"Thanks." I hugged her back. "Have a good day."

"One more question."

"What's that?" I asked.

"Who are you going to date? Sam or Brad?" Her eyes twinkled at my dilemma.

"Who's to say either will want to date me once things slow down here?"

"Oh, please, you're the best catch in town."

"Thanks, but tell my cousin Mindy that."

"Oh, I meant to ask you, how is Mindy? She's in the house, but she never says anything more than 'hi' to me or Kip."

"Something is up with her." I shrugged. "I don't know what yet, but she's made it clear to me and Grandma Ruth that she has her eyes on Brad."

"Ouch, how does that make you feel?"

"There isn't much I can say. It's not like I can tell her to stay away from him if I'm not dating him."

Tasha narrowed her eyes. "Well, I can."

I laughed. "Good friends . . ."

"Help you bury the body," Tasha finished.

The thing is that it wasn't Mindy's body I was worried about. It was the skeletons buried in her closet.

CHAPTER 12

Very early the next morning Grandma Ruth stopped by and sat down at the tiny table in the kitchen of Baker's Treat.

"Tim's been renting rooms in local motels at least once a week for the last six to eight months." Grandma drank the coffee I put in front of her along with a small plate of my latest cookies.

"No, he hasn't," I said. "I know for a fact he's been living with me since Mom died. Except for the last thirty days, when he moved into his own apartment."

"My sources say he usually used the room for a few hours then vacated it."

"That's ridiculous. Who are your sources?" I rolled out more dough. This time it was all sugar cookies, which would be cut into fun animal shapes then carefully frosted to a high-gloss sheen. Each sugar cookie would have a small hole punched in the top before baking so that they could be used as Christmas tree ornaments.

"A good reporter never exposes her sources," Grandma Ruth said with her mouth full of cookie. "Besides, I have access to printouts of some of the smaller hotels' registrations. Tim's name shows up quite often."

"Is that legal?" I shook my head and started cutting out giraffes and elephants. "Forget I said that. Just because someone used Tim's name doesn't mean it was actually him. Knowing Tim, he could easily have had his identity stolen. He never uses any precautions. He tells me that he's too much of a nobody. No one would want his identity."

"Not true," Grandma said and slurped coffee. "Small-town nobodies are the best targets to steal. No one knows them well enough out of their own town to even question if they are who they say they are."

"That's what I told Tim." I carefully transferred the cutout cookies from the slab to the cookie sheets. Any cookies that changed shape or broke apart were tossed back into the bowl to be rerolled.

"Besides, I already checked into Tim's credit record. There isn't any proof of identity theft. That said, no one seems to remember if it was Tim who rented the room. They see the name and Tim's face pops up in their mind's eyes."

"Eyewitnesses are notoriously unreliable."

"You know what I think?" Grandma crammed another cookie in her mouth.

"What?" I put the full cookie sheets into the oven and set the timer.

"If Tim didn't rent all these rooms, then someone else local did."

I drew my brows together. "What makes you think they're local?"

"People would remember a stranger. Even better, they would remember if a stranger used Tim's name." Grandma slurped more coffee.

"But if someone like Todd used Tim's name, they would know that, too. Wouldn't they?"

"Oh, they might or they might not. Think about it. If Todd stopped in and registered, would you verify he wrote his name and address? What if he says he has family coming in and he's paying? No one would turn down his money. They know where he lives."

"You are devious," I said.

"Thank you," Grandma said and grinned.

"What does Tim have to say about this?"

"Tim says he has no reason to rent rooms. He has his apartment and the house."

"That's certainly true." I rolled out more dough. "Didn't the police consider that?"

"It was one of the first things they considered." Grandma nodded. "According to my sources, there was drug paraphernalia left at each room site. Word around town is that Tim's been drug dealing out of these rooms."

"That's crazy!" I washed my hands, dried them on a towel and checked the cookies in the oven. It was time to switch them from middle rack to high and high to middle. "Tim never took drugs, let alone sold them."

"My sources tell me Tim's been making some big dents in his credit card debt lately."

"That doesn't mean anything." I cut out more cookies as the scent of vanilla and butter filled the air. "He deliberately stayed with me at the homestead to pay off his bills."

"The entire case is circumstantial." Grandma nodded. "But Tim is the best suspect so far. We need to find another suspect if we want to get the police away from Tim. Once they identify a person of interest, they can be like a dog with a bone. They'll stick with Tim until the bitter end."

"Poor Tim," I said and transferred cookies. "I wish I had more time to help."

"So you've decided not to help your brother."

"Wow, when you put it that way I sound like a horrible person."

"Don't worry, we all know how busy you are." Grandma kept up with the guilt.

I rolled my eyes. "I called Brad, didn't I? I'm letting Tim stay at the house, aren't I? What more should I do?"

"You could help me figure out who really did this."

"I love you, Grandma, but I'm up to my eyeballs in cookie orders."

"I can see that," she said and licked her finger to pick up the crumbs left on her plate and shove them in her mouth. "Cookies are good."

"Thanks."

"Is there any reason Meghan can't bake some?"

"Meghan has school finals this week. Her school has to come first."

"Is that why you've been sleeping in your office? Or is it because you think Tim is guilty and can't bring yourself to sleep under the same roof as a killer?"

"Grandma!"

"What? Isn't that a question the police might have for you? Have they interviewed you in depth yet?"

"No and no," I said, pulling baked cookies from the oven and putting in the new trays. I used parchment paper to cover the bottoms of the cookie sheets. It helps with slippage and cleaning the cookie sheets.

"Well, my guess is that Officer Bright will be contacting you to talk about Tim," Grandma said. "You are your brother's alibi."

"Grandma, I'm not his alibi. I didn't see him at all that night. He was at work and his apartment."

"Well, you certainly can tell them if Tim was home when any of these rooms were rented." Grandma lifted a stack of papers.

Curious, I went over and took the papers. She told the truth. She actually had printouts from several of the local hotels. "How did you get these?"

"You know anyone with a computer and skills can get online and discover everything about you, from what color underwear you wear to when the last time you tithed to church was." Grandma gave me the hairy eyeball.

"I go to church," I said. "Really, and if your sources are good enough they'll know that I do give ten percent."

"They did." Grandma sat up straight and sent me her oversized grin. "All my grands are good kids."

"Except Tim." I pointed to the papers in my hand.

"That's not Tim," Grandma said. "I don't know who it is, but it's not Tim. I'm hoping you can help me figure out who this impersonator is."

I looked through the records. You could tell which hotels were favorite places for Oiltop's relatives to stay. Some were filled with local names, while others—closer to the turnpike—had almost all strangers' names.

"It doesn't make any sense. If you were trying to impersonate someone, why wouldn't you make up a wide variety of names and stay at the trucker motels?"

"What do you mean, 'trucker motels'?"

"The ones closest to the turnpike, where people generally don't have reservations."

"Maybe because people would get suspicious if they recognized you coming in and writing different names down."

"I see. The smartest thing to do to hide in plain sight is to put down the name of a local."

"I'm going to find out who was on duty when this stranger rented the room. Maybe they can help me out."

"I've already been over this with Tasha," I said and handed Grandma her papers back. "She wasn't working the desk at the time the killer rented the room. And the Red Tile does not video its reception area."

"What about the outside areas?" Grandma asked.

"There's a camera on the corner of the outside. It basically covers the cars coming and going, not the people or which room they are staying in."

"But there is video. . . ."

"Yes, Tasha gave it to Officer Strickland the day of the murder." I tilted my head. "Wait, if they've looked at the video, then they know that Tim was never at the hotel."

"Rumor is that it's still being processed." Grandma waddled over to the coffeepot and poured herself another cup.

"Please ask me and I'll get it for you," I said and plopped three more cookies on her plate as she clutched chairs until she was back to the table. The kitchen was not that large. I had asked her not to drive her scooter around inside. Grandma groused but did as I asked, all the while making a big production over how hard it was for her to get around without her scooter. Still, what worked for her endangered anyone else who could not get out of the way of the scooter fast enough. So you see why I waited on her hand and foot. It was purely to save myself from injury.

"I will tell Brad about the video. He'll ensure he gets to see it," I said. "He gets to see all the evidence—right?"

"Only if they arrest Tim." Grandma bit into another cookie. She drew her eyebrows together and creased her forehead. "What's in these?"

"Why? Don't you like them?" I asked. For Grandma to not like a cookie, there had to be something very wrong.

"No, they're good," she said and studied the remaining part of the cookie. "Are they lemon bars?"

"They're lemon with a gluten-free sugar cookie crust."

"I wasn't expecting lemon at all," Grandma said. "Lemon bars are usually spring cookies."

"Really?" I tilted my head. "Mom made them every Christmas. She said they helped lighten the dessert tray filled with heavy cookie flavors."

"Talking about dessert trays"—Grandma popped the remainder of the cookie into her mouth then took a slurp of coffee—"I promised you'd cater the senior center's Christmas lunch. There are a lot of older people who have special diets. Can you make any of these diabetic-friendly?"

"I've been known to make cookies for people with diabetes as long as they watch the carbs in the rest of their meal. I won't be responsible for sugar comas."

Grandma waved her big flat hand in the air. "We're all grown-ups at the center," she insisted. "If we eat ourselves into a coma, it's because we choose to do so. You are free from all responsibility."

I put my hands on my hips and studied her. "I'll call Grace Ledbetter and ask her how many cookies you'll need. When's the Christmas luncheon?"

I grabbed a marker and went over to my working board, where I listed cookie orders and dates.

"Next Thursday," Grandma said. "We'll need at least four dozen assorted on a couple of big trays."

"That's a lot of cookies." I raised both eyebrows.

"Everyone comes out of the woodwork for the senior center party. Think of the exposure you'll get."

"Right." I bit my bottom lip and drew an arrow between two full days of baking and pointed it at the sideways words—*Grandma senior center, diabetic cookies, 4 dozen assorted*.

I could do it if I made the Thursday cookies two days early and stored them in the freezer to have a baking marathon on Wednesday. I studied the overflowing schedule. What I really needed was an employee who was good with sugar work. It would be awesome to give the decorating work to someone else.

Don't get me wrong, I loved to be creative in design, but at busy times like now, it would be nice to have help.

"Grandma, do you know anyone with experience working with confection?"

Grandma pursed her lips and moved them sideways in thought. "No, I don't, but I can ask around. Are you wanting to hire someone?"

There it was again: the problem of little to no cash flow. "I wish I could pay, but not yet. Instead I could offer them an internship and experience on their résumé."

"Then I'd go see Leslie Writ at the community college. She's the head of the cooking school. I'm not so sure they have anyone who can do more than flip burgers or make a mean milk shake, but it's worth a try." Grandma brushed the crumbs off her hands, hobbled over to her scooter, climbed aboard with a sigh, and backed around with a *beep, beep, beep.* "She might know someone from the culinary institute in KC."

"Thanks, Grandma," I said as I made a note on my scratch paper to make an appointment with Leslie.

"My pleasure." Grandma grabbed her overstuffed down coat from the coat tree near the door and put it on. "See ya, kiddo." She stuffed her orange-red hair into her favorite fedora, pulled down the ear flaps she'd sewn into it, and tied them neatly under her chin.

I walked over and gave her a kiss on the cheek. "It's cold out there; do you want me to have Meghan get you a ride?"

"No thanks," Grandma said with a twinkle in her eye. "I'm looking forward to doing donuts in the bank parking lot."

Grandma scootered out into the cold darkness of a winter morning. I watched as she hollered, "Yahoooo!" and did a couple donuts in the parking lot, barely missing the back of the van.

I was this close to calling the cops on her, but her excitement for the season was fun to see. I closed the door, locked it, and went back to baking cookies.

I rolled out gluten-free gingerbread to quarter-inch depth and cut out reindeer. Christmas carols played over the radio. As I slid another baking sheet into the top oven, the radio announcer came on. "Fourteen days until Christmas," his deep voice said. "If you don't have your gifts ready and wrapped, you're going to be left with empty stores. So be sure and come to downtown Oiltop this week and shop Gray's Hardware or Millie Green's Antique Store. The big day is rapidly approaching. Don't be left ordering things online. Trust me, a good wrench set the morning of Christmas far outweighs the best gift card under the tree."

Darn, I still hadn't gotten any Christmas presents. I looked at the busy kitchen. It smelled of spice and molasses mixed with vanilla and chocolate. Meghan had put up a three-foot artificial tree in the corner of the counter nearest my office. Its fiber-optic lights glowed through the construction-paper ornaments she had placed on it.

Christmas. I had only so much time to make cookies and fill orders. The regular fun of the season was lost in the sheer volume of work I was trying to get done.

The good news was that my family didn't mind the seconds that piled up haphazardly on plastic platters. Burnt sugar cookies always reminded me of Christmas. My mother tended to get distracted making cookies. Having six kids would do that.

My poor mother would be a wreck if she were alive today to hear that the police thought Tim was a drug dealer and a possible murderer. In fact I could feel her ghost standing behind me with her arms crossed, tapping her foot, wondering why I wasn't moving heaven and hell to see that Tim was proved innocent.

CHAPTER 13

"I saw Grandma Ruth trying to pop a wheelie on her scooter," Meghan announced as she came into the kitchen. With a smooth move she took off her camo green coat and hung it on the coatrack. Her hat and gloves were stuffed inside.

"I don't think that's possible on a Scootaround," I said as I crumb-coated the three cakes that had to be out the door this afternoon. Cakes tend to have crumbs that get into the frosting. Bakers use buttercream to make a light first layer all over the cake to catch all the crumbs. We called that the crumb-coat. Once frosted, the cakes went back into the fridge to set.

"All things are possible with Grandma Ruth." Meghan grabbed an oversized bib apron from the hooks on the wall and wrapped it around her slender figure.

Oh, to be nineteen and slim again. Not that I was curvy by any stretch of the imagination. When people described me they usually mentioned Popeye's girlfriend, Olive Oyl.

I guess that was better than being compared to Little Lotta. Still, it was hard to work with an attractive nineteen-year-old. Not that we would date the same guys or anything. For goodness' sake, I could be her mom.

I shook my head to clear my thoughts. I was tired. That was all. I finished the crumb-coats and put the cakes in the freezer. Meghan started on the giant pile of dishes. Her black hair was casually twisted into a messy bun at the nape of her neck. She wore a white tee shirt and black slacks. When she'd come in, she'd traded her snow boots for a pair of comfortable athletic shoes. When you spent eight to ten hours on your feet each day, you were glad for sensible shoes.

"Did you sleep here again?" Meghan asked.

I grabbed a coffee mug and poured the dark brew. Then I sat at the table and put my tired feet up on the chair across from me. "I'm still five orders behind." I rubbed the back of my neck. "It's good to be busy."

"Not if it kills you." Meghan glanced at me. Her thick black eyeliner accented the sparkle in her eyes. "Please take care of you. I need this apprenticeship."

I smiled at her and took a swallow of my coffee. "You want me to take care of myself purely for your selfish reasons."

"Yes." She nodded. "And because you haven't taught me how to make Danish yet."

"If I get these cookie orders done and delivered, I'll make Danish for the Saturday-morning crowd."

"Oh, cream cheese or jelly?"

"Both, plus lemon."

"You are my new favorite person." She turned back to the dishes. The doorbells rang. I glanced at the clock. It was after nine and the morning rush had already happened. Whoever had come in would get the morning leftovers. I hadn't had time to start on the tea and desserts for the late-afternoon crowd.

"I'll get it," I said and waved at Meghan to finish the

dishes. "I need those bowls to make more cookie dough. If I can get it in the freezer in the next hour I'll finally be on track to catch up."

"If you don't get caught up, it won't be because of me." She turned back to the sink.

"Hello?"

I pushed open the kitchen door to see Mindy standing in front of the counter. "Mindy, Grandma left some time ago."

"I wasn't looking for Grandma," Mindy said. She bared her teeth in an insincere smile. Pulling off her gloves one finger at a time, she looked around. "So this is your bakery."

"Yes." I put my hands behind my back to hide the rough, dry skin and supershort nails that were more than a little ragged.

Today Mindy wore a neat navy shift dress with black tights that showed off her long legs. Her coat was a knee-length wool overcoat in a classic beige with big black buttons. "The décor is . . . quaint."

"Thanks, it's supposed to be," I said and watched her circle the room taking in everything from the front windows to the yellow-painted walls to the wrought iron café tables and chairs.

"With a name like Baker's Treat—I would have thought you would have gone for a more English tearoom look."

"There are two cabbage-rose-print wingback chairs." I pointed to the two chairs in the far corner grouped around a wrought iron side table. "In the summer we'll put the wrought iron out on the sidewalk like a café. Then I'll get a few more English teahouse pieces," I said. "Can I get you a cup of coffee? We have organic coffees as well as other gluten-free, organic, and allergy-free products."

"Sure," she said and waved at me dismissively as she studied the paintings I had bought from students at the junior college.

I grabbed a fat oversized white cup and matching saucer

and set them on top of the glass counter. "The coffee is at the coffee bar." I waved toward the three containers of coffee and the one hot water for teas. "There's cream, half-and-half, skim milk, and soy or almond milk. There are also a wide variety of sugars. I recommend the agave. It tastes the most like sugar, but it's healthier."

"Thanks." Mindy put her gloves in her coat pockets, picked up the mug, and stepped over to the coffee bar. "Everything looks so . . ."

"Good?" I added.

"Hmm, I was going to say *professional*." She pumped coffee into her cup, added a splash of cream, and turned back to me. She raised the cup to her red-painted lips.

"What do you mean, 'professional'?" I drew my brows together and tilted my head.

"It looks like a real bakery," Mindy said. "Smells like one, too."

"It *is* a real bakery," I countered. "What did you think it was?"

"Oh, I don't know, some sort of hippie kitchen. You have this weird, granola-like diet."

"Gluten-free is not a granola, health-freak way of living. Lots of people live with food allergies. Just because they can't eat fried Twinkies doesn't mean they're hippies. Because I bake allergy-free doesn't mean I'm not a 'real' professional."

"Oh, did I sound insulting?" She batted her perfectly mascaraed false eyelashes. "I didn't mean to insult. I'm simply surprised. That's all. You've been busy since your mother died."

Mindy was my cousin and from New York, so I decided to believe her when she said she didn't mean to sound insulting. "I like to stay busy. It helps me work out my issues."

"Your issues?" She raised the cup to her lips.

I shrugged. "Between my divorce and mom passing on I've been reexamining my life."

Her head tilted and her shoulders dropped a bit. The mask of perfection slipped for a fraction of a second. "I'm sorry about Auntie. I have no idea what I would do if my mom died." In the next second she was back to her cool perfection. "Don't you feel stifled in Oiltop? I mean, you lived in Chicago for years. It's not New York, but it's a long way from Oiltop." She looked out the window to the windswept gray of Main Street in December. "There's nothing here. It's like being stuck in time." She turned her attention back to me. "Even the radio stations are still playing music from when we were kids and would come visit Grandma. Have you noticed that?"

I shook my head. "I listen for the weather and such. If I want music I'll put on my MP3 player."

The corners of her mouth lifted slightly. "The small town might be backward, but you work around it, don't you? How resourceful."

"Mindy, why did you stop in? I've got to get back to baking."

"I wanted to know more about Brad Ridgeway. Tim tells me he went to KU and was a basketball star."

"Why don't you come on around to the back? That way I can work while we talk."

She eyed the door skeptically. "Is it dusty? This is a designer outfit. I don't want to get whatever you call flour on it."

I shrugged. "Your choice." I turned on my heel and pushed the kitchen door open. In the back it was warm and the air was filled with the scents of yeast, cinnamon, chocolate, and ginger. The radio played popular music and Meghan danced while she finished up the dishes.

Mindy must have really wanted to talk, because she followed me into the back. "Oh, hello."

Meghan stopped and cautiously observed Mindy and her designer duds. "Hey."

"Mindy, this is my assistant Meghan. Meghan, this is my cousin Mindy. She's here to visit for a while."

"Hello," Mindy said again and stood just inside the door balancing on her sky-high stilettos as if she had suddenly entered a lion's den.

Meghan gave Mindy a small smile then turned to me. "I pulled the ingredients for the plum pudding that's next on the list."

"Thanks." I went to the small sink and washed my hands with soap and water. It was a bakery policy to always wash your hands when you entered the kitchen. I glanced at Mindy, who hadn't moved. She seriously looked scared. I had pity on her. "Mindy, you can sit at the table. That way we can chat and you won't be in the way."

"Okay." She carefully teetered her way to the table, pulled out one of the chrome-and–red vinyl chairs, and sat down. Her coffee cup rested carefully on the table while she maintained a wary distance from the surface as if it were covered in an invisible contaminant that might ruin her outfit.

"Can I take your coat?" Meghan asked her. "We usually hang them on the hooks near the door."

"No thank you, I'm fine." Mindy waved her away.

Meghan shrugged. "Suit yourself." She turned to me and rolled her eyes. Her silver eyebrow piercing wiggled when she raised an eyebrow. "I'll go change out the coffee."

"Thanks." I nodded. It was policy to change the coffee every hour so that it remained hot and fresh throughout the day. If the coffee was good, people tended to stop by more often, and if they bought coffee they were more likely to purchase something to go with it.

"She is certainly interesting to look at," Mindy said when the door swung closed behind Meghan. "Is she a Goth?"

"I think *Goth* is passé," I said carefully. "Meghan is highly creative and a hard worker. She's apprenticing under me so that she can move on to culinary school in Chicago and New York."

"Huh." Mindy raised her cup and refused to lean back

against the chair. She looked so stubbornly uncomfortable, but she was a grown-up and it wasn't for me to change her mind. Still, I couldn't help thinking how silly she was being.

I added ingredients to the spotlessly clean stainless steel bowl, my back to Mindy. I hated to be rude, but I was swamped and not ready to indulge her insults with my complete attention.

"So tell me about Brad," Mindy said as I measured vanilla and brandy flavors.

"What do you want to know?"

"Well, what is he doing here in Oiltop? Is he seeing anyone? Not that that matters—as long as he's not married, he's mine."

"That's a tad arrogant, don't you think?" I kept my voice bland and refused to look at her.

She laughed, a clear, bright, and lovely sound. "Dear, dear cousin, I'm from New York and I'm gorgeous. There's no way any man from little Oiltop, Kansas, could resist this." I caught her movement from the corner of my eye as she waved her hand over her outfit as if she were a living, breathing goddess.

Part of me envied her for feeling that way. Part of me wanted to slug that smug grin off her face. Mostly I took a deep breath and decided to be a grown-up about it. "As far as I know, Brad's not seeing anyone right now. He moved to Oiltop when his dad was terminally ill. As for why he stayed, well, you'll have to ask him."

"Oh, I will," Mindy said with a gleam in her eye. "Trust me. This time next week, that gorgeous lawyer will be putty in my hands."

"Didn't you say you were going back home? Why bother with an Oiltop man if you plan on leaving soon?"

"Oh, honey, it's no bother to have a vacation fling with a man like Brad. Besides, if things work out, neither one of us will be in Oiltop after the new year."

CHAPTER 14

Candy Cole came tearing back into the kitchen through the front door, Rocky Rhode on her heels taking pictures as he walked. "Tim's been arrested," Candy announced into her phone's recorder. "Did he really kill that poor man? Do you know why he did it?" She shoved the phone under my nose.

"What?" My hands were covered in rice flour from kneading sweet dough for cinnamon rolls. It had been a heck of a day. First Grandma, then Mindy, and now this. I glanced at the clock. It was nearly 7:00 P.M., and I hadn't had much of a break all day. The good news was that my to-do list was shrinking . . . some. The bad news was that Meghan had been taking more calls and clocking in the e-mails for web orders all day. As the old saying goes, *When it rains, it pours. . . .*

"Your brother Tim was arrested," Candy said with a salacious gleam in her eye. "Officers Strickland and Emry were seen going into the FedEx warehouse and they brought your brother out in handcuffs."

"What?" I asked again, unable to comprehend the full meaning of her words. "Why would they do that?"

Candy's eyes lit up. "That's what I'm finding out. My readers want to know . . . Did your brother kill that man?"

"They arrested Tim?" I felt a bit numb. I knew I was tired from working and a bit desperate due to my financial crunch, but I also knew Tim was innocent. They couldn't arrest an innocent man. Could they?

"Sit down." Candy looked at Rocky and motioned to the stool beside him.

Rocky went to sit down when Candy gave him the evil eye.

"Oh," Rocky said and pushed the stool toward me. He then had the nerve to photograph me while I sat down before my shaky legs caused me to collapse.

"Do you need water?" Candy asked, suddenly concerned for my welfare. I didn't believe it. She was concerned for her story and didn't want me to pass out before she got it.

"Candy, are we really friends?"

"Of course!" She handed me a glass of water. "I told you that we are. Didn't we meet for coffee two weeks ago? What about when I helped you with George Meister's killer?"

"Candy, you tried to prove I killed George," I pointed out and sipped my water. I had watched her get it from my sink; otherwise I might be afraid she dosed me with something.

"That was just me doing my job." She waved it off. "Just like I'm doing my job now. I'm a reporter, Toni. It's what I do, and I can't keep letting your Grandma scoop me. I'll be out of a job. Now, what do you know about Tim being arrested this evening?"

"I don't know anything." I guzzled the water. My thoughts ran wild. Did Brad know Tim had been arrested? What did they have on Tim? How did he go from being a person of interest to being arrested? Who was going to pay Tim's bail? How would they pay it? My stomach clenched.

"You're Tim's sister. He's staying at your house. Are you telling me you had no clue he murdered that man?" Candy moved her phone speaker from herself to me.

"I'm telling you, I saw the crime scene. There is no way my brother Tim or anyone I know could do something so violent and so horrific." I put the glass down on the counter. The scene in the hotel room flashed in front of my eyes, and my stomach was queasy at the idea that another human being would do such a thing.

"Tell us about the crime scene," Candy pushed. "Did you see anything that would incriminate your brother? I understand you called Tim the moment you found out his name was on the registry. Why did you alert him to the investigation? Did you suspect him?"

"I called my brother to see if he was all right," I said. "Whoever killed Harold might also have killed Tim. I was worried, that's all." I shook my head. "I don't ever impede the investigation. The law is the law and, for the most part, it works."

"You didn't believe that when you were a person of interest."

"It still worked," I argued. "Chief Blaylock never arrested me."

"They arrested your brother Tim. That means they believe that they have enough evidence to indict him. What do you know about the circumstances of the case? Did your brother and Harold fight? Was there a disagreement in the weeks before the murder? What evidence do you think they have against Tim?"

The shock cleared from my brain. I realized that Candy was recording whatever I said. I also realized that Tim needed help. I had to stall Candy enough to get to the police station and find out what needed to be done to help my brother. Suddenly my decision to trust the police to do their job felt weak and stupid.

I stood and went to the sink to wash the gluten-free flour from my hands.

"Come on, Toni." Candy followed me with Rocky behind her taking pictures. Rocky was the local photographer who did all the senior pictures, weddings, and such for the county. In his spare time he was the photo editor for the *Oiltop Times*. He told me once that photojournalism didn't pay the bills, but if he didn't do it he would feel as if he had wasted his talents. So he took studio photos to keep a roof over his head and worked for the newspaper to satisfy the serious photographer in him.

"I've got nothing to say." I grabbed a towel to dry my hands and Rocky took photos of me. "Rocky, stop taking pictures. You won't be able to use them. I won't sign a release."

"Oh, come on, Toni," Rocky said. "You make a good subject."

"Thanks, but no comment." I pushed through the doors to the front of the store, turned the OPEN sign to CLOSED, and locked the door.

"You can't close," Candy said. "Your store hours are until nine and it's only seven."

"My family comes before store hours," I said as I pushed back into the kitchen with Candy and Rocky trailing behind me.

"What about your family should my readers know?" Candy asked.

"Like I said, no comment." I pulled my coat off the rack, tossed a stocking cap on my head, and prepped for the brisk wind that blew the dry bits of snow around.

"You might as well tell me something. If you don't say anything publicly, then the story will be what other people think of you and your brother."

I paused a second before opening the door. "I'm not giving a statement until I talk to my brother and his lawyer and find out what is going on. Now, you can and probably will print whatever sensationalism you need to sell newspapers, but I won't say anything that anyone can take out of context. Do you understand?"

"I understand." Candy lowered her phone. There was disappointment in her blue eyes. "Look, I can't let your grandma scoop me on this. Ernie told me that he'll fire me if I can't do better than a ninety-something-year-old woman."

"I need to find out what's happening." I opened the door into the rush of icy-cold wind. "We'll talk later."

"On the record or off?" Candy asked as she stood in the door frame.

"Whichever my lawyer thinks is best."

"Someday you're going to have to trust me," Candy said with a shake of her head.

"That day is not today," I replied and locked the door behind us. I got in the van. The inside was cold as ice and my breath came out in a thick mist that fogged the windows. After five minutes to warm up the engine and brush the snow off the windows and mirrors, I took off toward the police station.

I had dialed both Tim and Brad but neither answered. Hopefully they were together getting this thing figured out. Luckily Tim's juvenile record would not be admissible in court. My brother was a good man, and I loved him to pieces, but after Dad died Tim had gone through a period of boundary testing. Unfortunately he'd ended up doing four weeks of community service for shoplifting a pack of cigarettes. Then there'd been a vandalism incident, after which Mom had sent Tim to a summer boot camp for troubled youth.

He met some shady characters at the camp. How shady could a fourteen-year-old boy be? Tim never said. He'd come home after three months of grief counseling and team building a changed boy. He never talked about camp, but he'd come home and joined the football team, the basketball team, and student council. He was fun to be around, kind and carefree. Tim lived his life as if each day were his last.

It was why he never married. Dad had been forty when he'd died. Tim figured he didn't have much longer to live so he never settled down. Then last year he'd turned forty—the same age as Dad—and Mom had died. It was Tim's wake-up call. At Mom's funeral he'd said his only regret was he'd never given Mom more grandkids to love.

My brother had gotten a steady job and worked long and hard hours. He'd moved out of my house a month ago and was saving up for a nice little house to buy. He'd told me he was counting on the *Field of Dreams* movie statement. If he built it, she would come.

I never had the heart to tell him marriage wasn't all it was cut out to be. I didn't want my experience to color his opportunity. Even though my marriage had been a disaster, in my heart I always believed everyone should try marriage at least once. For some people it was a life of sweet companionship. Marriage was a relationship where the good outweighed the bad when both partners did what it took to make it work through the bad times and into the good. Who was I to take away anyone's chance at a happy ending? So mine didn't work out. It didn't mean that all relationships were doomed. Did it?

CHAPTER 15

I put the van in reverse and rolled out of my parking spot, leaving a car-shaped bit of pavement showing. The way the snow was coming down, the bare spot would be filled in soon. I turned on the radio.

Lou Bradley was deejaying tonight. He currently spoke of the winter weather advisory and told truck drivers to be careful on the roads with the high wind warning.

The wind was shockingly strong as I left the protected area of the parking lot and turned onto Main Street. The van was built for space to deliver a cargo of baked goods, not to withstand hurricane-force winds. I put my hazard lights on and slowed way down. The roads were wet and slushy but passable. I only ever worried when we were hit by an ice storm. The van was pretty good in bad weather. This time the wind kept knocking it to the right and it was a fight to keep it on the road.

The police station loomed before me, like a beacon in

the storm. I pulled into the unpaved parking area and came to a crunching stop just outside the front door. Outside, the wind and snow tugged at my hair, froze my breath on my nose and cheeks. I struggled to open the station door. Finally I stepped inside, the storm slamming the door behind me.

"Auntie Em, Auntie Em," I muttered as a whirlwind of snow and ice blew me into the lobby.

"Can I help you?" There was a young guy at the registration desk. He looked like he was twelve years old. His blond hair was cut short to his scalp. It made his ears seem larger as they stuck out on the sides of his head. He had light blue eyes and a clean-shaven jaw that had that round babyish softness to it.

"Um, hi, I'm Toni Holmes. I was told my brother Tim Keene was arrested tonight. Is that true?"

The kid looked through a logbook in front of him. I noticed that his name badge said BLAYLOCK.

"I'm sorry. I just noticed your name tag. Are you Chief Blaylock's son?"

The officer blushed like a schoolboy. "He's my uncle." He pushed forward, ignoring his red cheeks. "According to the log, a Tim Keene was brought in on charges of second-degree murder and felony drug dealing."

"Holy cow! Murder and drug dealing? There's no way!" I exclaimed. "What kind of evidence do they have?"

"I'm not at liberty to say, miss." He closed the logbook and carefully folded his hands on top of it. He remained calm, his actions purposeful.

I realized that I might have been a little loud when Officer Bright came around from the back. "Calvin, why are they arresting Tim? Is it true he's being charged with murder and drug dealing?" I waved toward the officer at the front desk as if accusing him of lying.

"Toni, calm down."

"Those are fightin' words." I narrowed my eyes, my

temper flaring. "You have no right to patronize me. I want to see my brother, and I want to see him now."

"I'm not patronizing you." He remained calm and reached his hand out. "May I touch you?"

"Why?" I narrowed my eyes.

"Sometimes a touch can be soothing in an emotional time." He slowly put his hand on my bent elbow. Then he gently led me away from the front desk to the two benches where either family members or arrestees waited.

Right now it was only me and Officer Bright. We sat down together on the carved pine benches. "Do you want some tea or coffee?"

I shook my head. "I can't think of that until I know Tim is all right." I studied Calvin's sober expression, looking for a glint of hope. He gave away nothing.

"I can tell you Brad is with him. Tim lawyered up the moment he was taken into custody."

My eyes teared up. How could this have happened? "I trusted you to do your job." I went from sad to mad in a flash and balled up my hands. "I don't know what evidence you think you have, but Tim didn't do this horrible thing. He lived with me for six months. If he were dealing drugs and getting into the wrong crowd I would have known. Don't you see? I would have known."

He patted my forearm. "I did do my job, Toni." He didn't say anything else.

"Well, you didn't do it right." I pulled away from him and stood. "When can I see Tim?"

"He's spending the night here until the bail hearing in the morning. After that it will be up to the judge to determine how much a risk to society he is."

"He's not a risk to anyone. In fact, right now you are in more danger from me than Tim." My fists were still balled.

He stood and held his hands out palms vertical. "Violence solves nothing, Toni."

"Maybe not, but I'd feel better hitting someone. If you arrest me for it, I'll be with my brother tonight." It made sense in my head anyway.

"Blaylock, get Mr. Ridgeway out here right now," Officer Bright said with authority. At the same time he took a step away from me.

"Yes, sir." The kid at the desk fled to the back.

"The only way Brad is going to help is if he can get Tim out of jail. Seriously." I narrowed my eyes. "I'm tired of ya'll picking on my family. We are not murderers, thieves, or drug dealers, for goodness' sake." My voice rose in tone and volume. "I thought, since you were seeing Tasha, you would be on our side."

I hated how whiny that sounded, but he *was* supposed to be on our side. He was practically family.

"Toni, you know that I follow the letter of the law. If there was enough evidence to arrest my own mother, I would do it. Do you understand?"

"No!" If I weren't a disciplined adult I would have stomped my foot. "How could anyone arrest their own mother? What is wrong with you?"

"There's nothing wrong with me." Officer Bright's chin rose, his chest puffed out, and his hands went to his hips. "You need to calm down now."

Two doors opened at the exact moment. Tasha came flying in from the outside door while Brad strode through the door to the back with a calm fury.

"Toni! What's going on? I heard they arrested Tim." Tasha was beside me in a flash, her arms around my shoulders, her eyes flashing. "Calvin, how could you?"

Officer Bright held up his hands and took another step back. Maybe it was because we were a united front or maybe he recalled how together Tasha and I can put up a heck of a fight.

"I've got this, Bright," Brad said. He was four inches taller than Calvin and his suit was cut to perfection to show off his wide shoulders. Brad had the look of a Scandinavian Adonis. The crisp white of his dress shirt against the tan of his skin made me want to bury my nose in the crook of his neck and cling to him for comfort. The black suit coat he wore was made of fine wool and well tailored. I'd seen suits like that during my years of training in Chicago. A cut that good on material that fine cost a great deal of money. Brad's thick blond mane was cut and styled to perfection. He didn't get it cut in Oiltop. I was pretty sure no one in this small town was that up on current men's style. I could be wrong. I'd have to ask him sometime.

Brad stepped between Calvin and us. "Don't you have paperwork to attend to?" His tone was pure alpha male dismissing a lesser man. My heart rate sped up. Officer Bright narrowed his eyes and took a step toward Brad when the kid popped back behind the reception counter.

"Officer Bright, the chief wants you in the back," the younger Blaylock said.

I doubt he knew he'd just stopped a shoving match before it got started. Calvin's gaze remained narrow.

"We'll finish this later," he promised and left. The door slammed behind him and a cheap framed photo that hung on the wall crashed to the floor.

The noise startled me and I suddenly felt as if my last nerve had been hit. My knees buckled and I sat on the bench, put my head in my hands, and sobbed.

Tasha was beside me in a flash. She handed me a tissue and put her arm around me to comfort me. "How bad is it?" Tasha asked.

Brad sat beside me and put his elbows on his knees so that his head was on the same level as ours. The man was a giant, after all. I mean, I was considered tall for a woman, and Brad had a whole foot of height on me. There was something nice about a guy big enough to make you feel delicate.

"We'll know more in the morning, when Tim stands

before the judge for his bail hearing." Brad's deep voice soothed my nerves.

"What time is it? I want to be there. What evidence do they have? They have to have something in order to arrest him. Don't they?" My stomach hurt at the thought of my brother in a jail cell with a killer or worse.

"The hearing is at ten A.M. We'll know more then. In the meantime, he has his own private room. He'll be fine, okay? Try not to worry too much. Tim is taking it all one day at a time."

"Tim's taking it well? Crap, does that mean he won't look remorseful and they'll sentence him to life? Oh, thank goodness we don't live in Texas. I don't know what I would do if he got the death penalty."

Brad patted my hand. Tasha hugged me.

"I don't mean to be so dramatic," I said. "It's just that everyone told me to help investigate and I said no. I told them that the Oiltop police were good at their job. All we had to do was trust them."

"That's true," Brad said. His electric blue gaze tried to reassure me.

"But they arrested the wrong man. We all know Tim didn't do it."

"Do you have any idea who might have been renting rooms around town in your brother's name?" Brad asked.

"Not a clue." I shook my head in despair. "Why didn't the desk clerk notice that it wasn't Tim signing in?"

"I can answer that," Tasha said. "There are certain times of day when everyone wants to check in at once. If the imposter rented the room over the Internet, then all he had to do was show up with an ID with Tim's name and his own picture. We really don't check beyond what it takes to ensure we get paid."

"Wouldn't you know it wasn't Tim?"

"People have similar names all the time. I've signed in

a couple of Tasha Wilkeses myself. The name might sound familiar, but if the ID matches we just go with it."

"Wait, you think whoever is behind this watches the reception area and comes in when the customers are two and three deep?"

"That's how I'd do it." Tasha's eyes were wide. "That's why I'm surprised they arrested Tim. I gave them the videotape of the day the room was rented. We should be able to match the time they checked in to the number of cars in the parking lot. If Tim's car isn't there, then they can't prove the Tim checking in was your brother."

"That's right!" I looked at Brad. "They have video. You can't really fake that, can you?"

"There are a million ways to fake video." Brad's mouth was a thin line. "For that matter, you can scramble the video with a simple device in your pocket."

"Who knows this kind of stuff?" I asked, confused. "If people could fake the video, then why even have video?"

"Video is one more step in security," Tasha said. "It's not meant to solve crimes but to be a piece of the puzzle."

"Did they show you the video?" I asked Brad. "Can you tell who was in the parking lot?"

"I didn't see the video. I was told it was still being processed, which means it's not part of the arrest warrant." Brad ran his big hand over his square jaw.

"I thought you said you didn't know what they have to hold him." I studied his guarded expression.

"I said we'd have to wait until morning to see how compelling the information is." Brad took my hand in his. His hand was warm and his grip was firm. His thumb swept the back of my hand, gentle and soothing. "What I do know is they had Tim in a lineup after they brought him into the station. It sounds like at least one if not two witnesses confirmed that Tim was at the different hotels the days the other rooms were reserved in his name."

I shook my head. "How can that be? He was staying with me. He was saving money to get his own place. There's no way he'd have spent it on an unnecessary hotel room. Not when he has full access to the house."

"The final person to identify your brother was Maria," Brad said.

"Maria?" I couldn't believe it.

"You mean *my* Maria? The one who found the body?" Tasha asked in as much disbelief as I was.

"Yes, your Maria," Brad said, his eyes took on a darker shade of blue. "She claims to have seen a man leaving the room an hour before she went to clean. She identified that man as Tim in the lineup."

"How can that be?" I felt drained as if all the strength had gone out of my body.

"She has to be mistaken," Tasha said. "I was working that morning. I would have seen Tim if he'd been there."

"That's true," I said. "I stopped into the lobby before Maria started her shift. That room faces the clubhouse. In fact, I sat facing east most of the time I was there. I would have noticed Tim if it had been him leaving."

"Wait, a lot of drugs come out of Colombia, don't they? Aren't there Colombian drug lords? What if Maria is part of this frame-up? What if someone has her children and is forcing her to testify against Tim?" I looked at Brad. "What can we do? There must be something to do to help her and Tim."

"That's a lot of speculation, Toni," Brad said. "She could simply be mistaken."

"Oh, poor Maria," Tasha said. "I hope that none of this is true."

"I can't feel for Maria," I said. "She is accusing my brother. At this point we don't know why. So I say poor Tim," I reminded her. "See? This is what happens when I let the professionals do their jobs." I stood, filled with a sudden need to jump into the investigation.

"What are you going to do?" Brad asked as I put on my stocking cap and my gloves.

"What I should have done the moment we found that body," I said and wrapped a muffler around my neck. "I'm going to investigate."

CHAPTER 16

Brad followed me out of the station. I ignored him as I hit the UNLOCK button on my key and opened the van door. I climbed up into the driver's seat and tried to close the door before he could talk me out of my decision.

I was too slow. Brad's long legs ate up the ground, closing in on me. He grabbed the door when I did. There was a moment where we tussled for possession, then I gave up. He was bigger and stronger. I stuck my keys in the ignition and started up the van. If I had to I could simply put the van in reverse. He'd either let go or be dragged under.

Yeah, like I could hurt the man of my teenage dreams. I rolled my eyes, tossed up my hands, and turned to him. "What?"

"As your lawyer and your brother's lawyer I have to advise you not to investigate this," he said solemnly. "As your friend, all I can say is be careful. Don't go anywhere alone. Don't confront anyone; bring your evidence to Calvin. He will listen."

"Fine. Is that all?" I couldn't look at him. I reached out to close the door again when he stopped me.

"Look at me," he said softly.

I did and saw real warmth in his blue eyes. "What?" I asked.

He put his hand over mine. "Promise me you'll be safe. Okay, Toni?"

My heart softened at the plea in his voice. "I promise."

"Good." He gave a short nod and stepped away from the van. Shoving his hands in his pockets, he shivered.

"Go inside and get warm," I said. "I'll see you in the morning."

"Ten A.M. at the courthouse," Brad said.

"Ten it is," I said then closed my door, turned my heater on high, and pulled out of my parking space. The first thing I was going to do was find out more about Maria. We really didn't know anything other than what she had told us. I'd get Tasha to investigate the public records. Meanwhile I'd run a credit check on the maid. It should tell me at least when and where she entered the United States. I also needed to find out who the main drug dealer in town was.

If they thought it was Tim, then that meant they didn't know for sure who was dealing. Grandma might have her sources, but so did I.

My alarm made this horrible buzzing noise. Still half-asleep, I tried to hit SNOOZE. The buzzing turned into screaming metal rock music. Ugh. I hit the thing a third time. Finally, peace and quiet. . . . "Good morning, good morning, good morning, time to rise and shine . . . Good morning, good morning, good morning, I hope you're feeling fine. Get up, get up, get out of bed, get up, get up, you sleepyhead." It was the most annoying little ditty.

Now I was really awake and mad as a bear dragged out

of hibernation too early. I grabbed the offending machine
and yanked it out of the wall and threw it across my room
with a resounding smashing noise. I lay back down and
pulled the pillow over my head, but it was no use. My anger
had me fully awake. Disgusted, I sat up. It was dark out, but
I could see the snow driving through the light given off by
the nearby lamppost.

I remembered why I had set my alarm even earlier than
normal. I had hoped to go in and make cookies early so I
had time to do some investigating. After Tim's arrest, I'd
realized that waiting for the authorities to proceed with justice was foolish. And so I had finally decided to investigate
after all. With so many cookies to bake and money to earn,
the only time left to investigate was during my sleep time.
And so it was that I had set my poor abused alarm two hours
earlier than normal.

My eyes felt like they were filled with grit. I showered
and pulled my hair back into a ponytail. At least getting
dressed was easy when you wore a uniform. The longest
part of my morning routine was waiting for the coffee to
brew. I skipped the at-home coffee, wrapped my muffler
firmly around my face, and, holding my puffy down coat
close to my chest, I braved the icy wind and hurried to the
van. Once inside I started it up.

"You're up pretty early," a gravelly voice said from
behind me. I screamed with fright, and turned to find
Grandma Ruth lying in the backseat. I sometimes laid it flat
to add more cargo room. Grandma lay on the folded back
as if it were her bed. Her feet stuck out from a pile of knitted
afghans and were covered in fluffy pink bunny slippers.

My heart raced and all the spit dried up in my mouth.
"Holy Moses, you scared the stuffins out of me," I managed
to say. "What are you doing in my van at this hour of the
night?"

Grandma sat up. The blankets rolled down revealing her

thick down coat unzipped enough that you could see a black cable-knit sweater and a tee shirt underneath. Her hands were tucked inside two pairs of mittens. "I figured you were finally mad enough to do some investigating. I thought I'd wait for you in the van."

"Grandma! You could have frozen. What is the windchill outside, negative twenty degrees?"

"It's forty degrees in here," Grandma said. "Which is above freezing, so there is no way I could freeze, plus it's even warmer under my blankets."

"How do you know it's forty degrees in the van?" I wanted her to realize how silly she had been. For goodness' sake, she could have frozen to death. "And what would have happened if I hadn't gotten up early? Hmm?"

Grandma grinned and lifted her hand. "I have a thermometer." She showed me the small round indoor outdoor temperature gauge. "If it got below freezing I would have come inside."

"Grandma! There are plenty of beds in the house."

"And if I'd have slept there you wouldn't have woken me when you left. This way is far better." She crossed her arms over her chest and sat up, turning her legs toward the front. She reached over and hit the lever that bounced the backseat back into its L shape. "Now tell me what you're thinking of doing first."

I turned the key in the ignition. "If I had any sense I'd take you home first, but something tells me you'd simply drive your scooter through the snow to get to the bakery."

"You are a very smart girl," Grandma said. "You should really take the Mensa test. I'm certain you would pass it."

"I don't have time to be a genius, Grandma." I backed out of the driveway and turned on my windshield wipers. The snow was coming down sideways as the wind blew fiercely. It was tough to keep the van on the road in the storm. My vehicle was great for delivering baked goods, but

top-heavy for bad weather. The wind kept pushing us off
the road. I eased through the storm with my wipers going
full force, the heater blasting, and my semibald tires slipping
around corners.

All in all it was a harrowing journey to the bakery. I knew
my knuckles were white from gripping the steering wheel.
Meanwhile Grandma grinned from ear to ear as if she had
just gotten off a roller coaster and wanted to go again.

"Grandma, how is it that you're so brave?"

"Kiddo, at my age I'm happy to just be alive. I don't have
time to worry about dying."

I shook my head and opened the van door. "Stay put until
I unlock the bakery door. Okay?"

"What's that?" Grandma's grin widened. I shook my
head. Grandma was what we called "selectively" hard of
hearing. In other words she could hear just fine when she
wanted to otherwise she was deaf in one ear.

"Don't make me use the child safety locks," I warned.

"They don't put them in delivery vans," Grandma said.
"I checked. Did you know that all the car manuals are now
available online?"

I rolled my eyes and got out. The wind was what you
would call *bracing*. It pushed me back a good foot before I
got my bearings. With weather like this, it was going to be
a slow bakery day. Anyone with any sense would stay home
and off the roads.

That meant I would have more time to figure out what
the heck Chief Blaylock had on Tim that he could arrest him
and make him spend a night in jail.

I unlocked the door, stepped inside, and hit the lights.

"Is your coffee made yet?"

Startled, I turned to see that Grandma Ruth was out of
the van. She pushed her girth through the door, waddled to
the small table in the kitchen, and sat down. When she

wanted to, Grandma could move faster than I could. "Well, close the door. You can't afford to heat the entire outside." She waved her hand at me.

I closed the door and threw the lock shut. A glance out the peephole showed me that the van doors were closed. I hit the automatic lock on the key and the van's lights flashed at me, letting me know it was secure.

There wasn't anything in the van to steal, but I had gotten into the habit of securing everything when I lived in Chicago. It was a good habit to keep in Oiltop. Especially since a wheat-free bakery wasn't the most popular place in wheat country.

"So, what's the plan?" Grandma asked, rubbing her hands together.

"Besides figuring out how to help Tim make bail?" I asked. "There is no plan." I evaded the question. The last thing I needed was to get Grandma involved in whatever I planned to do. I made a show of filling the big perk pot with water and coffee.

"Oh, there's a plan," Grandma said. "First off, I can bail Tim out if need be. I have retirement funds."

"Grandma, you don't need to put your retirement funds on the line for Tim," I said. "We can put a lien on the house. It's what Mom would want."

"What if you lose the house?" Grandma asked.

"I'm not going to lose the house. Tim isn't going anywhere and if he were, then it would be better to lose the house than your retirement fund. Case closed," I said.

"Fine," Grandma said.

"Fine," I replied.

She sat in silence for a moment or two and watched me.

"What?" I asked, feeling weird that she kept staring.

"If you don't want to tell me your plan, then I won't tell you mine."

I mulled that over a moment. "Fine. Tell me yours first."

"Oh, come on, kiddo, you know I'm smarter than that." Grandma raised her right eyebrow and gave me the look.

"Fine." I put my hands on my hips as the coffeemaker perked, filling the air with the fresh, hot scent. "I plan on visiting all the local motels and speaking to the staff."

"Already did that." Grandma pursed her lips and crossed her arms. "They don't remember squat. Turns out you don't need a Mensa card to sit at a reservation desk and welcome people for eight hours."

I grabbed the second chair and sat down. "What did they say? Anything? Did anyone remember Tim?"

"You would know all this if you'd been investigating from the start like I told you to." Grandma raised both eyebrows and half lowered her lids.

"Grandma, I don't have a lot of time here." I stood. "I've got dozens of cookies to make and all the morning pastries."

"You don't have to make a full complement of pastries this morning. I listened to the weather. We're in a severe storm warning with blizzard conditions and such for the next twenty-four hours. No one's coming to buy donuts."

"Darn it, Grandma, I need people to buy donuts and pastries and breads. How else am I going to stay in business?"

Grandma shrugged nonchalantly. "I don't make the weather." She pointed at the coffeepot with her chin. "Coffee's ready."

Great. Grandma was as hard to open as a fresh clam. I poured her coffee. "Fine. If you aren't going to tell me what you know, then I'll just have to find out myself."

"You do that." Grandma poured a ton of pink packets in her coffee and stirred it with one of the spoons in a container on the table.

"I will," I said and pulled out the bowls of dough that had been in the refrigerator overnight. One thing to know about Grandma—she hated to be ignored. I did just that, sprinkling the marble countertop with cornmeal and dumping the cool dough onto the surface. The smell of yeast wafted up as I did a couple of turns kneading, shaped the dough into round mounds, and popped it in the proofer.

"The silent treatment isn't going to work on me," Grandma said. "I've got my smartphone. I'll just sit here and read the *New York Times*. Maybe even work the puzzle."

I continued with my usual morning prep work. My mind raced as I tried to figure out who I could talk to that would know anything about the dead man or the identity thief who framed Tim. Maybe other people's identities had been stolen. Maybe someone else local had been checking into hotels once a week. It was a start, anyway.

I turned my radio up and blasted Mumford & Sons. Grandma got up and poured herself another cup of coffee and snatched two day-old muffins from the bin where I put the leftovers at night.

"Don'tcha wanna know who I talked to?" she asked as I pulled out the ingredients for the cookies.

"I do, but you won't tell me," I said as I measured sugar and butter.

"Darned right I won't tell you. You have to tell me your plan first."

"I don't have a plan," I repeated.

"Oh, poppycock. We both know you have a plan, and I have information. Spill."

"I'm making cookies, Grandma," I said. "See that list on the wall? Those are the orders that need to be baked today."

"What does that have to do with your brother?"

"Not a thing." I blew out a breath.

"Humph." Grandma took her baked goods and coffee and went back to the table. A few more moments of music and Grandma started talking. "Allie May at the Motel 7 says her records show Tim was checked in twice a month, but she doesn't remember ever seeing him there. She'd remember, too, because she has a thing for your brother."

"Does she remember anyone else local checking in?" I asked the question casually as if I were talking to the cookie dough.

"She said she hasn't seen anyone from town check in. She has regulars that come for the fishing or the prairie chicken hunting, but that's it."

I finished creaming the butter and sugar and added the dry ingredients to my oatmeal raisin cookies. I reached up and switched radio stations to the one that played continuous Christmas music from Thanksgiving through New Year's Eve. I loved Christmas, but I had no idea why anyone would want to listen to nothing but Christmas songs for so long.

"Don't you just love Christmas songs?" Grandma said, her long fingers flying in the air as if she were conducting. "I could listen to them all year long."

"That's a lot of Christmas," I stated as I scraped dough onto waxed paper. I shaped the dough into logs, wrapped them in waxed paper, and froze them. Later I would pull out the frozen logs, cut out discs of cookies, and bake them. That way I always had warm cookies in the bakery.

"I bet Tim's not getting any Christmas in that cold jail cell he's stuck in." Grandma pouted. "All because his sister is too busy with cookies to help him."

"Tim is a grown man," I said, pulled out a clean bowl, and started creating more dough. This time it would be chocolate chip. "His time in jail is his business, not mine."

"He's being framed, and you're going to stand there and make cookies?"

I rolled my eyes, turned, and waved my hand to the door. "If you haven't noticed, there's a blizzard out there. It's hard to investigate anything in that kind of weather."

As if on cue, the radio stopped playing music and the disc jockey came on. "Good morning, ladies and gentlemen. It's Christmastime in Kansas, which means the winter wheat is in and the cattle are hunkered down because the wind is howling and the snow is falling. Let's hope you have nowhere to go today, because portions of I-35 are shut down. I-70 is a parking lot. Stay home, stay in bed, and let visions of sugarplums dance in your heads."

"This is the best time to investigate," Grandma declared and whipped out her smartphone. "People are going to be hanging around with nothing to do."

CHAPTER 17

She dialed a number and handed me the phone. I scowled but took it.

"Hey, this is The Hamilton Inn. I'm Terry, how can I help you?"

"Hi, Terry, it's Toni Holmes. My brother is Tim Keene. I think you were in his class in high school."

"Oh, sure, I remember you. You were skinny as a beanstalk and had the awful flyaway hair."

"Yes." I shook my head. "That's me."

"Hi, sugar, how've you been? Weren't you living in Chicago?"

"I moved back when my mom died last summer."

"Oh, I'm sorry to hear that."

There was a pause where I wondered briefly if she was sorry to hear I was back or that my mother had died. I chose to believe it was the fact that my mom had died. "Thanks," I said. Grandma motioned with her hands for me to get on with things. I gave her the evil eye and turned my back on her. "Hey, Terry, are you real busy?"

"Not right now, why?"

"I don't know if you heard that my brother Tim was arrested last night."

"Oh, sure, I heard," she said. "Terrible news, him killing that man and all—and right there at the Red Tile, where you and your friend Tasha were."

"You know, I don't think Tim killed anyone."

"Well, of course he did," she chided me. "The police wouldn't have arrested him unless they were pretty sure he did it."

Whatever. "Listen, I was wondering, did you have any registrations that belonged to Tim?"

"Excuse me?"

"No worries. I thought I'd help him pay his bills, so I'm calling around asking if he had run up any bills at the local hotels." I glanced at Grandma, who grinned and put both thumbs up.

"Oh, let me take a look in my computer." Terry did some fast typing and then some clicking. "It looks like your brother stayed here five times in the last two months. That's kind of weird since you have that big house and all. Were you having company?"

"No, no company."

"Huh, well, in any case he's all paid up. It looks like he paid in cash every time. He must be doing some work on the side. Nobody pays in cash anymore. What's he doing? Do you know? Because, if he's plowing, have him call me later. It's always good to have a backup plow guy. For instance Bill Western's our regular guy and he's on vacation this week. It would have been nice to have a backup snow-plow. Of course, with your brother in jail and all it wouldn't have helped much. But still . . . You know Bill saved up and took his whole family to Disney World. I always wanted to go to Disney World."

"Is that right?"

"Yes," she sighed. "I bet it's warmer in Florida, too. I mean if they had this kind of blizzard it'd ruin the orange crop or something, wouldn't it? I won't wish that on Florida, then, because I like my orange juice and I don't need it to get any more expensive."

"No, we don't," I said and widened my eyes at Grandma. She made the *wrap it up* signal with her index finger.

"Say, Terry, do you know if anyone else local has been staying at your hotel?"

"I don't know. . . . I guess it depends on what you mean by 'local.'"

"Well, you know anyone from Oiltop having a fight with their spouse or getting their place renovated? I mean, surely Tim can't be the only local guy renting a hotel room."

"Oh, honey, do I have the stories I could tell you. Why, just yesterday Junior Riley—you remember him, right? He was in your class, I'm thinking. Anyway, Junior came in and asked if we had any vacancies—which, of course, we didn't because it's the holiday season and people are visiting their families and all. Well, it turns out Allie May kicked Junior out of the house. She found out he wasn't going to those AA meetings like he said he was. Instead he was down at the Grey Goose playing pool every Monday. Boy, I would have loved to have been a fly on the wall when Allie May found out. That gal might be small, but she's feisty. I wouldn't be surprised if she waited for him with a shotgun in her lap."

"Right?" I agreed in an effort to keep Terry talking. "So really no one else local comes in every week?"

"Not to rent a room," Terry said. "We have a few regulars come into the restaurant and have supper or sit at the bar for a drink."

"Oh, I imagine you do see regulars; I hear the food there is good—especially Sunday-morning brunch."

"It is good."

"Too bad I can't eat there." I acted casual. "My needing to eat gluten-free and all."

"Well, you know, we don't get much call for people with allergies to eat here. I imagine if we ever did we'd be calling you to find out what all we had to do."

"I appreciate that, and Terry, always remember: if you need anything gluten-free, from donuts to rolls to sandwich bread and dessert, you can always call me. I give a discounted rate for small businesses."

"Now, that's good to know." Terry's voice sounded chipper. "I'm going to write that down on a big old notepad and stick it near the kitchen phone."

"Thank you. I appreciate all your help." I hung up after Terry said good-bye and frowned at Grandma. "The Hamilton Inn is like the Motel 7. They rarely see anyone from town except to eat at the restaurant or stop in at the bar." I worried my bottom lip. "How many of the places where Tim supposedly rented a room have restaurants or bars in them?"

"Give me my phone and I'll tell you." Grandma held out her hand. I studied her. It could be a ploy. She might dial someone else or she might have the list in her phone.

I suppose I could always refuse to talk to the next person she dialed. Yeah, like that was going to happen. I handed her the phone. She flipped through the icons like a pro. It made me sigh. Even my grandmother was better versed in smartphones than I was. I was still doing all my online ordering through e-mail, and that I checked from my desktop computer in my office. And here I was so proud to be modern and have a flat-screen television.

"A quick glance tells me half of them have restaurants and another third have bars."

"So they don't all have bars or restaurants?"

"Well, the Bait and Buckle is right next door to the Two-Hand Saloon." Grandma shrugged. "They don't need a restaurant or a bar. It's not like you get families staying at a place like Bait and Buckle."

"What other hotels are left?" I drew my eyebrows together. For goodness' sake, Oiltop only had twenty thousand residents. How many hotels did it need? No wonder Tasha had had a problem keeping her bed-and-breakfast going. I knew they were working on the new lake project and hoping to bring in race boats and sportfishing, but that meant there was a lot of summer campground business and such. Winter months were left to truckers and stranded motorists trying to get home.

"There's Paulette's Cabins on the other side of town."

"She's not even open. Why would she be on the list?"

"She's not. You asked me what other hotels were in town. Paulette's is down closer to the lake. It's a bit shady. The police blotter says they send someone down to break up the rowdies at least once a week."

"You read the police blotter?"

"It's an old habit. When I first started out I wrote the police report column. It was a completely boring exercise," Grandma said. "The dispatch writes down all the calls and the police blotter is a shortened version of dispatch notes. Sometimes the editor of the *Times* would tell me to keep something or someone out. But most of the time it was simply an address, a time, and a title—say, for instance, 'domestic dispute,' or 'disturbing the peace.'"

"Is that when you got the crime beat?" I always loved to hear Grandma's stories. I figured sooner or later she was going to pass on and then I'd share her stories with the family. That was if I didn't die first. Knowing Grandma, she just might live to be 120 years old.

"Yes, one night I picked up a blotter notice of a Peeping Tom on Locust Street. They sent a squad car down there three nights in a row and never saw anything. So I decided to go undercover. Now remember it was during WWII and things were rationed, so I was a bit thinner in those days."

"How old were you?"

"I was in my twenties. Just finished my college degree and was working at the paper so the men could be drafted. Anywho, I decided to go undercover and spend a night on Locust Street to see if I could catch the perpetrator of this crime. I dressed all in black and smeared mud on my face like I saw in the war movies. Then I took my flashlight with me and patrolled the street in a three-block radius of the calls."

"You patrolled the area?" After the usual early morning flurry of activity, the bread was rising and the cakes had come out of the freezer to thaw. I had set the mixer to low mixing powdered sugar and butter for buttercream frosting. I liked it to mix a while for a creamy result so I poured myself a cup of coffee and sat down at the table to hear Grandma's story. The wind howled outside, and I still had half an hour before I needed to open. "Yes, I did."

"What happened?"

"Well, I did all right up until three A.M. Then I sat down under Mrs. Rawlings's maple tree—you know, the one in her side yard—because I was tired. I dozed for a bit when something woke me up."

I leaned in closer. The scent of coffee filled the air and the steam swirled above my cup. "What was it?"

"The oddest thing I've ever seen. Two beady eyes staring at me. Gave me such a fright I jumped up and bit my tongue to keep from screaming. I turned my flashlight on the intruder." Grandma stopped to sip her coffee.

"And . . ."

"And the flashlight revealed . . ."

Grandma gave this dramatic pause until I was forced to say, "What? What did it reveal?"

"The Peeping Tom was no other than Mr. Maddox's

Great Dane. That was the biggest darn dog I've ever seen. When he stood on two legs he could grab whatever he wanted off the top of the refrigerator. It seems he'd jump the fence and go sniffing around, patrolling the neighborhood. Then before dawn, he'd jump back into his yard and lie down by the door as if he'd been there all night."

I laughed out loud at the story and got up to stop the mixer and test the frosting. "Only in a small town."

"Hand me one of those day-old donuts, would you?" Grandma asked.

The frosting was ready. I removed the bowl from the mixer, setting it down near the cakes. I took a small white plate from the stack on the counter and placed a spice donut with caramel frosting on the plate. "Aren't you supposed to be watching what you eat?" I asked as I brought Grandma the donuts. It was a conversation we had almost daily. I swear she ate just so that I would notice.

"I am," Grandma's blue eyes twinkled. "I watch it all the way into my mouth."

I shook my head and frowned at her. "Gluten-free is not calorie-free."

"Trust me, kiddo, at my age health is the last thing on your mind." She snagged one of the donuts and took a huge bite, washed it down with coffee. "There's a law," she said with her mouth full. "Once you hit ninety, all bets are off on trying to make a hundred."

"I want you here and well." I went back to the cakes. I knew the argument was more out of habit than real concern. Grandma was nowhere near dying, even if she smoked like a chimney and ate her way toward the three-hundred-pound range.

"Being alive *is* well." She cackled. "Now, where were we? I know there was a point to my story. What was I talking about?"

I grabbed a frosting knife and scooped up buttercream,

plopping it on top of a cake and making quick work of the crumb-coat. After that I covered half with marshmallow fondant and half with more buttercream. "I believe you were talking about Mr. Maddox's Great Dane."

"Oh, right." Grandma slurped her coffee and then reached for the pink packets to sweeten it further. "The point of the tale was that I broke the story wide-open simply by paying attention to the police blotter and then being in the right place at the right time."

"So you think I should go out to Paulette's Cabins at two in the morning to see what the police blotter is really talking about?" I whipped through the crumb-coats of the six cakes.

"Use your noggin, kiddo," Grandma said as she stuffed the second donut in her mouth. "What does Paulette's Cabins have in common with all the other hotels in the area?"

"The police blotter?" I raised my right eyebrow and made a flat line of my mouth.

"Close." Grandma lifted the plate and held it out to me. We both knew she wasn't giving it to me to put in the dishwasher.

I took the plate and, for a second, thought about pretending to mistake her motion as she was done.

"Chocolate chip ones . . . please."

I sighed long and loud as I put one chocolate chip donut on the plate. I could say no and not enable her, but she'd only run me over with her scooter and pile her plate with six donuts. "I don't understand," I said as I handed her the single donut. She gave me the evil eye for the lonely single donut. I answered back by raising my eyebrows innocently. "How is the police blotter close to the answer?"

"Think."

"Police? Blotter?"

"Yes." Grandma slurped the remainder of her coffee and held out her mug for more.

Now I was really confused. I filled her mug with hot

coffee. The scent filled the air as I thought over the conversation. The answer hit me the moment I handed her back her mug. "The police!"

"Exactly." Grandma added sweetener and cream until her mug overflowed onto the saucer.

"You think someone in the police department knows more than they're letting on."

"It might be how they have stayed one step ahead of us at every turn."

"I don't know." I sat down hard. "I can't see Chief Blaylock or Officer Bright involved in murder. There's no way Officer Emry is smart enough to stay one step ahead of anyone."

"Maybe." Grandma dunked her donut in the coffee until a portion fell off into the mug, splashing coffee all over. She dipped her head and slurped the drink until she could safely stick her fingers in it and dredge out the donut. "I don't have proof of anything. Sort of like the Peeping Tom. All I have is instinct. I bet if you start looking at the connection between the police and the motels you'll find something hiding in plain sight."

CHAPTER 18

Snow days in Kansas were rare, especially for the southeast corner of the state. We were much more likely to get an ice storm than actual large amounts of snow. But this time, the radio was calling it the storm of the century.

Grandma must have called Bill, because he showed up in his big fat Lincoln Town Car and escorted both Grandma and her scooter off to court. After last night's encounter at the police station, Brad and Tasha had both called me before 8:00 A.M. to suggest I not come out.

It had taken Brad giving Tim his phone so that I could hear from my brother's own lips that it was best if I didn't come down. I was disappointed and half-mad that everyone thought I didn't have the sense to behave properly in a court of law. Then I remembered how I had almost decked Calvin Bright last night and, with a sigh, I realized they were all right. Knowing it and liking it were two different things, though.

I'd only had one customer since Grandma Ruth had left.

John Emerson, a farmer/rancher who was dating police dispatcher Sarah Hogginboom, stopped by. He was a real regular and arrived on time to pick up Sarah's favorite breakfast Danish and a cinnamon roll for himself.

"How bad is it out there?" I asked him as he filled two thermoses with coffee from the coffee bar.

"The snow isn't bad. I've seen worse. But the wind's strong enough to blow semis off the road."

I winced. "The radio's telling everyone to stay home."

John tightened lids on the thermoses. "Probably for the best." He walked over and pulled out his wallet. "I was surprised to find you open."

"I got here before the storm."

He raised an eyebrow. "It started at eight last night."

I felt the heat of embarrassment rise into my cheeks. "Okay, so I came during the storm, but it was really early and the ride wasn't that bad. Besides, Christmas is baked-goods season."

"A woman as pretty as you should be at home snuggled up with her man on a day like this. Not working to make baked goods that won't be delivered until after the storm breaks." His brown eyes studied me with a steady gaze.

"Oh, fiddlesticks," I muttered. I hadn't thought about the delivery guys not working.

"Give me two dozen assorted of your donuts and such," he said. "I'll bring them to the police station for the guys who are out in the weather today."

"You are always so thoughtful," I said and quickly folded up two boxes and filled them. "When is Sarah going to make an honest man out of you?"

John laughed a deep sound that bounced off the bakery walls. "She's waiting for me to ask her."

I looked at him. "You haven't asked her yet?"

"Waiting for the right time." He put his credit card on top of the counter and took the boxes from me. "I want to be the last guy who asks her to marry him. It needs to be the right time, and from what I understand, these days it needs to be something big and unforgettable. I'm still working on the *unforgettable* part."

I ran his card through the card reader and ripped off the receipt for him to sign. "Trust me, how you ask isn't as important as asking."

He signed the paper and smiled. "Yeah, I know, but Sarah deserves a big, showy proposal." He winked, took his receipt and the donuts and coffee, and went out into the howling wind and icy snow.

My heart squeezed in my chest. Sarah was a lucky woman.

My cell rang and I answered it. "This is Toni."

"Hi, Toni, it's Meghan. The radio says the roads are closed and anyone found out on the street will be ticketed." She sounded upset. "The college is closed as well. Do you need me to come in? I'm thinking I could skate on down there."

I laughed at the idea of her skating down in one of her vintage dresses and her big black steel-toed boots. "No, stay home. I'm good here. John's the only one who came in." I glanced at the swirling snow. "I can handle any stragglers who show up."

"What about the cookie list?" she said. "We were planning on creating all the dough for the Saturday delivery."

"John tells me that all the deliveries aren't running today. Which means all the Christmas deliveries will be backed up by Saturday. If I do any baking, it will be to freeze it for deliveries later."

"Cool," she said. "Hey, do you want me to post on social media about the weather and the delay? I can get into the website from my phone."

"That would be helpful," I said and walked into the back of the kitchen. "Stay safe and warm."

"You, too."

I hung up the phone and placed it on the counter and stood in the early morning quiet of the kitchen. Scrubbing my hands over my tired eyes, I shrugged. First things first: triage the items that weren't baked yet. I popped the proofing bread dough back into the icebox. The cookies and muffins baking could be frozen and reheated later for a fresh taste. The paper with the long list of orders fluttered as the door-bells jangled. Who else was out in the middle of a raging storm? I wiped my hands on the tea towel I had tucked into my apron strings.

"Be right out," I called and closed the fridge door on the half-finished baked goods. When I pushed through the kitchen door, I saw that my mystery customer was none other than Sam Greenbaum. "Hi, what brings you out in this storm?"

"I had an emergency handyman call," Sam said. His hazel gaze eyed me warmly. The man always took my breath away. His dark brown hair was cut long and fell into his eyes like a little boy's. But there was nothing boyish about him. His strong jaw, wide shoulders, tight backside, and long legs came straight out of a romance novel.

"Who would call you out in this weather?" I leaned against the cash register to steady myself from the pure masculine onslaught of his smile.

"Mrs. McGregor's pilot light on her furnace blew out in the wind. She had to call. When I got there this morning, the inside temperature of her house was close to freezing."

"Oh, that's not good," I said. "Isn't she in her seventies?"

"Yeah." He sat his Stetson on the counter and brushed the hair from his eyes. "I lit her furnace pilot light and stayed with her until the temperature was over sixty-eight degrees. Once this storm clears, I need to go back and check her roof and air intake to see if there isn't some way to prevent that from happening again."

"You deserve coffee after your morning." I pulled a mug

and saucer from the shelf, turned it right side up, and handed it to him. "Help yourself. It's on me."

"You do make the best coffee in town—but don't tell my gram I said that." He winked and poured his coffee.

"How is your gram? Did she like the cookies and cakes you bought? Is there something else she might prefer?"

"She loved them. She always does. I was heading out to check on Gram when I saw your light." He wrapped his long, steady hand around the mug. "The prospect of a cup of this coffee had me parking in a no-parking zone." He nodded toward the front windows. I could make out the outline of his big black pickup truck parked next to the fire hydrant just north of the bakery.

"I doubt anyone will be out in this weather to give you a ticket."

"I left it running just in case." He winked. "I'll tell them I wasn't parking. I'm standing."

I shook my head. "Doesn't that waste gas?"

He took a drink of coffee and pure pleasure washed over his face. My hormones decided to take notice of his half-closed lids and had my heartbeat picking up. "Good coffee," he said. "Well worth the waste of gas."

"Thanks." For the second time today I felt the heat of a blush rush up my neck and into my cheeks. "Do you want to take a thermos?" I waved my shaking hand toward the thermoses for sale on the rack beside the coffee. "Otherwise I'll most likely end up dumping it. I like to keep a fresh pot, and there isn't exactly a stampede of customers in this storm."

"I'll take you up on that offer," he said. "But I want to pay for the thermos. And box me up a couple dozen assorted goodies." He waved at the glass counter. "I'll take them to Gram's and put them out in her lobby. It will make the seniors in her complex happy."

"Oh, okay." I turned from staring at his capable hands

and folded up three big boxes. "Everything is half price," I rambled on, trying to distract myself from the promise in his gaze. "I have a feeling it will all end up in the day-old section."

"My guess is more people will come out for your baked goods than you think."

I looked up at him and his smile dazzled. I swear he had to practice that smile in the mirror. It always sent shivers down to my toes. "I doubt they'll be as willing to waste gas as you are."

His grin widened. "Actually it's better to keep the car running in this cold. It keeps the engine warm. Therefore it's technically not wasting anything."

Okay, why did that feel like a double entendre?

"I told Meghan to stay home." I grasped for a subject, any subject, that felt safe and kept me from thinking about the fact that I was alone with a sexy man in the middle of a raging blizzard and there was a cot in my office. Ugh. Why had I had to swear off dating? All it seemed to have done was make me even more stupid around a good-looking man.

"I figured," he said and watched me stuff the boxes full of baked goods. "The radio said that the college campus was closed."

"I think everything is closed but me." I concentrated on closing the tops on the overfull boxes. "Even the roads."

"Definitely the highways," Sam said and snagged a donut out of the box I hadn't closed yet. He took a bite and closed his eyes. I couldn't help but watch. When he opened his eyes his pupils were wide and the look between us went straight to my stomach. "I can swing back by here if you decide to close up shop."

The spit in my mouth dried up. "Why?"

"Give you a ride home." He tilted his head. "I highly doubt that delivery van of yours can stay on the road in this wind."

"Oh, right." I rang up his order. "That will be twenty-five eighty-eight."

"Did you include two thermoses?" He waved the thermoses.

"That includes both," I said and took his card.

"I don't know how you can stay in business if you keep giving the store away." He winked at me.

I swallowed hard. "I consider today's baked goods a loss anyway." I stuffed a business card in each pink-and-white-striped box, then stacked them, one on top of the other. "Now I can consider this promotion as well." I pulled a flyer off the countertop and slapped it on top of the boxes. "I'm offering a buy one, get one half off on cookies."

"Just in time for the cookie exchange." He studied the flyer and pursed his mouth and nodded. "Smart."

"Thanks." It was my turn to brush the unruly hair from my face. A movement in the window caught my eye. A cop car with flashing blue and red lights pulled up behind his pickup truck. "Uh-oh," I said and pointed. "Looks like you'd better run."

Sam grinned and planted a warm kiss on my cheek as he gathered up the boxes and thermoses of coffee. "Call me if you need a ride home. I doubt I'll be going out to the ranch house any time soon. Storm time is prime time for handymen."

"Take care," I called after him. He put his Stetson on his head and went out the door backward to block the wind, gloved hands full of pink-and-white boxes.

He wore a heavy, lined duster made of brown leather. It opened at the front, revealing his denim-clad legs and sturdy cowboy boots. In my mind's eye I imagined he wore a colored tee shirt with some kind of flannel western shirt over the top.

I watched as he unlocked his pickup door, waved at the cop, shoved the boxes into the pickup, climbed in, and drove away. My jaw hung open. I couldn't believe he'd just left like that. If anyone in my family brazenly broke the law—not that we ever did—and then drove off, we'd be taken in handcuffs to the police station.

The thought reminded me that my brother Tim should be out by now. Grandma was going to pay his bail. I should probably call him and Grandma Ruth and see what was up. I took a step toward the back and pulled my cell phone from my apron pocket when the door jangled open. A gust of icy wind and snow rushed in as Officer Strickland pushed the door closed behind him.

"Hello," I said and dropped the cell back into my pocket.

Officer Strickland took off his plastic-covered police issue hat and brushed the snow off it and his shoulders. "Morning, Ms. Holmes." He wore a heavy leather coat with cream-colored shirred lining. A white shirt peeked out around his neck. His legs were clad in standard cowboy denim and his feet encased in dark leather cowboy boots. "I was surprised to see you open in this storm."

I stood my ground in front of the man who'd helped incriminate my brother. "I was here before it got too bad, and I felt it best to sit tight now that it's in full bloom."

He stuck out his lower lip and nodded in a quick agreement. "Sounds sensible. Do you have any coffee left or did Greenbaum drink it all?"

I glanced at the empty glass carafes. "I have some in the back. Hold on." I made my way around the counter, picked up the hot pots, and turned off the warmer plates.

"Do you have enough to fill a thermos?"

I whirled to find him right behind me. I took a step back and sent him an awkward smile. "Sure. I'll bring it out."

"Cool." His blue eyes had that flat cop look.

I was not going to let him intimidate me. I hurried back into the kitchen, put both pots in the sink, and grabbed the remaining half pot of coffee from the percolator. I took a deep breath to calm my nerves and pushed through the open door. "I've got enough left for two thermoses," I said with a fake smile plastered on my face.

"Great. I've heard you make the best coffee in town." He took the pot from me and filled his thermos. I chided myself for being wary. The man had done nothing to cause the wariness. "I'll take those last two bear claws, too," he said and pointed to the last of the morning pastries.

"Okay, is that for here or to go?" I pulled a wax tissue out of the box and paused.

"To go," he said and sipped coffee from his thermos. "Chief Blaylock has us all out working the streets. He doesn't want anyone stranded in this cold." He paused. "It might have been better if your brother had stayed in jail one more day."

"I doubt it." I put the two bear claws in a bag and closed it up. "No innocent man wants to spend time in jail—even in a storm."

"In a storm like this, he was lucky he got his hearing. If I were the judge I would have postponed it. Your brother has one darn good lawyer." He pulled out his wallet and handed me a twenty-dollar bill.

I went to the register to give him change, and the power flickered and died. My emergency power lights popped on in the far corner, but the register was toast. "Here," I said and handed him the twenty back. "Looks like this one's on me."

He folded his hand over mine, closing the bill into it. "Keep it. From what I've heard, you're going to need it."

I fought back the heat of anger. As a redhead my skin showed my every emotion, and I didn't need this man to see the blotches of anger on my face. The walkie on Strickland's belt squawked. He let go of my hand and pressed the SEND button. "Hi, Sarah, this is Strickland. Power just went out on Main Street."

I heard her answer but couldn't make out the words.

"Will do," he said and picked up his bag and thermos. "I've got to go. There's an accident on First and Central," he said. "Lock the door behind me. Sarah's calling KG&E about the power. Do you want me to send someone over to escort you home?"

"No thanks," I said and sent him a smile. "I've got work to do here."

He had his back to the door as he went to leave in the same manner Sam had. "Not a lot of work can be done without power."

"Enough work to keep me going," I said. "Go. Don't worry about me. I promise not to kill anyone during this storm."

"I didn't think you would."

"Just my brother," I said and folded my arms across my chest.

"My job is taking murderers off the street."

"Yes, well, Tim is innocent, so you haven't done your job."

"We'll let a court of law decide that," he said and tipped his hat. "Take care, now."

The case would never get to a court of law. Not if I had anything to say about it.

CHAPTER 19

Without power, the baked goods in the fridge would be lost if it didn't come back on in an hour or so. The freezer was good for up to forty-eight hours as long as I didn't open it. The back kitchen was pitch-black, with only the peephole in the door for light.

I pulled a box over and propped open the door to the front. The sound of the howling wind was much louder without the hum of the fridge and freezer. My radio was also out. I had a flashlight and batteries somewhere in my office. What I needed was a light to get back there and find my flashlight.

Noting the time on the battery-run clock on the wall, I had less than two hours to either get power back or discard everything I'd been working on today. I took a deep breath and let it out slowly. A single-day buy-one-get-one-half-off special on baked goods was one thing. I peered into the dark kitchen. Without power I could lose a week's worth of work. I tried not to think about disaster. Instead I concentrated on the positive. With the cold storm outside I could always put the dough in the van. As long as it didn't get above thirty-two degrees in there, the food would be fine. Right?

A knock on the front door startled me. I might have shrieked a little. I turned around to see Sam at the door with a large cooler in his hands. He motioned with his head for me to let him in.

I rushed across the floor and unlocked the door. He blew in with the wind and stinging icy snow. "You're back." I know it wasn't the brightest thing to say, but my heart still pounded from his knock.

"I was headed home when I saw the power's out all across Main Street," he said and set down the cooler. "The automated message at KG&E says they know about the power outage and it will be back on line the moment the storm is over."

I winced. "That will be too late." I hugged my waist and tried not to despair.

"I knew you were working really hard in here and I was afraid the power outage would mess with your baking. My aunt Mary was a food inspector. She drilled into our heads what the time limits were to keep food safe." He put the cooler down, then took off his hat and gloves and set them on the closest table. "I knew there was a cooler in the back of my truck. So I stopped back by in hopes I could help. I know it's not freezer-sized, but it's something."

"What about your gram?"

"I already brought her the stuff. She's good." He studied me. "Was I wrong to come back and offer the cooler?"

"Cooler?" It dawned on me what he was saying. A cooler would be best for transporting dough. "Oh! Thank you!" I hugged him. "I hadn't had a chance to form a plan about what to do with the power out. I was thinking about putting everything in the van somehow."

He smiled at my assault and hugged me back. "If I'd have

known I would get this reaction, I would have brought you a cooler sooner."

"Oh." I stepped back and clasped my hands. "Large family means you get a little touchy-feely when you're excited."

"I'm not complaining," he said. "But I think we should figure out what needs to happen to save your dough."

"Literally," I said and glanced at the black hole that was the open door to the back kitchen. "You wouldn't happen to have a flashlight on you, would you?"

He dropped his chin and gave me the *duh* look. Then he reached into his coat and brought out a large handyman-special flashlight. "As a part-time handyman I always have one for emergencies." He flipped on the switch and handed me the light.

"Wonderful. Follow me."

He lifted the cooler, which, while large, would still hold only a portion of my baked goods. Still, some was better than none. I led him into the back kitchen.

"You can put it down right there." I pointed with the light at the floor in front of the refrigerator. "The freezer should keep its temperature longer."

He set it down and straightened. His eyes glittered in the low light. "Is the fridge full? Because if it is, I don't think this cooler will do much to help."

I blew out a breath. "Yeah, it's full. But there's a cooler in my office as well. I use it for transporting cream pies. Hold on and I'll go get it." I turned the flashlight toward my office and hurried over.

"It's pretty darn dark," he called after me.

I flashed the light back into his face without a thought. He shielded his face with his hand.

"Oops, sorry," I said as I moved the light to the floor. "Yes, it's dark. I also have candles, batteries, and a flashlight in my office. Hold on."

I stepped into the small utility closet that passed for my

office. The cot was folded and stuffed in the back corner. Against the far wall was a set of shelves. On the bottom shelf was a large cooler. I had to push the cot out into the kitchen to make room so that I could pull out my cooler. I stuffed the large flashlight under my arm as I went through my drawers. In the far back I found my flashlight. It weighed nothing, which meant I hadn't gotten around to putting batteries in it.

Reaching back through the drawer, I found C batteries, candles, and a small, pistol-shaped lighter I had taken away from Grandma. Hands full, flashlight still tucked under my arm, I glanced at the cooler. It would be best to light up the place first, then drag out the cooler.

"Hello, are you taking a nap back there?" Sam asked. "It's dark out here." I heard him try to walk toward me and run into the corner of the counter. He muttered something dark under his breath.

"I'm coming," I called back.

The light caught him right in the eyes for the second time as I moved into the kitchen. He shielded his eyes and muttered another curse.

"Oh no, sorry. I didn't mean to do that." I adjusted my full hands and the flashlight slipped out from under my arm, bounced on the tile and then back up to knock against his shin.

"Ow!" Sam grabbed his shin and hopped around. The flashlight rolled under him, flashing light around the room like a strobe light on speed.

"Watch—"

He hopped onto the flashlight and went, arms and legs flailing, to the floor. I dropped everything as I tried to catch him. How I thought I could catch him or help in any matter was impossible to know. My flashlight went bouncing off with his flashlight. The package of batteries landed with a hard *thud* on the floor, followed by the handful of scented candles and Grandma's pistol lighter, which landed in his lap.

"I'm so sorry." I knelt down and went to pick up the pistol but thought better of it. "Are you okay?"

"No good deed goes unpunished," he muttered and held his hands up, palms toward me. "I'm fine."

"I'm—"

"Sorry, I know. I doubt anything is broken, but more than my pride might be bruised tomorrow." He sat up and snagged his flashlight, which had rolled to the kick step of the counter.

"Watch your head," I said and put my hands on his shoulder.

He froze inches from the sharp corner of the countertop. "What?"

"Sharp edge," I said, leaned over and put my hand on the corner.

"Thanks," he said and moved away from me with the flashlight in his hand.

"It's the least I could do, considering." I crawled on my hands and knees and picked up my flashlight and the batteries. Then I sat down and ripped open the package.

"What are you doing?" he asked and put me in the spotlight of his flashlight.

I blinked at the intensity of it. "Putting batteries in my flashlight so we can both see."

"Let me do that." He held out his hand.

"Thanks." I gave him the flashlight and the batteries. He stood at the counter and filled my flashlight, tested it, and then handed it to me as I got up.

"It sounded like you dropped a lot of stuff." He directed his light around the floor.

"Just candles and Grandma's gun thingy." I reached over and picked up the lighter.

He grabbed my forearm. "Don't point that thing at anyone."

"I won't," I reassured him. "Besides, it's a lighter. See?" I pointed it away from us both and hit the trigger. A flash of light and flame shot out the end. "I took it from Grandma Ruth when she was trying to quit smoking."

"Did she quit?" he asked.

"No"—I shrugged—"but, hey, I got a cool lighter." I picked up the candles and arranged them on plates on the countertop. Then I lit them one by one and set them around the room until we stood in an eerie twilight.

The storm raged on outside, rattling the door and pelting the siding. The sound reminded me of the time we had a blizzard in Chicago and my apartment was assaulted by blowing tree branches.

"I have an idea," he said. "Do you have any areas in the bakery that aren't heated? My gram used to put things out on her back porch when the temperature was below freezing."

I drew my eyebrows into a deep V. "Besides putting it in the van, I don't have a porch or a shed. At least, not here. Do you know if the power is on elsewhere? Maybe we can transport this stuff to the homestead and I can store it there."

"I'm not certain. Is anyone at your house? You can call and see. It's worth a try, right?" He shrugged.

"Right. I'll see if Tasha is home." I pulled out my cell phone and dialed.

"Hello?" Mindy picked up.

"Hi, Mindy, it's Toni. Do you have power at the house?"

"Yes, why?"

"The power's out here at the bakery. I was thinking about filling the van and bringing stuff home."

"Oh, right. Okay. Do you need me to do anything?"

"No, we're good."

"We?"

"My friend Sam stopped by to help when he heard the power was out."

"I see," Mindy said. "Can he drive in the storm?"

I glanced at Sam. He leaned against the counter with his arms crossed. "He's got a nice truck."

"Then don't be a fool. Bring the stuff here."

"Right." I hung up and looked at Sam. "The power's on at the house. My fridge isn't big enough to hold everything I need, but we do have a porch and it's cold enough to store anything."

"Sounds like a plan." He opened the larger refrigerator. "Wow, you stuffed this appliance." He ran the flashlight up and down, looking at the bowls of bread dough and cooling cakes and piecrusts.

"Baked goods are in high demand during the holidays," I said and opened his cooler. My flashlight showed me that the cooler was clean. I grabbed a dish towel and gave the interior a wipe-down. After all, it had been in his truck for an unknown amount of time.

"I'm pretty sure this cooler will only hold half a shelf of what you have here. What else do you have to carry stuff in?"

"I have a cooler, too, and a few boxes. I'm pretty sure it's cold enough out that we won't have to worry about things getting too hot."

Sam laughed at that. "Heat is not the first thing I would have worried about, unless we're talking about how hot you are in your baker's uniform."

I blushed. "Stop it!" I turned on my heel and ducked back into the office to drag out a handful of boxes and the second cooler.

"I mean it," he said when I came out of the office.

"You're distracting me," I admonished him. "I have to figure out what I'm doing about all the orders I have in the works. The freezer is made to stay cold for upward of forty-eight hours. Do you think the power will be back on by then?" I triaged the things inside the refrigerator. Several bowls of bread dough filled Sam's cooler and mine. Eggs, butter, and milk, along with almond milk, filled two boxes. Cookie dough came next, along with buttercream frosting. When those were full, I went back into my office and pulled out two more boxes that had held baking supplies. "I'm pretty sure this will take care of all the things in the fridge."

"You should think about a backup generator," Sam said. "The power is pretty stable here, but . . ." He closed the lids on the stuffed coolers.

"I know," I said, trying not to think of the money that would be lost should the freezer get to room temperature. "I just don't have the cash flow yet. It's on my list for next year."

"You're lucky the power loss was in the middle of a winter storm," Sam said as he lifted the two coolers at once. "It should stay cold enough in here. Come on, let's get these in the back of my truck. The sooner you get home, the better."

"Right, okay." I bent to lift one of the boxes and realized it was heavier than I thought. Sigh. Another reason to go to the gym. I mentally added a gym membership to my New Year's resolutions.

"I'll come back for it if you can't lift it," he said and lifted the plastic coolers as if they weighed a few pounds, which I knew they didn't.

"I can get this," I said and grunted as I struggled with the box. I unlocked the front door. The wind rushed in howling and attacking with icy needles. Sam's pickup was parked directly in front of the bakery with the hazard lights on.

I let him go in front of me. The wind whipped around us and I realized that Sam had his coat on and I'd left mine in the bakery. He set the coolers in the back of his truck, grabbed the box from me, and motioned for me to go inside. I was smart enough to do what he suggested.

Once inside I rubbed my forearms as a shiver went through me. I'm not sure what I would have done if Sam hadn't come by. I could have tried to fill the van and drive it home, but it would have been a real struggle. I pushed the next two boxes toward the door as Sam came in and grabbed them.

"Get your coat," he said. "And hat and gloves. The last thing you need is frostbite."

"Okay," I said and hurried back to the hooks on the wall by the back door. I dressed for the storm, grabbed my purse, blew out the candles, and turned off the flashlights.

Sam came back for the last couple of boxes.

"Thank you for thinking of me," I said as I checked the store one last time and turned the OPEN sign around to CLOSED. "I don't know what I would have done without you."

"It's my pleasure," he said. "Come on now. The truck is nice and warm. Let's get you home."

I followed him out into the storm and turned to lock the front door. I hated to admit it, but Baker's Treat was a start-up business, and that meant it was constantly in danger of failing. I didn't know what I would do if I lost the bakery. I turned and hurried to the pickup. I wasn't going to borrow trouble. For now, Tim was getting out on bail and Sam had rescued a full day's worth of work. It was time to count my blessings.

CHAPTER 20

"So, that was a nice-looking cowboy you just sent out into the storm," Mindy said as she wrapped her hands around a fresh cup of coffee. She looked well rested and offhandedly beautiful. She wore no makeup and had only brushed her hair and pulled on yoga pants and a pink sweatshirt. "I can't believe you didn't ask him to stay."

"I offered," I said with a shrug. "But he had a couple of calls. He works as a handyman and the seniors count on him, especially when weather's bad like today."

"Hmm," Mindy said. "I can't believe you opened the bakery in this mess. The television says that power is out all over the place and the highways are definitely closed. There is a huge pileup on the turnpike."

"I would think you were used to winter storms from being in New York."

"Oh, it might be east of here, but I'm not too sure it's any more north. The weather is milder on average." She stirred her coffee. Mindy liked coffee with a dash of creamer. No, that's not true. In reality she preferred a caramel macchiato with whip. But I wasn't a barista and I wasn't interested in spending money on a fancy coffee machine.

I checked the peanut butter cookies in the oven. Cookies could be baked and frozen for later shipment. So I baked. It helped me feel like I was accomplishing something in the storm. "I kind of thought maybe the weather was milder. I know New York has better weather than Chicago."

"It's that Midwest curse." She sipped. "Everything is extreme—too cold, too hot, too windy. That's what I like about the city. The buildings and concrete tend to hold in the heat and cold. It normalizes the extremes."

The cookies were done. I pulled two dozen out of the oven to cool and put a second set in. I set the timer for ten minutes. I'd learned that if you lower the oven temperature by twenty-five degrees and then let the cookies bake longer, it made for a soft, chewy cookie. Some people liked the crunchy cookies that crumble the moment you bit into them, but I found most people preferred the soft, chewy kind.

I blew out a long breath as I slipped the cookies from the cookie sheet to the wire rack. "I have to say I do miss the city—the theaters, the lyric opera, and the wide variety of restaurants and clubs."

"Oiltop is a backwater truck stop in comparison to New York," Mindy agreed. "Still you have the best-looking well-educated lawyers. Not to mention handyman cowboys. Why is that?"

"I told you. Brad moved back to be with his family." I shrugged. "Sam's family is here as well. Family means more than city life to some people."

"Grandma Ruth told me Brad's mom and dad have passed on." Mindy stared into space. "There really isn't anything keeping him here in Oiltop."

"I suppose there isn't," I said. "Nothing except his law office and the relationships he's built in town."

"If you're talking about his membership in the Chamber of Commerce, I'd hardly consider that 'building relationships.' I bet if he put out feelers in New York, he'd have five or six offers already."

"That's a lot of interest in a small-town lawyer."

A Cheshire cat grin spread across Mindy's face. "It's not what you know but *who* you know."

"Oh." I felt my shoulders lower in defeat. "I suppose that's true." I put together a batch of peanut butter fudge with chocolate chips. My recipe was gluten-free and no-boil. As long as you overlooked the amount of butter and sugar it was a real treat.

"You look worried that I might snatch Brad away to the city."

My cousin was as smart as I was. The difference was that she used her brain to strategize how to control people where I used mine to problem solve. "I have no say over whether Brad stays or goes." I plopped butter into the stainless steel bowl of the mixer and beat it to soften. "I worry that Brad is the only chance Tim has to stay out of jail. The other lawyers in town aren't as understanding when it comes to our crazy family."

"I'm sure some other hayseed will move into Oiltop and take Brad's place." Mindy brushed off my concern. "I'm surprised you stayed after your mother died. I mean, I know you got the house, but really? You'd prefer Oiltop to Chicago?"

"It grows on you."

The front doorbell rang.

We looked at each other, startled. "Who would be out in this blizzard?" I asked. Family never rang the doorbell. Mindy shrugged and we both moved to the front door.

The wind banged the storm door against the porch siding. There in the windswept drift on the porch were Tim and Brad.

"Speak of the devil," I muttered as I opened the door

wide and ushered them both in as quickly as possible. "Why didn't you just come in?"

"Someone locked the door," Tim said. He had his thin jacket wrapped around him, the collar turned up to keep the back of his neck warm. His jeans looked wrinkled and he had a thick five-o'clock shadow. For the first time ever I noticed the gray in his beard and the deep dark circles under his eyes. He stomped the snow off his boots as he entered the foyer.

"Who? The door's never locked." I glanced at Mindy.

She shrugged. "Big-city habit."

"Are you okay?" I asked Tim and hugged him.

He stiffened. "I survived."

"Bradley, you brought home our dear Timmy." Mindy stepped right up to Brad and unbuttoned his coat. "Give me your coat. Come in out of the cold. We have coffee."

I worked to keep emotion out of my expression. Tim and I both exchanged a look at Mindy's actions.

"Did the police station have power?" I asked my brother as we left the two lovebirds alone.

"They have a backup generator," Tim said. "If you don't mind, I'm going to hang up my jacket and go shower."

"Oh, sure, I understand. I'm making fudge and cookies. The bakery is without power."

"Yeah, I heard Greenbaum brought you home." He yanked off his jean jacket, hung it on the mudroom hooks.

"How did you hear that?" I asked.

"It's a small town," Tim said.

"Sheesh. He actually came back to bring me a cooler for the stuff in the bakery refrigerator. It was a good thing, too, because I didn't have a flashlight or batteries."

"I told you, you need to put one in the front under the cash register." Tim reached over me and snagged a coffee mug off the shelf. "I'll be down in five." He poured coffee in his mug and left me to my baking.

"I'm so impressed by your efforts to come out in this awful storm and bail my dear cousin out of jail." Mindy smiled her toothpaste-ad smile at Brad. "You didn't have to come into the kitchen. Go sit in the den. We have a fire burning. You can warm your hands and I'll bring a tray in."

"I wanted to see Toni," Brad said and pushed Mindy aside to step close enough to me to give me a hug. "How are you doing? How's the bakery? I understand there might be issues with the power being out. Do you have insurance to cover your losses?"

"Hi back." I reached up and hugged him. Then I stepped back to the fudge I was making. "The food in the freezer should be good for at least a day. I've got a thermometer in there so the health inspector can see what the temperature gets to without power."

"Do you need any help? I could scrounge up some coolers, and Tim and I could unpack the freezer and bring some of the stuff here and some to my place. I have a small chest freezer in my basement. I haven't used it in years, but it's on and we could ensure the baked goods remain at proper temperatures."

"Oh, I'm sure the power will come back on before the end of the day," Mindy said and turned Brad back toward the doorway. "Come on, Toni's working. Let's go sit by the fire and have a nice visit. Okay?"

"Sure." Brad followed her through the door and out into the hall.

I heard Mindy say something and laugh. The sound was a high bell-like quality. Followed by Brad's deep baritone laugh. My heart squeezed a little. When I was first separated from Eric I thought I would never want to be with another guy. I mean, who wants that heartbreak? I was done and done.

It seemed that something happened to your brain when you first got divorced. It fell out and caused you to remake the same mistakes you made as a young adult. I was not above knowing that I could do something just as tragic. And yet I cringed at the laughter I heard coming from the den.

"I don't need a guy," I muttered out loud and poured coffee into a carafe and put it on a tray with four mugs, a sugar bowl and creamer, and a plate full of cookies. I had told Brad he should ask someone else out. From the sounds of things he was taking me at my word.

I picked up the tray and brought it into the den where Mindy was curled up on the settee next to Brad. It was a cozy scene as she leaned against his broad shoulder and batted her eyelashes at him.

"Here's your coffee."

"Oh, you didn't have to bring that out here," Mindy declared. "But thank you."

I turned to leave and Brad called out my name. "Toni . . ."

"Yes?" I stood in the doorway conflicted.

"Why don't you join us? Cooking all day won't do you any good if none of the delivery trucks can pick it up and see it delivered."

"Thanks, but I'm going to go on the assumption that they'll be up and running by later this afternoon or early tomorrow. The weather guy says the storm is clearing in Western Kansas right now."

"It's more than a storm, and you know it," he said and stood, dumping Mindy off his lap. "If enough lines are down, the power can be out for days."

"Then I'll get a generator." I shrugged. "This is my busy season. I need to invoice orders. If that means baking and boxing in the homestead kitchen, then so be it."

"That's dedication," Mindy said. "Think of all the good you could do if you had become a doctor or lawyer. Why, you might even be able to prevent poverty."

She kept her expression neutral, but I knew sarcasm when I heard it. There wasn't anything I could do. If I called her on the sarcasm she would blink at me innocently and ask what I meant. So I let the issue go. I figured someday Mindy would get her comeuppance. Karma happened that way. As for those who were mean and didn't seem to get their comeuppance, well, I believed they lived very unhappy lives.

"Thank you," I finally said. "Sometimes it's good to be stubborn."

"You're most welcome." Mindy preened like a puffed-up bird.

"You two stay and talk. Brad, Tim said he'd be down after a quick shower. I'm sure you two have a lot of things to discuss—like who might be framing him and why."

"Wait." Brad stepped toward me, but Mindy took hold of his hand and pulled him back. His electric blue gaze looked concerned and uncertain. I read once that if a man is conflicted about how he feels for you, then you should let him go. Because it's true that a man always knows if he is interested. If he's waffling, then he's just not that into you.

"I've got fudge in the mixer," I said to hold him off. "Have some coffee. Tim will be right down."

He sat back down, his gaze uncertain like that of a small child who had just gotten a smack and didn't know why.

I shook off the image. He was five years older than me. Time was ticking for both of us. If he wanted to date silly girls like Mindy, then let him. Goodness knew I was up to my neck in enough troubles.

Tim walked into the kitchen as I scraped the peanut butter fudge into the lined pan. He poured himself some more coffee. I ran a knife through the fudge and then put the pan into the refrigerator.

He leaned back against the counter and wrapped his hands around his mug. Tim was tall and lean—a good-looking man with an attractive devil-may-care attitude. There was a time when he could have had any woman he wanted, but it had taken him a while to come to the realization that maybe there was more to life than charm and wit and parties.

Don't get me wrong, I love my brother. I hated that he had moved out. I hated that he was in the mess he was in now. I kind of figured he was mad at me for not investigating. I turned to face him and let him get it out.

"How was jail? I hear you get new clothes and three square meals." I joked with him.

He looked at me with a grim gaze. "It sucks." He scowled. "I did not do this, Toni. I don't know how the heck my name got on all those hotel rooms. You know I've been working hard to get my life together. I want things before I die. I want a home and a wife and kids, and heck . . . I want grandkids." His shoulders dropped. "Who wants a felon for a husband, or for that matter, who wants a criminal for a dad?" His gaze went through my heart. "I want to be the kind of father and husband that Dad was. There's not a whole lot of time left to be that."

I hugged him tight. "You are the kind of man Dad was," I reassured him. "Everyone with a brain knows you're being framed."

"They have enough circumstantial evidence to arrest me." A tear came to his eyes. "Brad says I'm innocent until proven guilty, but it sure as heck feels like I'm guilty and need to prove otherwise."

"Was it bad in jail?"

He shrugged. "It was weird, cold, and hard. I teased them by running my cup along the bars and chanting. 'Attica, Attica. . . .'"

That made me smile. "How's the sense of humor in the station these days?"

"Stinks." He stared into his mug of coffee. "How the heck did a murderer get away with using my identity? How could none of the desk workers notice that it wasn't me? They've got record of me checking into hotels twice a week for the last eight months. I know people know who I am. They have to know it wasn't me."

"Grandma has me investigating," I said. "I'm sorry I didn't do it sooner. I'm in a bit of overload with the bakery and I really thought Calvin would clear up this terrible misunderstanding."

"Yeah, well, the prosecutor's the one who wants me doing time."

"Why?"

"It's Dan Kelly. He was elected last October to the position of district attorney."

"Dan Kelly . . . Why does his name sound familiar?"

"He was that skinny kid who I beat out as quarterback. He was a senior and I was a sophomore. He thought he was a shoo-in because he had the best throwing arm in his class."

"But yours was better."

"And"—my brother looked at me—"he was dating Mary Ellen."

"Wait." I tilted my head. "Didn't you and Mary Ellen go out for two years?"

"Yeah." He got this sheepish look on his face. "Mary Ellen was the head cheerleader. She wanted to date the star quarterback. When I won the spot from Bill, I won her, too."

I winced. "So you think he's still harboring thoughts of revenge? It's been like twenty-three years."

"Twenty-*four* years—the man has waited a long time and now he's dancing around with glee at the idea of sending me to prison for the rest of my life."

"Oh, come on." I crossed my arms. "You're both adults. He's the prosecutor. That means he has a good job, a good education, and probably a nice house and a wife and kids. Why would he risk his reputation to get revenge on you?"

Tim ran a hand over his face and pushed his hair out of his eyes. "I don't know. Maybe it's not him. It has to be someone important. Who else could steal my identity and not get caught? Some of those places have video cameras. The cops have the video from the Red Tile, and as far as Brad knows there is no evidence that I entered the check-in area."

"Well, that should exonerate you right there."

"But there's also no evidence I didn't," he said. "They've got records of my name and my signature on all those records. According to them, I paid my bills in cash. Who has that kind of cash? What the heck were they doing checking into a variety of hotels using my name?"

"What are the reasons anyone checks into a hotel?" I asked.

"To sleep," Tim said, "or to get laid."

"What about the drug angle? Why would the cops come and search your apartment and the house for drugs?"

"They think I was dealing out of those hotels." Tim's mouth went flat and his gaze turned grim. "Who would be stupid enough to put their own name in a ledger that could prove they were dealing dope out of hotel rooms?"

"Exactly," I said and patted him on the arm. "You are not stupid, and Chief Blaylock knows that."

"Yeah, well, Calvin Bright and Joe Emry worked me over for eight hours straight."

"What did you tell them?" I rubbed his arms to comfort him. Being grilled for eight hours must have been awful.

"The first thing I told them was I wanted my lawyer."

"Thank goodness for Brad," I said and meant it. "Did it take him long to get there?"

"Only about an hour. He had to do a bunch of paperwork and such before they let him in to see me."

"Then what happened?"

"They kept trying to get me to admit to being at the Red Tile Inn that day. They even tried to say they caught me on tape walking through the parking lot toward the room." He shook his head. "It wasn't me, Toni. I swear."

"Did you see the video?"

"No, Brad asked for copies of the clips, but as far as I know they didn't produce them. Brad says until they produce the videos and share them with him, they can't use them in a trial."

My heart squeezed. Trial? Would this mess really go that far? I looked into my brother's eyes and for the first time ever I saw fear. What the heck was I doing worrying about cookies when my brother was in this much trouble?

CHAPTER 21

I slept fitfully that afternoon as the storm worked itself out.
All the things I'd brought to the house had been baked.
Brad and Tim had moved from the den to the front parlor
with the pale blue–and–white settee and sateen curtains. It
was such a feminine place for two men to work.

Somewhere along the way Mindy had given up flirting
with Brad and gone up to her room. I think it was the quiet
that woke me from a dream where my bakery failed and
everyone in town laughed and told me they knew I could
not be successful with such a silly bakery. I mean, who
didn't eat wheat?

Sitting up, I rubbed my eyes and shook off the terrible
dream. I hated to nap, and even worse, I hated the way I felt
after a nap—you know, as if taking a nap only made you
feel worse.

There was a scraping noise coming from outside. I went
to my window, lifted the sheer white curtain, and saw that
Tim was outside, shoveling snow and ice off the driveway.

A quick glance at the time told me it was nearly 6:00 P.M. The winter night sky was clear and black. Without a clock it could have been 4:00 A.M.

I stretched and went to the bathroom to wash my face and run a brush through my unruly red hair. Tim was in deep trouble and, while I trusted Brad would do his best, I had come to the conclusion that if I saved Baker's Treat only to lose my brother I would never be able to live with myself.

Putting on my heavy coat, hat, gloves, and boots, I went out to give Tim a hand. The snow was about eight inches deep and had drifted to about a foot or two in places. The worst part was the layer of ice that crusted everything like the crumb-coat on a cake.

"Hey," I said and grabbed a shovel from the open garage. "How long have you been out here?"

"What time is it?" he asked and scooped up a block of snow and tossed it to the growing mounds on the side of the driveway.

"Six," I replied as I dug my shovel halfway into the drift and lifted the snow up and over the side of the drive. It was what some people termed "heart attack snow"—heavy, wet, and difficult to clear. "What time did Brad leave?"

"He left around four," Tim said, effortlessly lifting and tossing twice as much snow as I could. "I came out shortly after that."

I looked around and saw that in two hours he'd gotten two-thirds of the way down the driveway. The streetlights were coated in ice and sparkled more than they actually lit the road. The pavement in front of our house was still paved in brick. It was a quaint reminder of the oil boom days, when people built grand Victorian homes and proudly filled them with china and silver and fine linen.

The street was as filled with snow as the drive. Clearly the side streets were not a priority for the snowplows. "How did Brad get out?" I asked, noticing that there weren't even any tire tracks in the snow.

"He has a Jeep four-by-four," Tim said. "The snow filled in his tracks." Tim shoveled up more snow and tossed it. I noticed that he worked up a sweat. His heavy jacket was unzipped and the tee shirt underneath dripped with sweat.

"How are you doing?" I asked and continued to shovel snow until my arms shook with the effort.

Tim shrugged and kept working. "Until we know for sure what evidence the prosecutor has against me, there's little we can do."

I stopped with a half-lifted shovel. "So, what, you simply wait?"

"Brad says they have to schedule a hearing in the next week or so. Then we'll know more about the case." He stopped and leaned on his shovel, the picture of a man in despair. "When you live alone and work the night shift, there aren't a lot of ways you can prove you were where you say you were."

"Isn't it on the prosecution to have to prove you were where *they* say you were?"

Tim shook his head. "It's a small town, sis. People tend to make up their own minds without regard to facts."

"Is Brad going to ask for your trial to be moved to Sedgwick County? I mean, it seems only fair to try you in an unprejudiced area."

"Brad said he thought maybe Oiltop wasn't a bad place for the trial. I'd be close to home and he'd paint me as a local boy, a high school quarterback who led the school to two state championships, blah, blah, blah."

I tilted my head. "Do you think that will work?"

"Who knows?" He shrugged and went back to shoveling. "High school was a long time ago."

I left it alone and worked side by side with him until my shoulders ached and my hands were numb. We got the driveway cleared, and the front and back walk. The night sky twinkled with starlight and the Christmas lights I'd had Tim hang around the wraparound porch twinkled and illuminated the white snow. It was as if someone had painted the homestead in white icing. Postcard pretty. I reached into my pocket, pulled out my cell phone, and snapped a couple of pictures.

"You know, I never asked how you are with Harold's death. I know you two were pretty close growing up."

"Yeah," Tim said, his expression grim. "I hadn't seen him in over a year. Still, it hit me hard. First Dad, then Mom, and now Harold." He shoveled snow as if his life depended on it. "I went to his funeral."

"You did?" I asked. I was so busy with the bakery that I hadn't even paid attention to Harold's funeral. I felt pretty low right now.

"Yeah," Tim said quietly. "His cousin Jeff asked me to leave."

I stopped short. "He did not."

"Yes, he did." Tim nodded his head. "So much for losing an old friend."

"You said you hadn't seen him in a year," I said. "What happened?"

"We had a fight," Tim said as he shoveled. "It was over something stupid. He was all hot over this new business he started. Harold had this surefire investment program he'd bought into. He was looking for a partner." Tim grimaced. "There was no way I was buying into one of those business schemes you see on late-night TV. Harold got pissed. He said it would look bad to people if his own best friend didn't invest. I told him I didn't have the capital, and if I did I wasn't going to spend it on a 'surefire' scheme. Dad taught me better than that. He got pissed and stormed out. We hadn't talked since."

I reached out and put my hand on Tim's shoulder. "I'm sorry."

He looked up at the night sky and studied the stars. "Thanks."

I gave him time to think about his loss before I went back to shoveling. The twinkle lights from the house across the street had me thinking. "It's so strange to think it's the holidays," I said. "I've been so busy baking and you've been arrested—and now this storm. I'd nearly forgotten that this season is about peace on Earth and goodwill to men."

"How can you forget when you have 1972-era decorations in the basement year-round?" Tim grinned at me. It seemed he'd gotten most of his frustrations out shoveling the snow and ice. We were both physically and emotionally exhausted. Just as we turned to put the shovels away and go in for warm drinks, the street plow came through and filled the bottom of the driveway with a knee-high drift of snow.

"Oh, now, that was simply mean," I said as he drove out of sight.

"Merry Christmas to all and to all a good night," Tim muttered. We both turned back, got our shovels, and attacked the drift. It's funny how at one point of exhaustion you feel warm and relaxed and almost happy. And yet if you have to continue past that point your muscles scream and you are filled with frustration and anger, wanting to rail at the unfairness of it all. The newly plowed drift, my loss of power and work time, and Tim's terrible arrest was almost too much to bear.

As Tim scooped up the last shovelful and tossed it on the head-high mound of snow I heard a faint whirr of wheels. I noticed an orange triangle waving in the air around the drifts. Grandma Ruth came tearing around the icy road on her Scootaround. She had strapped a flashlight between her handlebars, giving anyone coming at her just enough light to notice her in the middle of the road.

"Grandma! Get off the road. You are going to get killed. At the bare minimum the snowplows will run you over."

Grandma zipped around the corner into the driveway and stopped by the back door. She wore goggles and an old-fashioned leather pilot's flight hat strapped under her chin. Her torso was wrapped in a thick leather coat with lamb's wool inside. She had on a butterfly patterned skirt, thick striped over-the-knee socks, and heavy combat boots.

"I'm going to have to rig a headlight for her scooter, aren't I?" Tim muttered as we walked in tandem to the garage to put away the shovels.

"And reflectors," I added. "The triangle doesn't work so well in the dark."

"Hi, kids. Nice work on the driveway." Grandma slowly swung her hefty body off the seat of the scooter. "No worries, Toni, I won't drive my scooter into the house . . . just yet. I know how fussy you are about a little snow and salt on your wood floors."

"Grandma, what are you doing? It must be at best twenty degrees out. You're going to catch your death of cold."

"Honey, by now I've figured out that death is more worried that I will catch it than I am of it catching me." She used the rails on either side of the steps to hang on and lurch up them. Grandma had had both knees replaced in the last ten years. She also had a new hip. They worked well enough, considering Grandma had refused to go to physical therapy afterward.

When I'd mention PT, she'd shake her head and tell me she didn't have time for such silliness. Besides, she got around just fine with her scooter.

Grandma stopped at the top landing and pulled a half-smoked cigarette out of her skirt pocket. Her lighter clicked as she created a flame and lit the remaining bit of tobacco.

"Grandma." I coughed and waved my hand through her smoke. "It's a law that you have to be fifteen feet from an entrance to smoke."

"That's a public entrance. This is a private residence."

Grandma drew in a deep breath, held it a second then blew a long cloud of smoke straight up. "Bring out a can, will ya? The butt collector is buried under the snow somewhere and I don't want to pollute."

"You're always so thoughtful." Tim gave Grandma a kiss on her cheek. "Go on, Toni, get the poor woman a butt can."

I narrowed my eyes at my brother and he laughed. Lucky for me, the mudroom shelves held a wide variety of cans and vases and miscellaneous containers—some empty and some full. I picked the least valuable one and handed it to Grandma.

Tim took his boots off in the mudroom and hung up his coat and hat. I did the same and moved in stocking feet to make a fresh pot of coffee.

"I heard on the police scanner that the power has been restored to Main Street." Grandma waddled into the kitchen and sat down with a huff and a cloud of smoke.

I grabbed three mugs of coffee and brought them to the table, where Tim and Grandma sat. In my family some of the most important conversations happened over cookies and hot beverages. I put a variety of cookies on a plate along with the fudge and set it on the table.

"You've been busy," Grandma said as she snagged three cookies.

"I'm a day behind on my order list." I sat down. "I managed to get some of the orders filled here. I need to get back into the bakery and see what survived the power outage."

"Didn't that nice boy Sam Greenbaum drive you home this morning?" Grandma asked.

"How do you—never mind." I sighed. My neighbor Mrs. Dorsky was number one on Grandma Ruth's senior watch call tree. "Yes, the van was too unstable in the wind."

"How do you intend to get back to the bakery?" Tim asked as he stretched his long legs out in front of him and absently played with his cup of coffee.

"I suppose you could drive me," I said. "Or I could take Grandma's scooter."

"Hey, keep your mitts off my scooter." Grandma talked as she chewed the cookie, spitting crumbs all the while giving me the stink eye for even suggesting such a thing.

"The only way I'd drive you there is if I stayed," Tim said. "Brad advised me to never be alone night or day. I need solid alibis in case the identity thief strikes again."

"I have a cot in my office," I said with a shrug.

"Why can't Brad take her?" Grandma asked.

"Brad has a date," Tim said. "Our cousin is on the hunt for a new man, and I think she's set her eyes on Brad."

Grandma eyed me. "You okay with that?"

"I have to be." I shrugged. "Brad's free to date whoever he wants."

"You don't sound happy about it," Grandma pointed out.

"No, I am," I said truthfully. "If he and Sam find other women to date before I'm ready, then I have to be okay with that. Besides, I have a business to concentrate on."

"So, Grandma, you can tell me," Tim said. "What's up with Mindy? Why is she suddenly back in Oiltop and picking up men?"

Grandma Ruth concentrated on picking up crumbs off her ample breast. "She's going through a bit of a rough spot. The last thing I need is for you two to reject her."

"We're not rejecting her," I stated.

"We're curious." Tim put his arm around my shoulders. "Aren't we, sis?"

"Curiosity did nothing for the cat," Grandma said and bit into another cookie. "I can tell you she'll be here through Christmas, so you'd better have something for her under the tree."

"Ugh, Christmas." My shoulders fell along with my mood. "There are only a few days until Christmas and I don't have half the cookie orders ready." At this rate I would have to work night and day and perhaps split myself in two so that I could sleep and still get things done.

"Never fear, I got you the coolest present."

"That's great," I muttered. "I haven't even started shopping for Christmas."

"So, Grandma, you're telling us that Mindy came all the way to Kansas for Christmas presents?"

"I hope not, because I don't have the budget to buy her one," I said.

"As far as I can tell, Ridgeway is her present."

I rolled my eyes. "I'm glad she's here. She can decorate the parlor Christmas tree. A tree someone hasn't purchased yet." I eyed Grandma. She usually insisted that she get to go and pick out the perfect tree. This time she was quiet on the subject.

"I'll take her with me to find the perfect tree. Bill's going to bring his little hatchet and make everything go smoothly. I know Mindy won't mind letting us cut down the tree. This year we'll cut down the tree she picks." Grandma yawned and stretched her arms. "Besides, Tim, you should be happy to have Mindy around. She can be your shadow alibi until we figure out who's trying to frame you."

"Yeah, well, I won't be going anywhere for a while," Tim stated. "I got a call this afternoon. I'm fired."

"What?"

"Can they do that?"

"I missed a shift last night. That gave them the excuse they needed to fire me. They don't want a killer employed with them."

"Wait," I said and held out my hand in a stop sign. "This is America. You're innocent until proven guilty."

Tim ran a hand through his light brown hair. "I was fired for missing a shift without calling in."

"How could you call in if you were in jail?" I put my hands on my hips. Tim had been working hard at his job and had finally gotten some seniority. It made me so mad that all his hard work was worthless. A single suspicion and they'd dropped him like a hot potato.

"That's terrible," Grandma said and patted Tim on the shoulder. "Too bad your sister didn't investigate sooner and clear up this entire misunderstanding."

"Grandma, I am not responsible for Tim losing his job." I tossed my hands up in the air. "I've been busting my hump trying to keep from losing *my* job."

"Oh, pish." Grandma waved her hand, dismissing my concerns. "I love you, kiddo, but your brother's life is far more important than a bunch of Christmas cookies."

"To begin with, my gluten-free cookies might be the only thing that makes a newly diagnosed person feel as if they're normal. Second, the bakery is my life. Third, I thought it was time to allow the professionals to do their jobs."

"I get it, Toni." Tim shoved his hands in his jean pockets. "You're busy. I'm a screwup."

I rolled my eyes. Those two could really lay on a guilt trip.

"What's going on?" Tasha walked into the kitchen with Calvin Bright right behind her. Aubrey followed along at their heels. The puppy loved Calvin and never let him out of sight when Tasha's date was at the house.

"Tim lost his job," Grandma said and gave Calvin the evil eye.

"I'm sorry to hear that," Calvin said evenly. "Are you moving back in for good?"

Tim winced. "I've been advised to never be alone until the murderer is caught."

Calvin and Tasha exchanged a look. "I think that's smart," Calvin said. "Look, Tasha and I are here to let you know she and Kip are moving into my place."

"What?" I stood. "Are you sure?"

"It's sort of sudden, isn't it?" Grandma asked, her expression one of concern.

"We feel it's best for Kip," Tasha said. She looked at my brother. "No offense, Tim, but I can't have Kip living with a man out on bail." She then looked at me. "I also can't have him staying in a place where someone is hiding drugs. I hope you understand."

"You know we didn't hide drugs on my mother's property," I said, oddly hurt by Tasha's words.

"I'm not blaming anyone," Tasha said with her hands up. "I'm thinking about Kip. You know how he takes everything so literally. It's been hard to explain what's going on here."

"That someone is framing Tim?" I asked and crossed my arms in front of me.

"We hope you understand that this isn't about Tim," Calvin said. "It's about what's right for Kip."

"And moving in with you is what's right for Kip?" I said, my gaze going from Calvin to Tasha. My best friend had the good grace to blush.

"For now, yes," Calvin said. He was so calm and sincere it was hard to get mad at him.

"Fine," I said. "You're a big girl. You know what's best for your son."

"I do," Tasha said. "Thanks for understanding. There's just one problem." Tasha held Calvin's hand and I noticed a reassuring squeeze.

"What?" I asked.

"We can't take Aubrey." The pup looked from Tasha to me. It was as if he knew we were talking about him. "Calvin's apartment complex doesn't allow pets over thirty pounds. Can Aubrey stay with you until I can save up enough to get our own home with a yard?"

Aubrey reached up and licked Calvin's hand. The officer rubbed Aubrey's head and the pup closed his eyes in joy.

I felt sad at the sight of the pup's delight. Little did he know that Calvin was ditching him. "Of course Aubrey can stay," I said. Maybe if I kept the dog, Tasha would come to her senses and move back home.

"Good," Calvin said.

"Thank you," Tasha said.

"What about Kip?" I asked, my arms still crossed in front of me. "He loves Aubrey. They're best buddies, aren't they?"

"I told Kip that Aubrey needed to stay where he was safe and had a yard to run in."

"And the kid went for that?" Tim asked.

"It took some convincing, but we were finally able to get him to understand it was for the best," Calvin said. "Part of good pet ownership is putting the pet's needs first."

"Plus, we told Kip he could come visit Aubrey any time he wanted, right?" Tasha winced a bit.

"Of course," I said. "You and Kip are family. The homestead is always open to family."

"When are you moving out?" Grandma asked.

"Tonight, if possible," Calvin stated and tightened his fingers around Tasha's.

"In the snow?" I asked. "Do you have power at your apartment? Can you get through the roads?"

"We have a backup generator," Calvin said. "I've been patrolling all day. The drive won't be a problem."

"You seem to be in a bit of a hurry," Tim said, his eyes at a lazy half-mast. I knew that look. My brother had figured out Calvin was using him to get Tasha to move out.

"It's been a long time coming," Tasha said. "I felt so bad imposing on you the last couple of months."

"You weren't imposing," I said. "You paid rent and did chores. I like seeing you every day, and Kip, too."

"We promised Kip that he could come over to feed and walk Aubrey every day," Tasha reassured me. "Now is a good time to move. That way Kip and I and Calvin can have the Christmas holiday as a new family." She looked up at Calvin with adoring eyes. "It's really for the best."

"At least let me make you a farewell dinner," I said and stood to put on my apron and see what I had in the house to cook.

"No need," Tasha said. "Calvin's mom filled the kitchen for us before the storm. Plus I have lasagna in the Crock-Pot."

"Oh." I tried to keep the disappointment off my face. "So this is it? You're packed already?"

"Yes," Tasha said. "Kip's on the stairs playing his video games."

"I didn't hear you pack," I whined.

"You've been working very hard lately and when I saw you were sleeping I didn't have the heart to wake you. You understand, right?"

I swallowed the emotion in my throat. "Sure." I hugged her and kissed her cheek. "Remember, you always have a home here."

She squeezed me tight. "I know, sweetie. This is really for the best."

I walked them to the door. It was then that I noticed the suitcases waiting by the door. Calvin had pulled up in front of the house and the side doors to his crossover were open, along with the hatchback.

"Come on, Kip." Tasha reached out and touched her son's shoulder. Kip pulled away at her touch.

"I'm nearly to the next level."

"You can finish the level in the car," Calvin said. His tone was straightforward. "Plus you'll win a sticker for following instructions immediately."

"Cool." Kip moved toward the door.

"Say good-bye to Auntie Toni and Uncle Tim and Grandma Ruth," Tasha chided him.

Kip stopped and turned toward us, his gaze never leaving the screen of his game. "Bye."

"See you soon," I said. "Don't worry, we'll take good care of Aubrey." I held the big pup by his collar. He sat on his haunches as if he knew he was not going with Tasha. His loyalty to me warmed my heart. Here was a creature who was happy to stay with me through thick or thin . . . as long as I had treats, that was. I knew even dogs had limits to their devotion.

"Bye, Aubrey." Kip stopped long enough to give the dog a hug around the neck then rushed out the door to the waiting car.

"Zip up your coat!" Tasha called after him. She smiled and hugged me again and then she and Calvin picked up the suitcases and left us to stand in the door and wave good-bye.

The car was packed, the doors closed, and Calvin drove off into the darkness of the quiet snow. I closed the door and saw the despair on my brother's face and the disappointment on Grandma's. We all knew that this was a last-minute decision. Calvin was a police officer and couldn't afford to be seen with a suspected murderer.

"I still need a ride to work," I muttered as I walked to the kitchen to give Aubrey a dog treat so that he wouldn't feel the loss of his family as much as I did.

"Sam brought you home. Call him to take you back." Grandma's eyes sparkled as she sat down at the kitchen table. "Or better yet, call Officer Strickland. Then, while you're in the car, try to find out what, if anything, they have on your brother. We can't defend what we don't know."

"Like that won't be weird," I said. "I might as well call Officer Emry. He's more likely to tell me things than Officer Strickland."

"Officer Emry will do," Grandma said. "If that's who you want to ride to the bakery with. There's no accounting for taste."

I rolled my eyes. "So that's it now?" I asked. "I'm supposed to call up the police department and get them to drive me to the bakery so that I can spy on the enemy?"

"Just bat your eyes and act helpless," Grandma Ruth advised. "Either one of them might just let some important information slip."

"If you can't do it for me," Tim said as I handed the dog a gluten-free doggie biscuit I'd been experimenting with, "do it for Baker's Treat. Because if your own BFF can't stand to be near me, imagine what your customers will feel."

I scowled at my brother. "Sometimes you are so mean."

He shrugged. "Guilty by association, Toni."

The worst part is I knew he was right.

CHAPTER 22

"Thanks for picking me up and bringing me into work," I said to Officer Strickland as we sat at the corner of Third Street and Central waiting for the light to turn green.

"Not a problem," he said smoothly. "I'm glad you called. The power might be back, but the roads are still rough."

I sat for a moment and tried to figure out how to ask a question. Deciding to try to be subtle, I asked. "So, what happens to all those people stranded on the highway?"

"We pick them up, mark the car, and call a tow truck."

"But tow trucks aren't running in the snow, are they?" I played with the handle of my purse and studied his profile.

"No, we advised them to stay off the roads so that the plows could get their work done. The fewer people on the roads, the better for the plows to come through and move the snow and attack the ice with salt."

"So what do you do with stranded people? Is there like a Red Cross shelter or something?"

He glanced at me then turned down Central Avenue. "We take them to a central location and have volunteer staff who match them with local hotels, or, if they have family in the area, we connect them. Once they have a place to go, we dedicate a van to take them to their various shelters."

"Huh, so like hotels and such."

"Yes."

I sat silent for a moment. "Do you find that crime goes up when people are in unexpected places or does it go down because of the *we're all in this together* feel?"

"Generally people are less likely to make trouble in times of crisis," he said. "That said, it's the department's policy to at least drive by all the hotels and check on the residents. If a storm lasts too long, employees get tired and food becomes scarce and then trouble can brew."

"What can the police department do about it?"

"We keep an eye on things and bring food donated by the local food pantries. Pretty much we walk through the hotel or motel and answer questions. A lot of times, just having a presence keeps people in line."

"Wow." I widened my gaze. "Do you only do that during a crisis?"

"Pretty much." We stopped at a red light on Central and First Street.

"Do people like to see a police presence at hotels only when there's a problem?"

"Most of the time we keep our presence to times of crisis. If a hotel is a known magnet for trouble, we usually schedule someone to check on the security once a night."

"I had no idea," I said as we sped up and headed toward Main and the back alley of the bakery. "What are some of the places you patrol the most?"

He glanced at me.

I kept my expression innocent. "I have a lot of family

who come into town. They can't all stay at the homestead. I don't want to put them up in a known trouble spot."

"Right." He gave a short nod. "The Super 7 is one, Paulette's Cabins, usually any one of the places right off the turnpike. People like to stop when they get tired and rest for a short time. So these places see people come and go pretty quickly. That leads to an unstable environment, and some criminal elements take advantage of that."

"Huh, see, I would have never thought of that. Who pays for you all to patrol the hotels? Is that a taxpayer service or is there like a security package the hotel can pay for?"

Again he glanced at me, suspicious of my motives. My heart raced. I stilled my fingers and smiled at him. "Tasha and I are thinking of turning the homestead into a bed-and-breakfast. What's a single gal like me going to do with all that space, anyway?"

"I doubt your house is in an area zoned for hotels," he replied.

"Oh, no, it's not. I need to get down to the zoning and planning department to see whether or not I can even do it. But I thought since I had you here, you might know."

He pulled up to the back of the bakery. I wasn't surprised to see that snow had drifted to a couple of feet high in front of the back door.

Parking, Officer Strickland put his arm over the top of his steering wheel and turned toward me. "Do you need me to check out the store before you enter?"

"Oh, no thanks." I unbuckled my seat belt. "It looks like we're the only ones downtown right now, anyway." I smiled at him. "Thanks for the ride."

"Not a problem. Call the department anytime," he said.

I opened my door and climbed out into the sharp, cold night. The breath froze in my nose and the snow crunched under my feet as I turned to the warm interior of the car, my hand on the edge of the door. "Thanks again."

"You're welcome." He peered up at me. "As for the answer to your question, the hotels are responsible for their security. Marcus Blackmore runs a team of security guards."

"Really?" I tilted my head and leaned toward the warm interior. "Are they trained security people or just random hourly workers?"

"A lot of the police force works for him on their off time," he said. "A first responder's salary is notoriously low. We pick up extra jobs when we can."

I winced. "Wow, I'm sorry."

He laughed and shrugged. "Just remember that the next time you're voting on a budget increase for the county. We know that you don't want to raise taxes, but those taxes pay for things like police and firefighters as well as other first responders."

"I'll remember," I said. "Thanks again." I closed the door and walked through the drifts to the back door of the bakery.

Inside was warm with a blaze of lights on. With the power off there had been no way to tell which lights were on and what were off. The hum of the freezer and refrigerator were music to my ears. I opened the freezer and was happy to see the temperature was still below freezing.

The refrigerator was another story. It was humming overtime in an attempt to cool itself again. I hung up my coat, stuffed my hat and gloves in a pocket, and put on a fresh apron. Then I grabbed a plastic bucket and made a vinegar-and–baking soda cleaning solution. Sliding on my pink rubber gloves, I turned to take a clean dishcloth off the linen pile on the baker's rack that sat with its back against the fridge and faced the table and chairs.

I used dishcloths instead of sponges because they were easier to keep clean. I'd use the cloth once, then rinse and toss into the laundry. On warm summer days I would hang the linens out in the sunshine. Sunlight was the best way to kill bacteria. In the winter I added bleach to the wash. They didn't smell as sweet, but they were virus-free.

It took me about an hour to properly clean the refrigerator, but it was completely worth it. It would be months before I'd have an empty icebox again.

I stood back and eyed my appliance with pride. The glass shelves sparkled and the sides gleamed. Suddenly the back door to the bakery opened. Startled, I clutched the bucket in my hands, ready to throw the dirty water—my only defense— in the face of an intruder.

"Wait! Wait!" Meghan held her hands up. "Don't douse me. I swear I took a shower before I came in."

I put the bucket down and slumped my shoulders. My heart still raced and my mouth was dry. "Holy goodness, you scared the *p* out of me."

"Sorry." Meghan grimaced. She was dressed in a navy ice-skater coat. Her legs were encased in black leggings and she wore knee-high lace-up steel-toed boots. She had on white knit gloves, a white knit scarf, and a white knit beret with a red-and-green stripe in the front slanted on her pitch-black hair.

Her lovely winged eyebrows had red and green jewels in the piercing. Her cute nose had a nose ring and her ears had studs all the way up and around the outside.

"What are you doing here?" I asked and glanced at the clock as it read midnight.

"If figured you might need some help, since the power was out for almost ten hours." She took off her gloves, unbuttoned her coat, and revealed a Betty Boop pop art tee shirt and black pleated miniskirt underneath.

Every time I saw her in a new outfit I wished I were nineteen years old again and could wear cool clothes. The sad truth was that I was in my forties. I worked so much that three-quarters of my closet was filled with standards like black slacks and white button-down shirts.

Even if I was young and could afford the cute clothes Meghan wore, I simply didn't have her dramatic flair. Today she wore thick black eyeliner, mascara, and nude lipstick.

"Wow, you cleaned the fridge?" Meghan peered into the empty appliance. "Cool! What did you do with everything inside?" She glanced around. "You didn't bake it, did you?"

"No, Sam Greenbaum stopped by and brought me a cooler. With that, plus the Styrofoam cooler in my office, and a few empty supply boxes, we were able to dig out everything of merit."

Meghan looked around. "Where are the coolers?"

"We took them to the house. I did a lot of baking there. Which means we're only a day behind, not days.

"That said, why don't you start the coffee? I think it's going to be a long night of baking."

"Cool," she said and moved toward the coffeepot.

"How'd you get here?" I asked as I put eggs and milk and butter out to reach room temperature. "Don't tell me you walked. It's like minus twenty outside."

Meghan laughed. "You're such a mom. And the answer is no. No, I didn't walk or ride my bike here. My boyfriend, Andre, brought me. He works the snowplows in between classes, so he knew all the roads that were safe to travel."

"Oh, huh." I set up for the next two batches of baked goods. "Who exactly is this Andre and why haven't you mentioned him before?" I asked and put a hand over my heart in a silent apology at the scolding way the words came out. "What I meant was where did you meet? A bar? The roller rink? The bowling alley?"

Meghan laughed and the sound was like tiny bells in the air. "No, nothing so cool as the roller rink or bowling alley. We met in church, actually."

"In church?" I drew my eyebrows down in confusion. Meghan never talked about her religion, and I realized that I didn't know that much about her. I mean, I knew that she was young and on her own. I knew that her parents believed that their job was done when the kid turned eighteen and graduated high school. I knew that she was struggling to pay her rent and go to school.

But one look at the piercings and kooky vintage wardrobe along with the pitch-black hair and the wild-colored streaks and the last thing you thought of was small-town church-goer.

"Yes, I sing in the choir. Andre plays guitar." She went right to work making coffee.

Now I felt horrible for being so self-involved that I could work with her every day and not know this simple fact. "That's really awesome," I said.

"I know, isn't it?" Meghan said with a dreamy look on her face. I remembered that look. I'd had it once. "Wait, how'd *you* get here?" she asked, her dark brows pulling together. "It looks like the van hasn't been driven since the storm started."

"I got a ride with Officer Strickland."

"Really?" She looked more confused. "Why not your brother or Uncle Sam or even that hunky Brad guy?"

"Well," I said as I started a fresh batch of chocolate chip cookie dough, "first of all, my brother Tim was arrested yesterday and spent the night in jail."

"Oh no, I hadn't heard." She put her hands on her hips. "That's terrible. What are they accusing him of?"

I flattened my mouth and shook my head. "They arrested him for suspicion of murder."

"What? No!"

"I know, right?" I finished up. "He had his bail posted and Brad worked tirelessly to get him out. He was able to convince the judge that Tim was not a flight risk."

"They did this in the middle of that storm?"

"Well, they can only hold you so long without a hearing. Brad worked it so that the judge and prosecutor all Skyped into the jail. Tim was let out on one hundred thousand dollars bail."

"Ouch." Meghan crossed her arms. "Where did he get the money?"

"Grandma Ruth offered to pay, but I let him put the homestead up for collateral."

"Good thing he didn't do it. What would you do if he skipped town and you lost the house?"

"I suppose I could stay with Grandma until I figured out other accommodations."

"You wouldn't close up Baker's Treat, would you?"

"No," I reassured her. "Baker's Treat would not close because I lost my home." I didn't mention the fact that I had several bills at the ninety-day point and that I needed to deliver an unreasonable amount of Christmas baked goods to pay them off. It was always best to tackle one problem at a time.

"I suppose you could always rent the space above the bakery," Meghan said thoughtfully.

"I think it would take Mrs. Melcher a year to move all the stuff she has stored up there."

"In the meantime, you always have the cot in your office," Meghan said. Her smile lit up the room.

"Saw that, did you?"

"You work too hard." She added, "You need to go out and have fun. When was the last time you were on a date?"

"Oh, now, don't you start in on me," I said and went to the front to pull out all the day-old pastries from the glass cabinet.

"You know what they say about all work and no play. . . ."

"I'll play when the holidays are over. For now this is our prime time," I said as I pulled out a tray of cupcakes and put them on the day-old rack in the back.

Meghan grabbed the remainder of the baked goods and piled them all on one tray then stacked the used trays for washing. I eyed the pile. There were three trays of day-old baked goods. All a loss. The thing about gluten-free was that unlike wheat flour, gluten-free flours tended to crumble in a day or two. Baked goods had to be eaten soon or frozen to preserve the taste and texture.

"Well, I'm glad I came into work," she said. "If we both work all night then we can get caught up."

"Hmm, that is if the delivery guys will show up tomorrow."

"We're going to say they will."

I was cheered by her youthful enthusiasm. Right now I felt exhausted from worry. Maybe spending the night baking with a teenager would help turn around my lack of holiday spirit. One could hope.

CHAPTER 23

"Did you know that there is a security company that patrols the hotels in the area?" I asked Tasha the next morning.

"Sure, the Red Tile uses them." She dunked her tea bag in her mug. It was after the morning rush and Tasha had come into Baker's Treat to see me and make sure our friendship was okay after her moving out.

"Is there only one in town?" I asked as I wiped down the coffee bar and replenished the creams and sugars. I'd made Meghan go home at 5:00 A.M. after we'd caught up on cookie dough making, leaving the yeast dough to proof and the cakes to cool. She'd been a trouper, working through the night, but she was still only part-time help and I had to ensure she watched her hours. Thank goodness she didn't have any classes this week. She'd admitted that her final was a cake-off, so I'd let her look through my recipes. She decided on a delicate cinnamon raisin cake with orange filling and cream cheese frosting. Tonight I would let her practice making it. The actual final had to be made in the school's kitchen under the watchful eye of the instructor.

"There used to be two security companies," Tasha said. "But the competition was fierce and Blackmore Brothers Security won out."

"Was it competition or was there some kind of mafia thing going on?"

Tasha laughed. Her pretty blonde hair bounced and her blue eyes sparkled. She looked good. Calvin had a positive influence on her and I hoped that he was as wonderful as he seemed. Tasha deserved that and more. "You have such a criminal mind, Toni. No, there was no mafia or payouts. Blackmore underbid the other company at every turn. Their business model was better. They use only part-time guys and don't offer any insurance or benefits. Everyone is a subcontractor.

"The other security company was Haverson. They were a family business and had two crews of five that worked full-time. Full-time pay and benefits are expensive. They simply couldn't compete."

"That doesn't seem right." I hung the washcloth on a hook behind the counter to dry then poured myself some hot cocoa and sat with Tasha. She wore a lovely flowered blouse under a Christmas green sweater and fresh dark-wash jeans. It made me self-conscious of my black pants, plain white tee and pink-and-white bib apron. Perhaps it was simply that I was exhausted. I'd managed to sleep two hours in my cramped office before the alarm went off and I opened up.

"I agree it doesn't seem right," Tasha said. "But this is America and capitalism is king. The best business model wins. Blackmore has that. If you look at it from the hotel management point of view, cheaper is better. It's not like Oiltop is a hotbed of crime. Most of the time the security presence is there only to give the customer a sense of safety, not to actually do anything."

"That's pretty clear." I stretched my legs out and slumped in my chair. "If the Red Tile had real security, then the murder would have never happened."

"Oh, I don't know." Tasha's expression turned serious. "Legally we can only keep an eye on what goes on in the public areas. What happens in the rooms is private."

"So there was no way to prevent the murder?"

Tasha shook her head. "Not really. By law we have to allow anyone who can pay to rent a room. We can't discriminate. After that we can call the police if they are disturbing the peace or if we notice any illegal activity."

"What kind of illegal activity?"

"Prostitution or drug dealing." Tasha played with the rim of her mug. "The Red Tile is a family hotel. We call right away if we notice anyone shady. That's why this murder was such a shock. It's been really bad for business. We've had several reservations get canceled. I may need to let some of the staff go until things pick up again."

"Ouch." I winced. "I hadn't thought about the effect it might have on your business."

"Thankfully, this time it isn't my business but my boss's. He promised me that I will be the last one to be laid off, but I had to agree to do whatever needs done—from cleaning toilets to changing lightbulbs."

"Oh." I made a face. "So he's working you like you own the place, but you don't. Is he at least paying you well?"

She lifted one shoulder in a slight shrug. "It's a job. In this economy I'm happy to have the work."

"Tim lost his job," I stated and ran my hand over my face in exhaustion. "I'm racing the clock to get orders out so that I can bring money in. I've got bills ninety days past due that could sink me if the holiday business doesn't go well."

"I wondered why you look so tired. I bet this storm set you back."

"I worked all night and I'm almost caught up." I sent her

a small smile. "Now I need my delivery guys to show up and send things out."

"Oh, I hadn't thought about the highways being closed. Christmas is only two weeks away. Will they arrive on time?"

"I'll have to overnight several orders for free." My mouth flattened at the memory of the price of overnight shipping during the holidays. "But so far so good. Plus I'm keeping my fingers crossed."

"Lots of people are taking second jobs," Tasha said. "Calvin talked about picking up a security shift with Blackmore." She smiled brilliantly. "He thought he could work security for the Red Tile Inn while I'm on shift. That way we can be together and make money."

"Officer Strickland was telling me that several of the Blackmore employees are on the police force."

"It's true."

"Then that makes the identity thief/murderer even more brazen if he did this under the noses of the local police."

"Unless . . ."

"Unless what?" I leaned in.

"Unless he *is* one of the security guys." Tasha's eyes grew wide.

"Oh." I sat back, my thoughts a whirl. "If he were a part-time security worker, then he would be able to go from hotel to hotel without anyone noticing."

"Yes, we don't think twice about it when a Blackmore uniformed guard comes in. In fact, we've been known to comp them a room if things are slow or they're working late."

"Do they sign in when you comp them?"

"Yes, but we don't really pay attention to the names." Tasha's fingers tightened around her cup. "We see them all the time. We just assume they're putting their own names down." She paused. "You know what else? Lance Webb works part-time for Blackmore. Funny, but I hadn't thought about him in years and then suddenly there he is working for Blackmore." She shrugged. "It's a small world."

"Someone from Blackmore could be putting my brother's name down and staying in the rooms."

Tasha looked at me with surprise and horror. "I suppose they could. For that matter, they could put down anyone's name. We see so many strangers that we don't really pay attention to the names and faces."

"Do you think Lance has anything to do with Harold's murder?"

"Oh, I don't know," Tasha said. "I don't think they really knew each other."

"What if they did?" I reached into my apron pocket and pulled out my cell phone.

"Who are you calling?"

"I'm calling Brad," I said. "He would know what to do with this information. Maybe he can check out Lance as well."

"Good idea." Tasha leaned in toward me, concern on her face.

I listened as the phone rang and Brad picked up. "Ridgeway."

"Hi, Brad, it's Toni Holmes."

"Hi, Toni." His voice had that confident male tone that made me weak in the knees. "What can I do for you?"

"Thanks for helping bail out Tim."

"That's my job."

"Any luck on getting video from the Red Tile incident?" I asked and Tasha drew her eyebrows together in confusion. I held up one finger to let her know I had a plan.

"No, the video seems to be in analysis hell. No one's seen it since Strickland took it to the IT guys. We all know it could be months before they get to it. The legal system is overwhelmed and understaffed."

"Can they go to trial without the video? It seems as if everything they have on Tim is completely circumstantial."

"It's hard to tell at this point. I'm still waiting on the evidence. It takes a while for the court system to gather it, make copies, and ensure I get them."

"I'm glad Tim made bail. It would be horrible to incarcerate him while the judicial process takes its sweet time."

"I'm sure Tim appreciates the fact that you put the homestead up as collateral."

"Quick question . . ."

"Sure."

"Have you checked for video from any of the other hotels on the nights when Tim supposedly stayed?"

"I requested it," Brad said. "The judge had to issue a warrant to collect it. That went through this morning. Officer Emry is out collecting that information right now."

"That means you won't see those images for months." I frowned at the idea of bumbling Officer Emry collecting CDs of the videos. "Is there any way you can download the files and look at them right away?"

"Maybe," Brad said. "I could ask the judge if I could establish a private Dropbox file where all shared evidence is stored online. It's unprecedented at this time, but it doesn't mean I can't ask."

"One last thing." I watched Tasha move her hands as if to signal for me to get to the point.

"Sure."

"Do you know Blackmore Brothers Security?"

"Vaguely . . . The company is part of the Chamber of Commerce. I might know the owner. Why?"

"Tasha tells me that the security guys will oftentimes rent a room."

"What are you saying?"

"It could be one of Blackmore's men who is staying at the hotel and using my brother's name to register."

"Huh." He was silent for a long moment.

I chewed my bottom lip and squirmed to keep from breaking the silence. I needed him to conclude what I had concluded earlier. If he didn't think it was absurd then maybe I was on the right track.

"I'm not certain if we can prove any real connection between Blackmore Brothers Security and whoever is framing your brother," he finally said. "The charges for Tim are murder two and drug possession with the intent to distribute. From what I understand, Blackmore hires a lot of off-duty cops. Oiltop is a small town; if a cop were distributing drugs people would know about it."

"But Tim doesn't do drugs."

"The stash they found in your garage gave them enough evidence to arrest him."

"That was planted. I'm certain. The garage is never locked. Anyone could have put that in there."

"You think that maybe one of Blackmore's men is dealing drugs out of these hotel rooms?" I heard him scratch his chin.

"It would be a great cover," I said "The security guard assigned to keep drug dealers out would have the perfect opening to deal themselves. Tasha tells me Blackmore overworks and underpays his guys to keep costs low so that he is able to outbid any competition."

"Hmm," Brad said. "I had a vague sense that he seriously underbid the competition when I attended a couple of Chamber coffees. By the way, why haven't you been attending lately? You need to keep up on your inclusion in the Oiltop community. It's a small town, Toni. You need to get involved until you fit in as a native."

"I *am* a native," I protested. "I was born here and went to school here. My parents are buried here and my grandmother lives here. I'm hardly a stranger."

"You haven't been a part of Oiltop in years, Toni. You

can't expect to come back and have everyone treat you as if you never left. It's a small town with a closed community. You have to show them why you fit in, not just tell them."

"Right," I said and frowned. "I'll get involved as soon as I get some free time."

"Now is better than later," Brad pushed. "There's a coffee at ten A.M. Why don't you come and mingle a bit. You can't let it seem like you only joined for the ribbon cutting and the newspaper article. Okay?"

"Yes." What he said made perfect sense, but frankly I had no idea how to spend time mingling with the country club set and still have time to investigate this murder and keep my sustainable, environmentally friendly gluten-free store. "Okay, I'll try to be there."

"What do you mean by 'try'?" he pushed. "If you want to fit in, you need to attend. Whether you like it or not. Trust me on this, it took me three years of Chamber outings and a stint on the board of directors before I was truly accepted in the Oiltop community."

"But, wait, you were the high school jock. Everyone was so proud of you."

"Yes, but then, like you, I left. When I came back people were certain that I was only around until my father died. It took a lot of hard work and schmoozing before they understood that I wanted to make Oiltop my home."

"Why did you want to make Oiltop your home, Brad?" I asked. "Mindy tells me you could easily work for a large firm in New York or Chicago."

"I've been to New York, Chicago, and Los Angeles, Toni. I like Oiltop and its small-town ways. You do, too, or you would not have stayed."

"I stayed because of the homestead."

"No, you didn't," he said. "You could easily give the house to your brother Tim or any one of your cousins. You didn't. You stayed and opened Baker's Treat. Now you need to make an effort to fit in. Come to the coffee. Blackmore might be there. You can ask him about the shady characters he hires."

"Okay."

"Good."

"Fine." I hung up and looked at Tasha. "I got scolded."

"How so?"

"He said I needed to make an effort to fit in." I frowned. "He said I should attend more Chamber of Commerce coffees."

"He's right, you know." She wrapped her hands around her warm cup. "You can't just set up shop and hope people come to you. You have to reach out to them as well. Show them you care and you're in it for the long haul."

My shoulders slumped as I sat back suddenly exhausted. "I'm barely making ends meet now. It's going to be very difficult to lose two more hours to the Chamber coffee."

Tasha reached out and put her hand over mine. "Look at it this way: attending the coffee may not only strengthen your business but save your brother. While you are schmoozing you can do some snooping. Blackmore might be there, or one of his managers. If nothing else you can bring some baked goods and remind everyone how you can make their holidays brighter."

"Speaking of the holidays, I need to check on the delivery guys. If I can't get my orders out today, the entire season is sunk."

"I'm here if you need any help," she said. "Kip's on winter break after today. I've got my work schedule set up to accommodate him. So I'll be around to help."

"Thanks." I stood and hugged her. "You and Brad are so right. I need to quit being so self-involved and start connecting with people, or any success I have will be worthless."

"It really is smart." Tasha paused. "Are we good?" She looked at me with concern. "I know I sprung moving out on you. It wasn't personal."

"I know. Calvin only has your best interests in mind."

"It's not like he's forbidding me to see you. Leaving Aubrey with you means you'll see us every day."

"Somehow I sense a well-thought-out plot."

"Ha!" Tasha laughed. "You're good."

"Yes, I am."

"So we're good."

"Yes."

"Great! Go get your delivery guys on the phone. I'm going to finish my tea and go to work. Call me if you need me."

"You do the same," I said and went to the back office to look up the number for the shipping guys. My thoughts turned to the Chamber coffees I'd missed. It wasn't that I didn't like the people at the Chamber. It's just that after Chamber darling Lois Striker's murder and Grandma Ruth's suspected involvement, it felt awkward to go. Once that situation was straightened out, I was out of the habit of going. Perhaps it was time to get back into the habit. Schmoozing was a practiced art. The more you practiced, the better you got. Or so I was told.

CHAPTER 24

I walked into the Chamber coffee with two trays of baked goods.

"Oh, Toni, Daylight Donuts catered this coffee." Sherry Waters Williams stopped me at the door. Her blonde hair was in a soft straight blunt cut that swung with ease across her shoulder. Her makeup was Miss America perfect along with her navy suit and green-and-red pin-striped blouse. Her long legs were encased in the soft sheen of a pair of sheer hose, and she wore four-inch beige stilettoes. Her every motion was grace and beauty.

"Hi, Sherry, I know. I'm not trying to upstage Daylight. I called and checked with Doug Asher and he agreed I could bring in a few gluten-free items to complement their offering."

"Oh, okay." Sherry's attitude changed from that of a *you aren't following the rules* busybody to a welcoming host. "Then put them over here behind the donuts." We walked through the Chamber offices to the conference room. It had one giant table and chairs and then two credenzas, where the donuts were artfully arranged along with coffee, tea, and juices.

"Hi, Doug." Sherry stopped in front of Doug Asher, the owner of Daylight Donuts. "Toni says she called you about bringing some gluten-free items out to complement your spread."

"Oh, yes. Hi, Toni." Doug held out his hand and I adjusted my trays and shook it. "Thanks for bringing those." He took one of the trays off my hands and maneuvered around Sherry. "Come on. I'll show you where to put them."

Sherry's feathers seemed a tad ruffled as she narrowed her eyes at us. But in the next second her attention was caught by Brad walking into the room. She went off to coo and flirt. I tried not to roll my eyes.

"Thanks for saving me," I said as Doug put down the tray next to his pastries. "Sherry is a stickler for rules."

"I know." He lifted the corner of his mouth. "She gets kind of crazy whenever anyone acts differently than she thinks they should."

Doug was a nice, middle-aged man with a soft jaw and bald head. His hazel eyes showed intelligence and understanding of my perceived social awkwardness. When you worked in the back kitchen like I did, you didn't have need for social graces. Unless you were at a Chamber coffee trying to get the rich and powerful in the county to notice you.

A quick look around the room and you could tell the bankers and lawyers from the other small business owners. They dressed in perfectly pressed shirts with matching ties along with suits of gray and charcoal with four-hundred-dollar Italian shoes that were well polished.

There were a few women here. Sherry, of course, who tended to host these things. Then there were her other Chamber mates—Pete Hamm, Chamber president, and Alisa Thompson, an older woman with champagne blonde hair and the chubby body of a woman in her fifties who was too busy to get to the gym. Alisa was community liaison and tried to come visit Baker's Treat once a month if for nothing else than to ensure I kept the small plaque declaring Baker's Treat a part of the Chamber in plain view.

"So, Doug." I rearranged the goodies so that they looked like part of his display. "How long have you been a member of the Chamber?"

He crossed his arms as if uncertain what to do with his hands. "For six months now."

"Has it been helpful?"

"I'm not really certain," he said with a shrug. "I signed up to cater four times a year, but Sherry keeps forgetting my days." His mouth tightened. "It's like I don't exist unless I make a fuss."

"But if you cater, then they have to know what you do."

"Every time I come to one of these I have to remind Sherry what I do for a living. It seems that unless you're part of the country club set you are easily dismissed."

"I'm sorry," I said. "I know what that's like, and I went to school with her."

"As warm and welcoming as the community is, it takes them forever to accept you."

"That's the thing about small towns, isn't it?" I said. "Everyone knows everyone, and anyone they don't know everything about is suspect."

"Speaking of suspect, I heard your brother was arrested for that murder. How are you handling that?" He stuck his hands in his pockets when he asked.

"Wow, gossip really does travel fast," I said. "I would have figured the storm closing down the highways would have trumped the news about my brother."

"The opposite happened," Doug said with a shrug. "Everyone was stuck at home with nothing to do but call each other."

"Tim's innocent."

"Yeah, I figured you'd say that. What's with all the sinister goings-on in your family?"

Okay, how do you answer a question like that? "Once a suspect, always a suspect?" I shrugged.

Doug laughed heartily and people turned to look at us. I felt the heat of embarrassment creep up my cheeks. "I suppose that's the easiest answer." He grinned. "I don't know what the family did to the police, but I hope you're able to straighten things out."

"From your mouth to God's ears," I muttered. Lucky for me Brad stepped through the door at that moment. "Take care." I left Doug standing near his donuts.

"Good, you're here," Brad said as he gave me a quick hug and a kiss on the cheek.

"Sherry tried to kick me out because I brought gluten-free treats. Luckily I had prearranged with Doug to bring them in."

"Sherry's a stickler. As much as she can be a pain to deal with, it's good to have a person who enforces the rules or the entire world would run amuck."

"Yes, we wouldn't want everyone bringing in their baked goods and upstaging the sponsor."

"Did you mingle?"

I winced. "You know I'm terrible at the whole mingle/schmooze thing."

"Toni, it's a necessary part of being a small business owner."

"Fine, but before I wander around aimlessly butting into conversations and pretending I belong here, did you find out anything more about the videos?"

"No, but I do have a phone message in to the judge. Don't worry, I'm on good speaking terms with him." Brad gave me a sincere look. "I met him at a Chamber coffee and we hit it off at the Chamber charity golf tournament."

"Okay, okay, I get the point." I blew out a breath and

turned to face the clusters of people in the room. There was nothing for it but to square my shoulders and butt in. I took a step and decided that I needed a cup of coffee so that I didn't stand around wondering what to do with my hands.

I made a beeline to the coffeepots. There was a short, square bald man filling his cup with hot water. "Tea drinker?" I asked as I grabbed a white mug.

He eyed the coffee I poured into my cup. "Not really," he said. "But my doc says no more than a single cup in the morning. So I'm stuck with herbal tea." He ripped the paper off a packet of orange zest herbal tea and dunked the tea bag in the hot water.

"Oh, you have my sympathy." I poured half-and-half into my cup. "I don't know what I'd do if I couldn't have coffee." I held out my hand. "Toni Holmes."

"Mark Blackmore," he said and shook my hand.

Okay, wow, talk about coincidence. "Hi, I've heard good things about you."

"Oh, really? Like what?" He used a spoon to squeeze the tea bag into his cup and then discarded the bag in the trash can.

"You have a really good business model." I sipped my coffee and burnt my tongue. There was nothing to do but swallow the superhot liquid, and it burnt all the way down my throat. My eyes watered.

"Hot?" He chuckled.

"A little." I grabbed a napkin and dabbed at my mouth. "Excuse me, I need ice water." I stepped around him and poured a glass half full of ice water and downed it quickly.

Sherry stepped up while I cooled my throat and took Blackmore by the arm, cooed something about using his services for the Chamber's security, and walked him away.

"That went well," Brad said as he poured his own drink.

"Right?" I watched Mark Blackmore enjoy Sherry's attention. "Is there any way we can get his company records so that we can compare the security guard list to the hotels at the times that Tim supposedly did business out of them?"

Brad shook his head. "No, there's no evidence that there's a connection."

"That's the point," I said. "If we had the list, we'd have the evidence we need."

"Toni, if we don't follow the law, then that list and any other evidence we find could be thrown out of court. That would actually hurt your brother. You don't want that, do you?"

"No, no, I don't." I sipped my cooled coffee, but with a burnt tongue the joy was gone. "Mindy's really hooked on you." Brad looked shocked and surprised at that statement. I bit my lower lip. You see, I have this very bad habit of blurting out the wrong thing at the wrong time.

"Your cousin is a very beautiful woman." Brad tilted his head to the side and eyed me like a curiosity. "Are you jealous?"

"What? Me? No," I said. "I can't be jealous. We're not dating."

"No, we aren't. That hasn't changed, has it?"

"No." I tried not to express the regret I felt. "That hasn't changed. I'm still trying to get my life in order."

"Then you don't mind if I take your cousin out to dinner."

I swallowed hard. "No. I don't mind."

"Good, because we're going out tonight."

"You didn't waste any time there," I muttered under my breath.

"What's that?" he asked, his electric blue gaze watching me knowingly.

"I said have a good time." I sent him an insincere smile. "I'm off to mingle. See if you can't get Mark Blackmore to give up the info we need to save Tim."

"Trust me, Toni, I'm doing everything I can to help your brother."

"I certainly hope so."

CHAPTER 25

"So you weren't able to get anything out of Blackmore?" Tasha asked. It was after nine and the bakery was closed. Tasha was working the front desk of the Red Tile Inn. Kip was asleep on a cot in the manager's office.

"No." I shook my head and rolled the wheeled desk chair I sat in over to the office doorway to help keep an eye on Kip. "I wish you would move back in with me," I said wistfully. "Then Kip wouldn't have to come to work with you."

"I can't impose on you anymore," Tasha said. "Kip loves being with me. Besides, if Calvin weren't working second shift he'd watch Kip. He is good to us both."

"Yeah," I said sincerely. "I know he's one of the good ones."

"It's so strange to say that and really mean it. I was afraid I was falling back into the same old bad judgment. But then I looked into his eyes and saw this big heart. For the first time ever, I knew it was going to be all right."

"Good for you," I said and patted her hand. I kept my

fingers crossed that Calvin Bright was the good man Tasha deserved.

"As for Blackmore Brothers Security, I can tell you who came in the night of the murder," Tasha said as she went to the front desk computer.

"You can?"

"Sure, the guys all have a code. We mark them in and out. It's a fail-safe for the company. If something goes wrong while his guys are on duty, Blackmore knows who to contact."

"Wait! You mean you know who was on duty while the murder happened? How come you are only just now mentioning this?"

"Oh, I did mention it to Calvin." She did some typing and a name popped up on the screen. "It's security guard number eight-two-six-seven-four."

"Okay." I drew my eyebrows together in confusion. "Do you have a name to go with the number?"

"No." Tasha pursed her lips and moved them to the side. "All we ever get is the number. I know most of the guys by name, but I don't pay attention to their numbers or who comes in on certain days. Their schedules seem odd. So we just swipe in their numbers and move on. As long as someone swipes in, we're happy."

"So anyone with a Blackmore badge could come in and swipe the number and pretend to be security."

"Well, I hadn't thought of it that way. The security guys are always local. It's one of those things you take for granted."

"So number eight-two-six-seven-four was on duty that night." I wrote the number on a piece of notepaper with *Red Tile Inn* and the address on it. "It's something," I said. "Calvin knows this number?"

"Sure, it was all part of the investigation that night." Tasha shrugged. "I trust Calvin to check it out."

"Okay." I folded the paper and put it in my pocket. "What are you doing for Christmas? Can you come over Christmas Eve or Christmas Day?"

"We have church and Christmas dinner with my mom on Christmas Day."

"I'm having an open house Christmas Eve. You and Kip and Calvin are invited. The house opens at six P.M. and I'll shut it all down at eleven thirty so that anyone who wants to can go to midnight service."

"Okay, sounds like fun."

"There's something under the tree for Kip," I said with a smile.

"You were able to Christmas shop during all this?" Tasha looked surprised.

"Thank goodness for online shopping," I said. "The stores are always open."

"I love to shop online," Tasha said with a dreamy look in her eyes. "Right now I'm saving pennies." She straightened. "There's this small house on Second Street I'm looking at. Calvin knows a banker who can get me a good mortgage at a rate I can afford. It would be good for Kip to have an anchor in his life. A house would help with that."

"What about Aubrey?" I asked.

"There's a fenced-in backyard—perfect for the dog."

"Oh, well, wonderful," I said. "Then Kip will get to take his puppy home."

"Wait, you're going to miss him, aren't you?" Tasha came over and hugged me. "You can come visit him anytime. Okay?"

"Sure, thanks." I patted her back. In a few short weeks I had gotten used to the big dog wandering underfoot and leaving giant fur balls that needed to be vacuumed every day. I tried not to imagine how quiet the house would be without Tasha, Kip, or Aubrey. "I've got some work to do." I rose. "Thanks for the visit. I'd love to see the house sometime."

"Oh, I'd love to have you do a walk-through with me. We can think about decorating it. You do like to paint, right?"

We both laughed. Tasha had helped me paint the soft fat stripes on the front walls of Baker's Treat. My stripes were a mess, as I relied on painter's tape to keep my edges clean. Meanwhile, Tasha barely colored out of the lines. Her stripes were done twice as fast and twice as well.

I pulled on my hat, puffy coat, gloves, and scarf. It hadn't snowed since the big storm, but it was still bitter cold. The windchill was in the negative numbers. The last thing I wanted was to get frostbite on top of everything else.

All bundled up, I waved my good-byes and got into the van. One of the first things I was going to do after making tomorrow's baked goods was a little investigation. I had the list of places where rooms had been rented in Tim's name. Maybe, just maybe, security guard number 82674 had worked those nights. There had to be a pattern to this madness. If there was, then I was determined to discover it.

Funny thing about the days after a storm that closes the roads: everyone has to get out and see the damage. The sun shone brightly against the snow, producing a terrifying glare. The sky was an honest blue—one so clear you could almost see the stars. Luckily the bakery was busy. People needed a place to go after being cooped up for so long.

Meghan made coffee and worked the counter while I made up extra batches of donuts, muffins, Danish, and tarts. The pie and cake orders rose to a record level. It gave me hope, and I tried not to think about how I would get it all done by the requested pickup time. I'd worked twenty-four hours straight before and I could do it now.

Sam came in during a lull just after lunchtime. He teased Meghan about her vintage day dress and combat boots. Then he walked into the kitchen and all the air went out of the room. I smiled like a fool.

"Meghan said I was family and could hang out in the kitchen with the cool kids," he teased. Then he helped himself to a coffee mug and poured thick black brew into his cup.

"You are her uncle," I said casually. "I suppose that makes you family."

He reached over and snagged two chocolate cookies off the day-old trays. His presence made the kitchen feel small and had my entire body tingling in anticipation. Which was silly, I told myself. It was all because I hadn't slept. Then I turned to find him standing right behind me. "Oh!"

"Sorry," he said, giving me that practiced smile.

"No, you aren't," I accused him. The heat from his body teased my senses. It really had been a long time since I had been so close to a man. There was something tempting about it. I wanted to lean into him and rest my head against his broad shoulder and take comfort in the touch of another human being.

"You're exhausted," he said, his sexy gaze taking in every inch of my face.

"It's the busy time for the bakery."

He reached up and tucked a wayward lock of hair behind my ear. I stood very still. It took a lot of effort not to curl into his touch like a cat. "Hire more help," he said firmly. "It does no one any good if you exhaust yourself."

"I know, but honestly . . . I can't afford to hire anyone. I'm barely making the bills."

He frowned. "Ask your family to help. It's why you have a large family."

"I suppose you're right."

"You know I'm right. What's kept you from asking for help? Hmm? Pride? Are you too proud to ask for help?"

I winced and this time pressed my forehead into his

shoulder so he couldn't see the tears that welled up in my eyes. He put down his cup and the purloined cookies and held me against him. Running his hands up and down my back, he worked magic, and the stiffness and worry melted off me. I sighed. "Eleanor has been waiting for me to fail. Joan thinks gluten-free is a fad that will fade. Richard advised me to not invest in a storefront in a small town."

"And you're worried they were all right," he finished as he rubbed my back.

"Any start-up has its up and down moments," I said as I eased farther into his sturdy warm body. "You have to expect to not make a profit for at least three years."

"You won't make three years if you exhaust yourself in the first six months." He walked me over to the kitchen table and pulled a chair out for me. "Sit."

I opened my mouth to protest.

He placed his index finger on my lips. "The world won't end if you take a fifteen-minute break."

I sat down and he poured me coffee, put in a splash of cream, and brought over a small plate with my fiber-rich apple cinnamon muffins.

"Here, drink this and eat these. I happen to know from a very reliable person that these particular gluten-free muffins are a good source of protein, fiber, and carbohydrates."

I couldn't help the smile that crossed my face. "You are a good man, Sam Greenbaum."

"I'm a handyman; it means I'm handy to have around." He winked and sat down beside me.

I laughed and teased back. "I've yet to see how good your hands are."

He threw his head back and laughed. It was a full, deep, wonderful sound that warmed me to my toes. "Well, now we're going to have to fix that." He reached over, took my hand, kissed my fingertips, then waggled his eyebrows. "Ready to date yet?"

"Oh, I'm ready," I said with a long sigh. "But the year isn't up yet."

"Why a year?" he asked.

"Because I wanted to take the time to get to know myself again. I think maybe you need time to undo all those bad habits that got you into trouble the first time."

"So it wasn't all Eric's fault?"

"Oh, Eric was a cheating, lying, bad guy," I said with no bitterness in my voice. "But I refused to see it. I believe in seeing the best in people. That gets me into trouble—especially when I shrug off the truth."

"And what truth is that?" His gaze was warm and interested.

"The truth that while everyone has good parts, they also have bad. I have to face the good and the bad when I'm in a relationship. I need to figure out how those good and bad parts fit in with my good and bad parts."

"You have bad parts?" His mouth twitched and his eyes shone.

"I do." I smiled back, then got serious. "The trick is to find someone who helps you make the bad parts better. You know?"

"You are an intelligent woman, Toni Holmes." He took a big bite out of his chocolate cookie. "And an excellent baker."

I laughed. "It would be even better if I could be both things at the same time."

CHAPTER 26

"Well, have you discovered who the real killer is yet?" Grandma Ruth rolled her scooter into the bakery's back kitchen door in a whirlwind of cold and the beginning of another snowstorm.

"Grandma, what are you doing out in this weather?"

"Oh, please, I got tired of being stuck with the old people down at the center. There is nothing worse than old people . . . always complaining about this or that ache or pain. Always saying, *Who knew you lived this long?* Well, let me tell you, I knew. I'm here to tell you that old saying is true."

"What saying, Grandma?" Meghan closed and locked the door behind her, then got out the mop to wipe up the snow that had melted into puddles on the floor, leaving perfect scooter tracks.

Grandma snagged an oatmeal cinnamon chip cookie off the fresh rack before I could say no. She put it in her mouth for safekeeping and scootered over to the table. Pulling the cookie out, she took a bite. "That saying that goes something like this: *Who wants to go to the grave perfectly preserved? I plan on partying, eating, smoking, and drinking until the last moment. You only have one life, chickie. You should live every day to the fullest,* which means I'm not going to let a little snow and ice keep me from all the fun." She popped the rest of the cookie in her mouth. "Now tell me how the investigation is going."

"Are you kidding me?" Meghan said. "We've been baking twenty-four/seven to cover all the orders. We lost an entire day due to the power outage and the last storm."

"Well, see, there you go." Grandma shook her head and waved her hand in Meghan's direction. "Worrying about all the wrong things, while my grandbaby faces certain jail time."

"Tim won't go to jail," I said, then took the coffee out of her hand and replaced it with herbal tea. "Brad won't let it happen."

Grandma gave me the stink eye, sniffed the orange zest calming herbal tea, and made a face. "I wasn't asking what Brad was doing. I know that boy's working hard on Tim's case. What I wanted to know is what *you've* found out. Don't tell me you haven't been investigating. Not after I practically handed you the solution."

"Handed me?" I put my hands on my hips, my arms akimbo. "All you did was tell me to keep an eye on the police blotter."

"Which leads you to the security firms that patrol Oiltop's best hotels and motels." Grandma pushed the teacup away and folded her hands on the top of the table. "That should have led you to the fact that only one company runs security in Oiltop."

"So you knew about Blackmore Security?" I narrowed my eyes and pursed my mouth.

"Of course I knew. Everyone in town knew." Grandma waved her hand as if it was a simple fact and I was missing the bigger point. "What else do you know about Blackmore?"

"That his became the only security company by outbidding everyone else."

Grandma tilted her head and nodded. "And . . ."

"And he only uses part-time subcontractors so they work on ten-ninety-nines and he doesn't have to pay them full-time wages or cover their taxes and insurance. It was the only way to undercut the competition."

"Good, good, you're on the right track." Grandma slapped the table and grinned.

I jumped back when her hand hit the table, the sound and motion startling me.

"Then what'd you find out?" she pressed.

I swallowed. "Then I learned that each employee has a code that the hotels use to clock their coming and going for the night. Blackmore coded all his workers so that no one would have a set routine. He keeps them all on their toes by using a computer random generator to determine who goes where every night."

"Huh." Grandma sat back. "He has to use a random number generator? That's ridiculous. What a waste of a good generator. Why, I could set up a fairly random pattern in excel for a tenth the price." Grandma rubbed her bristly chin. "So did you ask why he wants to use only random schedules?"

"No." I pouted. "I figured he didn't want his guys to be predictable, that way they couldn't be eluded by criminals."

"Maybe he does it for more nefarious reasons."

"And what would those be?" Meghan put the mop away and stood with a wide stance, her arms crossed in front of her vintage, cherry-patterned, 1950s dress.

"Maybe he was doing something illegal and didn't want anyone to know," I filled in. "Is that right?"

"Bingo." Grandma tapped her index finger on the end of her nose.

"That's silly. Marcus Blackmore is a churchgoing man. I see him every Sunday right there in the front row with his wife and three kids," Meghan said.

"Some of the best criminals are churchgoers," Grandma said.

"You think it's Blackmore who's framing Tim? How would he even know who Tim was?" I asked and leaned in over my coffee cup. I pushed the tea back toward Grandma.

"That's the part I've been waiting for you to ask." Grandma's blue eyes glinted with secrets. "How does anyone know anyone in Oiltop?"

"It's a small town," I replied. "Everyone you meet is somehow related to anyone else you might run into or accidentally cut off at a corner," I said.

"So Blackmore must have a thing against Tim," Grandma said and pushed the tea away. She got up and grabbed a mug and poured herself some coffee.

"Caffeine isn't that good for you," I said as I watched her add her packets of sweetener and creamer.

"The latest studies beg to differ with you," Grandma said and maneuvered her way back to the table, managing to snag two more cookies.

"Don't you think it's rather random to assume that Mr. Blackmore is framing Tim?" Meghan asked. She had her right hand on her hip and the left hand held a wooden stirring spoon. She'd started to make brownies but had turned around when Grandma's story got interesting. "There has to be some real hatred there to do this to someone. Tim seems like a nice guy. Who would hate him that much?"

"Tim is a nice guy," I said. "Whoever is doing this is crazy. That's something we haven't looked into. . . ."

"What?" Grandma asked.

"Whoever is doing this has to be a psychopath or something similar. That means they don't have to have a reason to frame Tim. Maybe Tim is simply convenient."

"That's a scary idea," Meghan said. "To think that you might be going about living your life and some psycho decides to frame you and bam! You're in jail for the rest of your life."

"Tim is not going to be in jail for the rest of his life," I said, trying not to panic over the thought.

"What about Harold?" Grandma Ruth asked. "What has Harold been doing? Has anyone looked into a motive to murder him?"

"They say that Tim murdered Harold over a falling-out after a drug deal went bad," Meghan said.

Grandma and I looked at her.

She shrugged. "I heard it from one of the girls at school."

"Well, they're wrong," I said as I poured dry ingredients for pie dough into a mixing bowl then added cut-up cubes of butter. "I talked to Tim about Harold. He said they had a fight about a year ago and haven't spoken since."

"What was the fight about?" Grandma asked.

"Tim said it was something stupid. Harold wanted Tim to invest in this scheme he said was a sure bet. Tim said no way and Harold never forgave him."

"Well, I've done some checking up on Harold," Grandma said. "That boy has had a falling-out with more than Tim. He and Lance Webb started an investment business in Wichita last year. They talked some pretty wealthy people into investing and the business went bust. It seems Harold blamed Lance and Lance blamed Harold. Needless to say, the investors demanded their money back. When they didn't have it, there was talk about fraud charges. But for some reason they got dropped. It's why Harold was back in town."

"So that must be why Lance is working part-time for Blackmore," I said. "I wonder if that was the scheme that Tim didn't buy into?"

"Rumor has it the initial investments were bold but made a lot of money," Grandma said. "But like any gamble, things went south fast when they put all their money into a sure thing that turned out to be nothing more than sand dunes in Mexico. All my sources can tell me is that the business went bust and both men have been scraping by ever since."

"That's sad for Harold and Lance," I said as I slowly added cold water to the mixture. "But I don't see what any of that has to do with Tim."

"You're right. We need something definitive." Grandma scowled and crossed her arms over her ample chest.

I let the dough mix. The thing about gluten-free dough is, unlike regular flour, you couldn't overknead it. "Whoever murdered Harold could have been an investor."

"Or even Lance Webb," Meghan suggested as she poured the brownie batter into a pan and put it into the oven.

"I'm sure the police must have thought of this and already looked into it." I turned off the mixer. The dough was a nice rounded ball. I plopped it onto a cold marble slab and let it rest. "I mean, even knowing this, they must think Tim had the best motive and means or they would have charged someone else."

"There has to be more to the story," Meghan said and stood with her hands on her hips.

"I agree," I said. "I find it odd that whoever it is seems to be one step ahead of us. I mean, they planted that cocaine in the garage, so they had to know a warrant was in the works."

"That brings us back to Marcus Blackmore," Grandma said.

"I don't follow your line of thinking," I said and drew my brows together. "How could Marcus know about the warrant and get to the house before the police could serve it?"

"Easy," Grandma said. "There are a lot of off-duty cops working for him. He could have a snitch inside the courtroom."

"But I never saw him around the house," I pointed out.

"In fact, I'd never met him until I went to the Chamber coffee yesterday."

"He could have sent one of his henchmen to do it," Meghan said, her eyes sparkling. "Someone who lives in your neighborhood so you wouldn't think twice about seeing them walk by your house."

"I still don't understand why Marcus would kill Harold and frame Tim," I said with a shake of my head.

"Maybe Marcus is the one running the drug deals and Harold found out about it," Grandma said. "As you said, it would be easy for Marcus to do with his guys patrolling the hotels."

"Why frame Tim?"

"Maybe Harold was working for Marcus all along," Meghan said. "Grandma said he needed money. Maybe it was Harold using Tim's name to sign into those rooms and sell drugs. After all, Harold was pissed at Tim. He might have blamed Tim for not helping him when his business went south."

"Well, now, that is the first thing that makes sense. Harold would use Tim's name just to get back at my brother."

"Marcus would have to know," Grandma said. "Say Harold tried to pull a fast one on Marcus. Marcus killed Harold and then pinned it on Tim because he was the only other person to know that Tim's name was on all those hotel registrations."

"How can we prove any of this?" I asked.

"You can talk to Lance Webb," Grandma said. "It's odd that he and Harold ended up working for Blackmore. Maybe Blackmore was an investor who demanded his pound of flesh when things went south."

"That's something we could check," I said, suddenly relieved to have something concrete to look in to. "I'll do some research on Harold's business. If they went bankrupt, then all their financials are public record."

"Cool," Meghan said. "You should go do some sleuthing online."

"Well, my work here is done," Grandma said and slurped up the last of her coffee before standing.

"Oh, no, you're not getting off that easy," I said. "Your job is to see if you can find out who knew the judge was going to sign the warrant for the search of our house. I'm sure the senior network knows what's going on with judges. They tend to be older, right?"

"Right." Grandma nodded

"What about me?" Meghan asked.

"You're helping me keep up on my bakery orders," I said and waved my hands toward the work on the table. "I really can't investigate and bake at the same time."

"You know you can get your cousins to help," Grandma said. "Lucy and her girls are great cooks."

"Lucy has her hands full with the diner," I countered. "I feel guilty asking for help."

"That's what family is for," Grandma said. She reached into the pocket of her brown corduroy pants and pulled out her cell phone.

"What are you doing?"

"I'm calling your cousins. You may be too proud to ask for help, but I'm not."

I swallowed my embarrassment and went out to my office to fire up my computer. There was no time to argue. I had to find a connection between Blackmore and Harold. Right now it seemed like the only hope we had in cracking the case.

An hour later, I had dug up a list of Harold's investors. It was surprisingly long. The problem was that Blackmore was not on the list. Still, there were several investors listed under corporations. Which meant Blackmore was not off the hook yet. I had to dig into the corporations to see if there was a hidden connection.

Meanwhile the back kitchen was full of cousins. Lucy had come and brought her two oldest girls. I took time off from sleuthing to hand out aprons and set up the back kitchen in workstations. Then I divvied up the to-do list and turned on the satellite radio to pop music. My quiet kitchen was now a madhouse of activity.

The ovens were working full speed. The proofers were full of dough. Amber had the cake station and was busy rolling fondant and covering the crumb-coated cakes with the proper color base.

I had a big batch of buttercream frosting and bags and tips and was taking the fondant-covered cakes and finishing them off with buttercream skirting at the bases of the cakes and personalized decorations on the top.

Outside the snow fell in fat flakes and the Christmas lights in the front of the shop blinked. It was a blast working with my cousins and teasing the girls about their boyfriends, joking with Lucy over who was the most experienced baker, and making the work easier with creative competitions.

The afternoon flew by. For the first time in weeks, the entire day's list of baked goods was finished by dinnertime. Lucy and I let the girls go home with boxes of goodies that didn't quite make the grade to sell in the front. I had to stay at the bakery to man the front of the store until nine. Plus the deliverymen were set to come and pick up the stacks of boxed baked goods at six thirty.

"Thanks for all your hard work today. I don't know what I would have done without you and your girls."

"Anytime." Lucy brushed back her lovely blonde hair. It was thick and had those beachy waves everyone wanted.

Except hers were natural. Like me, she wore black slacks and a white tee shirt. But instead of BAKER'S TREAT her shirt said GRANDMA'S DINER. That was the restaurant that Lucy owned and ran. "That's what family is for."

"Yeah, Grandma Ruth said the same thing. I guess I worked so hard to be independent that I'd forgotten how to ask for help and work as a team." I rotated my cup of orange zest tea between my hands.

"How's Tim holding up?" Lucy asked.

Lucy had a slender figure that was the envy of all the other women in town. She had five kids and still looked as beautiful as the day she got married. The best part for her was she had curves while I was as thin as a beanpole. I suppose the happy thing was that we both had the same blue eyes—a genetic gift from Grandma Ruth.

"He's holding it together as best he can," I said.

"I have to wonder how single people prove their innocence. I mean, we live alone. How can we find anyone to alibi us?" Lucy traced the lip of her cup with her fingers. "Isn't it supposed to be that you're innocent until proven guilty? I mean, isn't it the prosecution's job to prove you're guilty? Beyond a reasonable doubt?"

"Yes." I nodded enthusiastically. "What the prosecution discovered was that Tim had been renting hotel rooms around town at least once or twice a week."

"Oh, come on, where would he get the money to do that?"

"Why would he do it?" I asked and sipped the tea. "Someone came up with the idea that Tim was selling drugs in those rooms. Now, who would be stupid enough to use their real name when they signed into a room? Especially if they planned on doing illegal things?"

"So, Tim is in the clear because Brad will ask that question and point out that Tim was not stupid."

"And yet they discovered a rather large bag of cocaine in the garage."

"Well, if anything they should arrest you, not Tim, for possession."

"With intent to sell," I added. "The amount of drug was too big to be someone's recreational stash."

Lucy's mouth flattened. "So someone is framing Tim and doing a bad job of it. Do you have any idea who it could be?"

"There are a couple of suspects." I sipped more of my tea, savoring the tangy taste of orange zest. "But again, nothing concrete to tie them to the murder. And if I merely go off circumstantial evidence I'm no better than the police."

"Yeah." Lucy sighed. "I can see the problem."

"Murder investigation aside, can I ask you a business question?"

"Sure, honey." Her lovely eyes held concern.

"How was your cash flow the first year you were in business? Mine seems to come and go, hovering around my must-pay-the-bills line. Is it true you have to stay afloat three years before you see a profit? I mean, that's a lot of time and effort invested if the business never really takes off."

"Oh, I remember those days. There were some months where I thought I'd have to close and then somehow the money came through. People became regulars and I learned what the bestsellers were. I adjusted my menu for the best-sellers with one or two chef specials a day to keep my cooking skills fresh and to ensure that I'm not missing out on a new 'favorite.' I mean, there is comfort food and then there is boredom. Sometimes it's a fine line. People like the same thing, only different." She laughed. "That's the key, honey. If you can figure that out, then you're golden."

"I think I know what you mean. I already have some best-sellers that I've begun to stock daily. And yet there are seasonal favorites like pumpkin pie in November, chocolate peppermint pie in December, and dark chocolate in January."

Lucy smiled. "Don't forget angel food cake with straw-berries in March and April."

"But of course." I giggled. "So keep on doing what I'm doing as long as I can?"

"As long as you can," she agreed. "If you're persistent, it will all work out."

"Well, that's a good thought," I said. "Because if I don't significantly increase profits this month, I may have to close the doors next month."

"Oh no, don't think that way. I mean, you can always have fund-raisers."

"Fund-raisers?"

"You know," she said with a glint in her eyes, "you can have a bake sale over at the senior center. Old people love their sweets."

"Right?" I shook my head. "Grandma puts so much sweetener in her coffee it has to have as many calories as a donut. She's just fooling herself that there aren't any calories in a whole box of zero calorie sweetener."

Lucy laughed. "Grandma's brilliant, which means she can argue herself into getting what she wants every time." Lucy leaned in and studied me.

"What?"

"Are you dating yet?"

A wash of embarrassment went through me. "No. I promised myself I'd wait a year from my divorce."

"Oh, honey, you're punishing yourself."

"What?" I tilted my head and tightened my fingers around my mug.

"You feel guilty for divorcing Eric and you're punishing yourself for doing it."

"No, I'm not." I drew my eyebrows together. "I've seen too many smart women get divorced and marry again quickly. It never works out. So I'm giving myself time to grieve."

Lucy patted my hand. "A woman has needs." Her expression was full of concern and had tears welling up in my eyes.

"It's no sin to date a handsome man . . . or two. You don't have to marry them, you know."

"Wow." I sat back, stunned by her point of view. The thought that I could date Sam or Brad and not do something stupid never crossed my mind. I had been so dead set on my "rule" I hadn't thought of just how lonely living alone could get. Trust me, even with a large family coming and going a person could be alone.

"So." Lucy pulled back and looked down at her hands then back up at me. "Who are you going to date first?" There was a twinkle in her eye.

"I don't know," I said coyly. "The world is full of eligible men."

"Stop it! I happen to know two who are interested in you, and possibly three."

"What do you mean, three?"

"Didn't Officer Strickland bring you back into work the day after the storm?"

"Yes." I chewed the inside of my mouth. "But that doesn't mean he wants to date me. Grandma made me call him and ask for a ride so that I could question him about Tim."

"And did you question him?"

"I tried," I said and it sounded lame to my own ears. "I'm not very good at that."

"No problem—you're a baker, not a sleuth, right?"

"Finally, someone who understands," I said and smiled.

"Of course I understand. I'm your favorite cousin. So who are you going to date first?"

I took a deep breath and blew it out. "So many men so little time," I quipped.

"Toni! I'm serious. You need to treat yourself. You've been working hard for months."

"Okay, let's leave it up to fate. I'll date the next eligible man who comes through the door."

"Oh, you may regret that. . . ."

I leaned back. "How can I regret that?"

"Officer Emry is eligible. . . ."

"Oh, no!" We both broke up laughing.

The door bells jangled, and Officer Strickland walked through the front door. I was more relieved than I wanted to admit. The chances of my dating Officer Strickland were null and none. "Hi, I'll be right with you."

Lucy giggled even harder. I gave her the stink eye, and that only made her laugh even harder.

It was hard to keep a straight face as I got up and sent Officer Strickland a sunny smile. "What can I get you?"

He took off his police hat and pushed his hair out of his eyes. I noticed how square his hands were. His jaw was a little soft and his mouth thin, but his shoulders were wide.

"What can I get you? Coffee, tea, or dessert?" Okay, that sounded wrong. I bit my bottom lip and accepted the blush that raced across my fair skin.

"Hi, Officer Strickland," Lucy said and waved from the safety of her seat at one of the small wrought iron tables. "I recommend the pecan pie. It's to die for."

"I bet," he said and his confused gaze went to my face. "I'll take a thermos of that good coffee and a croissant."

"Of course, for here or to go?"

"I'm on duty tonight, so I'll take it to go." He leaned over and placed his thermos on the counter as I grabbed a clean tissue paper and put a fat croissant in a paper bag. "Are you still working through the nights?"

"What? Oh, no. My cousin Lucy and her girls came out to help."

"Nice." He turned to Lucy and sent her a smile. "It's great to have a large family."

"Any news on the murder?" Lucy asked.

His expression turned solemn. "We're building a case."

"You know my brother Tim is being framed," I said.

"Yes, I've heard that's your theory," he said. "I take it you're investigating."

"She is," Lucy said before I could get the words out. "We have a few suspects of our own."

"Really?" He looked from Lucy to me. "Care to share?"

"No, I think we'll wait until we have more than circumstantial evidence." I filled his thermos full of coffee and capped it tight. "There's enough false evidence in the case already."

"You think the case against your brother is circumstantial?" he asked.

"That's seven ninety-nine," I said and put his goodies on the countertop. "Yes, I do."

"Why's that?"

"Because I know my brother. He doesn't deal drugs and he certainly would never stab anyone."

Officer Strickland's gaze was intense. "What's your theory on how Harold died?"

"I won't say until I have proof," I said and crossed my arms. "It's not good to unjustly blame someone without proof. That's what's happening to my brother. I wouldn't want to do that to anyone else."

"Smart girl." He gave me his credit card. "Do me a favor, would you?"

"What?" I asked as I swiped his card and handed it back to him.

"Call me first if you find any evidence. I'd like to be the first to nail the true killer. Deal?" He held out his hand.

I took hold of his hand and shook it, conscious of the heat and grip. "Deal." I nodded.

"Thank you." He tugged his hat on, picked up his thermos and bakery bag. "Take care tonight. Don't stay too late. I heard another big storm is on its way."

"Bye now," Lucy said from her seat and waved her fingers.

"Ma'am." Officer Strickland touched the brim of his hat and stepped out. The wind blew in strong and icy. The sky was that low-hanging black of winter clouds and early sunset.

"Is it really supposed to storm?" I winced at the idea of losing another day of delivery.

"Hold on, I'll Google the weather." Lucy pulled her smartphone out of her pocket and tapped on the screen. "Huh, looks like there is a storm, but it's fast-moving." She turned the phone toward me. "With any luck it will be here and gone by morning."

The back doorbell rang. "And that's the delivery guy," I said with relief.

"I'll walk back with you." Lucy got up and bussed our table. "I've got to get on over to the diner and see how things are going. I promoted Emmi to lead waitress. So far she's done a bang-up job."

"You're coming for Christmas Eve, right? I'm putting up a buffet and having an open house so people can come and go when they need to. Grandma Ruth and Bill will be spending the night at the homestead."

"We wouldn't miss it for the world." Lucy dropped a kiss on my cheek, put the glasses in the sink, and grabbed her coat as I checked the peephole to see that it was indeed the overnight delivery guy in his brown suit. "Is there anything you want me to bring?"

"Oh, bring your Christmas brisket. I love that. I don't know how you make it so tender." The doorbell rang again and I rolled my eyes. "Hold on," I said and waited for Lucy to be bundled up before opening the door.

"It's a secret recipe," Lucy said. "Don't worry, I'm sure it's gluten-free."

"Thanks." I opened the door and Lucy left as the delivery driver walked into the kitchen. Sharp, icy air blew in with them a sharp contrast to the warm sweet scent of baked goods.

"I hear there's a storm coming," I said as the delivery guy checked off packages with his scanner.

"Yeah, we know," he said as he worked smoothly through the piles of boxes filled with baked goods. "No worries. Delivery is guaranteed this time—power or no power."

"Cool," I said and signed his scanner. "With Christmas only a few days away, I need to guarantee my delivery times."

"We understand," he said and gathered up the boxes and stacked them on a small dolly he'd wheeled in behind him. "My boss says we have to have the packages there and on time, even if it means we work through the night and have to walk through darkness, sleet, and snow."

"Like that old postal service saying," I said and smiled as I opened the back door and let him go out into the swirling beginnings of the storm.

I watched as my baked goods left my custody. These deliveries were do-or-die for Baker's Treat. It was out of my hands as to whether they arrived or not. I closed and locked the back door, rested my forehead on the cool wood and said a little prayer that nothing more would go wrong between now and Christmas.

CHAPTER 27

"I got it!" I shouted and stood with excitement. No one heard me because I was in my home office in the homestead and it was after midnight. Mindy was still out with Brad and Tim went to bed early to mope about his loss of his job and his apartment.

Excitement washed through me. I printed out the list I had so carefully put together. I still needed to double- and triple-check the findings, but if they were right I had proof that it was indeed the same security guard number that coincided with all the nights that Tim had supposedly checked into the hotels.

I grabbed up the papers and ran down the hall to Tim's bedroom. The lights were out. I raised my hand to knock and then thought better of it. He hadn't slept since the day he was arrested. I didn't want to be the one to continue his streak. I looked at the papers with dates and numbers. If he was sleeping, then it would take him a while to wake up enough to decipher the meaning of the numbers.

Deflated that there was no one to share the evidence with, I heard the front door open and close. Mindy was home.

I rushed downstairs, spurred on by my discovery. "Hey, hi, how was your night?"

"Fine." She sounded the opposite of fine.

"What happened?" I hit the bottom of the stairs and stopped her in the foyer.

Mindy burst into tears.

Oh no, my news was going to have to wait. I put my arm around her and walked her into the kitchen. "Come on, I have a special drink that I make at times like these."

Mindy sobbed, covered her mouth, and hiccupped, trying to stop. "I'm sorry."

I snagged a box of tissues on the way into the kitchen. "Here, let me take your coat."

Mindy took the tissues and let me take her wool dress coat off her. I shook the remaining snow off of it and hung it up in the coat closet near the front door. By the time I returned to the kitchen, Mindy sat at the kitchen table, her elbows on the surface and her head in her hands.

"Don't say anything yet," I advised when she looked up at me. Her face was red and splotchy, her nose ran and so did her mascara. She hiccupped again. "Let me fix that drink first."

I pulled out two mugs and poured hot cocoa mix in each cup, then added hot water and a good thumb's width of amaretto. I finished it off with whipped cream. The drink was far from calorie-free, but there were times when you needed chocolate and alcohol and whipped cream. From the look on Mindy's face, this was one of those times.

"Here," I said and placed the drink in front of her. "Be careful—it's hot."

"Okay," she whispered and pushed the stack of used tissues aside to wrap her fingers around the warmth.

I sat down across from her and sipped my drink and

waited. It never did any good to rush someone when they were as upset as Mindy was. I had to admit I was a little worried. This was the first time in my entire life I'd seen Mindy cry.

It couldn't be Brad. She barely knew him. You don't get this upset about someone you barely know. I quickly deduced it was not the date that had her so worked up. Maybe, just maybe, I'd finally find out why she was here in Oiltop and not back in New York City at her high-powered law firm.

She took a sip of my concoction and sighed. "Yes, this is good. Thank you."

"My pleasure."

"I'm surprised you're still up. Don't you go into work at the bakery around three or four A.M.?"

"Yes, but I was busy with something and lost track of time."

"Oh." She hiccupped again and took a sip of the cocoa, leaving a white whipped cream mustache on her upper lip. What a tragic figure she looked, all red and splotchy with mascara running down her cheeks. I took careful note of this. It was the first and I suspect the only time I'd ever see Mindy look anything but perfect.

"Tell me what's going on? Surely Brad didn't hurt you." I leaned in close and spoke softly, calmly.

"Oh, Toni, my whole life is a mess." Mindy's face grew red and her eyes watered. "I'm in deep trouble."

"What happened?"

"I discovered one of the partners was embezzling from the firm."

"That's terrible." I tilted my head and scrunched my eyebrows. "But how would that ruin your life?"

"You're not going to like me anymore when I tell you." She inhaled sharply and held it, then exhaled, and tears rushed down her cheeks in an elegant stream.

Poor Mindy—how could I tell her I didn't much like her

before whatever happened in New York? I bit the inside of my mouth to keep from speaking. We were family, and family loved family unconditionally. The truth was we loved but we didn't have to like. I had a huge family—fifty-two cousins—I loved them all, but there were many I didn't like much. It's simply the way family works.

I kept my mouth shut and patted her hand.

"I did something awful. It was the reason I went out with Brad tonight. I've been trying to figure out how to fix things."

"You couldn't have done anything so bad that you can't fix it," I said.

"I don't know." She was resigned. "I broke the law and the trust of the partners."

"What did you do?" I felt my eyes grow wide and worked hard to keep from pulling my hand away from hers.

"When I confronted the embezzler, he offered to pay for my silence."

"You said no, right?"

She shook her head, tears welling up. "Well, I did at first, but then he offered me more money than I'd ever seen. I could pay off my student loans and buy a new car and stuff my retirement account and splurge on a couple of pairs of Manolo Blahniks."

"How much money did he offer you?" I was curious.

"I guess every person has their price." She hiccupped. "I didn't think I did until it was offered to me."

I wasn't going to ask her again. She either would tell me or she wouldn't. The amount was a moot point anyway. The real point was if she took the money or not. "Please tell me you didn't take it."

"I did," she whispered and hung her head. "But the moment I did, I realized how dirty I felt, so I demanded that he take it back."

"Did he?"

"Yes," she whispered. "But then he laughed and said I could never go to the partners about his crimes because he had proof that I had taken money from him."

"Wait." I held her hand. "You gave it back."

"Right." She looked up, her gaze pleading with me. "But he said it didn't matter. The cops would trace the money to my account and then I would be just as guilty as he is."

"That can't be right," I said. "What you did was human. But you didn't keep it."

"It's why I came home," she said. "I told the big bosses that Grandma Ruth wanted me here for Christmas. But I came to talk to Grandma about it. She is the smartest person I know."

"You told Grandma?" I took a sip of my cocoa. The amaretto warmed my throat and uncurled the pit in my stomach.

"Yes, she advised me to get a lawyer and then tell the truth."

"Did Brad tell you to ask for amnesty?"

Mindy looked up. Her large eyes filled with tears. "No, he was not happy with the fact that I took the money."

"I see." My mouth was a firm line. I might not like her much, but Mindy was family. The fact that Brad wouldn't help her brought him down a notch in my esteem.

"No, no." Mindy took my hand and squeezed. "You misunderstand. Yes, he didn't like the fact that I took the money, but he understood. He promised to help me. I dug out my bank records, which show the two transfers of funds. Tonight we went over everything I knew, what all I had proof of, and then the bribe. In the morning, Brad has a Skype meeting with me and the partners and the local authorities."

"So you're going to tell them everything?"

"Yes," she said and pulled back. Her shoulders slouched and she hugged herself. "Brad thinks that—depending on New York State law—I may receive a hefty fine and possibly a year in jail but not much more." She took a deep breath in and out. "I am going to plea bargain. If this were to go to a jury I may come out owing nothing, but then they could also convict me as a felon. The amount of money that went into my account was . . . um . . . quite large."

"I don't get it." I scrunched up my face. "How could they transfer a large sum without the bank telling the IRS? I happen to know that transfers over ten thousand dollars get flagged."

"My name was put on an overseas account," she explained. "That account was set to transfer ten thousand dollars a month for the next five years into a charity fund that paid me directly in cash. It would all be under the table—so to speak."

"Wait, I'm confused," I said. "If it was supposed to be under the table, then how could he have record of cash transfers to hold over you?"

"I work for some highly educated men whose families have been twisting finances for centuries."

"Did he show you his proof or simply threaten?" I frowned and sat back.

"Oh, he has proof." Mindy wrapped her hands around the warm mug in front of her. "Even Brad said it was pretty solid evidence of my wrongdoing. That said, he thinks I have a good shot of having my weakness dismissed as long as I testify in the embezzlement trial." She looked down at her mug. "Toni, I'm scared." The last came out a whisper.

I got out of my chair and went over and hugged her. "Don't worry. Brad is the best lawyer I know. He will help you."

She leaned her head on my shoulder. "I'm going to lose my job over this. That means no more New York, no more cool apartments and great shopping and wonderful sophisticated parties." Mindy closed her eyes. "Toni, my life is over."

I got a chill down my spine at the tone of her voice. "Your life is not over," I insisted and hugged her tight. "It's just changing course, okay?"

"That's what Brad said, too. Why, then, does it feel like it's over?"

"It's natural," I said. "When I divorced Eric and moved back here I felt as if my life was over as well. It was so hard not to simply crawl into bed and throw the covers over my head."

"You're different from me," she said. "You're strong and resilient."

"So are you," I said. "Ask Grandma Ruth to tell you how she felt when her thirty-year marriage was over. It's a great story."

Mindy grabbed a tissue from the box I brought in and blew her nose. She took out a second and wiped her eyes. As soon as she did that she looked lovely again, while I look swollen and red for two days after a crying jag.

"Thanks, I feel better." Mindy drank down the last of her cocoa. "I think, once I come clean with what I know, I'll feel even better." She put her elbow on the table and leaned her cheek into her palm. "Brad really is a doll. I'm surprised some smart Oiltop gal hasn't snatched him up yet."

"Any idea what you'll do after this all goes down?" I changed the subject. "I know you have connections in New York. I can't imagine you'd be happy here in Oiltop."

Mindy straightened. "Oh, gosh, no. I would never move to this antiquated town. I have a friend with a walk-up in Brooklyn who wants to rent out a room. I'll stay with her and look for something new. I know my life in the paralegal field is over. No one will hire a paralegal with a felony on her record."

"You don't know you'll be charged with a felony."

"Oh, I won't have to be charged," she said. "My firm is so well known when this goes down I'll be a felon, and worse, a whistle-blower."

"What will you do?"

She smiled. "I have a friend who's a PI. I'm going to see

if she's hiring. I think being a whistle-blower might be an advantage in the private investigator business—that's my hope, at least. But first I have to get through the scandal." She stood up. "I'm exhausted. Tomorrow is a big day and I need to look my best. Good night, Toni, and thanks!" She dropped a kiss on my cheek and left the kitchen. Her perfume lingered. She didn't even think to take her cup to the sink.

I shook my head. Some people can't see the world past their nose. Mindy was one such person. I got up and took our mugs to the sink and studied my reflection in the window. I really had to wonder, was all the crying and sadness just a show? Mindy seemed to have her plan all worked out—what with Brooklyn and her PI friend. I tended to take people at their word. It had gotten me in trouble so many times that I second-guessed everyone now. I sighed. I didn't want to be that person—the skeptic, especially when it came to my family.

I rinsed out the cups and put them in the dishwasher.

I picked my list up off the countertop where I'd laid it and went upstairs. Work started in five hours. Then once Meghan arrived, I would take my suspicions about the security company to the police department and Officer Bright. With only two days until Christmas, my sincerest wish was that there would be more than the two pairs of Goldtoe socks I'd bought Tim. With any luck, his freedom would be there are well.

CHAPTER 28

The next morning, the front door bells jangled, letting me know I had a late-morning customer at Baker's Treat. I pushed through the kitchen door to the shop space to find Sam pouring coffee into his thermos. "Hi," I said, my heart aflutter. He looked all male in his suede coat, blue jeans, and plaid button-down shirt. The man could make a feed sack look good.

"Hi, Toni," he said, then took off his Stetson and laid it on the counter. "Thought I'd stop by and see how you are."

"I'm good," I said and tried hard not to mess with my hair. Really, a gorgeous male should give a girl notice before he barged into her bakery and took up all the air. "Are you ready for Christmas?"

"I certainly hope so." He laughed. The happy sound echoed through the bakery. "We're closing in on it." He put his thermos on the counter. His gorgeous eyes were bright and filled with excitement. "Are you ready?"

"Oh, I'm never ready." I laughed at myself. "This year is

worse than ever. I've been so busy trying to keep the bakery afloat and help with Tim's investigation that I haven't had time to do more than pick up a few things online."

He leaned in close and smelled of spicy cologne and clean man. "What'd you get me?"

It was my turn to laugh. "Oh, that's easy. For you, a couple of gluten-free cherry tarts." I raised my right eyebrow. "Those are what you like best in the bakery, right?"

"Almost," he said and smiled that toothpaste-commercial grin.

"Almost? That's all you buy unless you're getting a platter for your grandmother."

"There is one thing in the bakery I like better than cherry tarts."

"What's that?" I asked.

"The baker," Sam said and leaned in close and planted a sweet short kiss on my shocked mouth. "I'm going to this shindig at the country club on New Year's Eve. I know you had other plans, but I'm still going to ask in case you change your mind. Would you do me the honor of accompanying me? We don't have to call it a date, if you're still stuck on the date thing."

I looked into his sincere gaze and thought, *Why not?* "Okay," I said, surprising us both. I shrugged. "I can cancel the other thing pretty easily, plus I think I'm over the no-date thing."

"Cool." His eyes deepened in color. "How about before then?"

"Well, okay. Christmas is only a few days away. How about after that?"

His entire face lit with pleasure. I don't think I'd ever seen his smile turn into such a big, toothy grin. "How about Boxing Day?"

"Boxing Day?"

"It's what they call the day after Christmas in England." He leaned his elbow on the top of the glass counter, bringing him in closer. I could smell his cologne mixed with the scent of warm male skin and leather.

"I think I have to work," I said as my mind went blank. "I mean, I usually have to work. I mean . . . okay."

"Good," he said. "Do you ice-skate?"

"What? No . . . Do people ice-skate in Kansas? I mean, people ice-skate in Chicago, but I don't remember ever ice-skating in Kansas."

His eyes twinkled. "There's an indoor rink in Wichita. We'll go, rent some skates. It'll be fun."

"As long as I don't break anything."

"No worries, I'll be there to catch you when you fall." He winked and the heat of embarrassment rushed up my cheeks.

I fanned myself. "I'll bring extra padding."

"What, you don't trust me to catch you?" He leaned back, offended.

"Oh, I think you'll catch me, but I'm not a small girl. If I go down you'll go down. At least one of us should have extra padding on when that happens so they can drive the other home."

He laughed. The rich tone of it echoed through the bakery. Then he grabbed his bag of treats and his thermos. "It's a date and a date." He winked again. "Can't wait."

"Me neither." I watched him put on his hat and walk out into the soft gray of winter sunrise. He was a gorgeous man in a Stetson. My heart beat rapidly. I had a date. I hadn't had an actual date in five, or was it ten years? I counted the years I'd dated Eric and added our marriage to the toll and realized it had been twelve years since I had last dated. Talk about rusty—I wasn't sure what people did when dating these days.

The door bells jangled and I looked up to see Lance Webb coming in with his hat in his hand. "Good morning, Toni. How are you?"

"I'm good," I said with a nod. "What can I do for you?"

"I came for coffee and to see you." His big hands played with the brim of his hat.

"Oh, okay. The coffee's fresh; I just replaced it. Did you want it to go?"

"Yes," he said. "Oh, I brought my thermos." He pulled the silver thermos out of his coat pocket.

"Great, why don't you pour the coffee. If you want, I can wrap up a bear claw."

"Um, okay—do they taste real?"

"I've been told they are good by people who don't eat exclusively gluten-free."

"Okay, then yes, thanks." He poured coffee as I grabbed a baking tissue and pulled two bear claws out of the counter and put them inside a pink-striped bag we used on the smaller orders.

I set the bag on the counter as he stepped up. "That's five dollars," I said.

"Great." He pulled a bill out of his wallet.

"I'm also collecting money for the food bank." I pointed to the small jar on the top of the counter next to the cash register. "I'm using it to purchase gluten-free essentials. It's not something people think about, but people who are homeless or out of work can have celiac or a gluten sensitivity. What can they eat out of a food bank?"

"Not much, I'd guess." He handed me the cash and then reached into his wallet and pulled out a second five-dollar bill and stuffed it in the jar.

"Thanks," I said and sent him a warm smile. "It's kind of a big deal to me. When one out of every one hundred people needs to eat gluten-free due to celiac, you have to remember special needs when you give to food banks."

"One out of every one hundred?" He picked up his paper bag. "That seems inflated. I mean, you're in the breadbasket of America."

"I know, right? It's a tough issue for farmers and families."

Lance studied me.

"What?" I asked and wiped at my face in case I had frosting on it, or chocolate.

"I was wondering if you might want to go out sometime."

For a moment I froze, not sure what to say or do. My long pause must have meant something to him, because he lifted his right shoulder in a half shrug and gave me a smile that didn't reach his pretty blue eyes. "Don't worry about it. It was a spontaneous invitation. I understand you're a busy woman."

"Oh, I'm so sorry." I reached out and touched his hand. "I was surprised and that almost always ends with me looking blankly at someone."

This time his smile reached his eyes. "Surprised you, huh?"

"It's been less than a year since my divorce was official. Why, just this morning I realized it's been years since I was on a date. Dating is a skill that takes practice. I'm terribly rusty."

"Wait, you have the time counted?" he asked.

"I promised myself I'd concentrate on me and Baker's Treat the first year. That means no dating for a year."

"Ah, yeah, I'd be counting the weeks, days, and hours if I had to wait a year to kiss a pretty woman. How do you do it?"

The heat of a blush rushed up my neck and into my cheeks. Really I was the only person to blush so much as an adult. I fanned my face. "Sometimes I'm not sure if it was a good idea—I've lost weeks of practice time."

He laughed and leaned in so close I could feel his warm breath whisper along my cheek. "I promise, I'll go easy on you." Then he winked. I took a step back.

"I just told Sam Greenbaum I'd go out with him on Boxing Day."

"So?" Lance asked. "You can't date more than one man at a time?"

"I can't imagine having the time to date more than one."

"That's right." He reluctantly stepped back. "I heard that you've got a lot going on. You're not only baking, you're investigating. How's that going, by the way? Need any help?"

I chewed on my bottom lip and debated if I should tell him what I knew. I made an instant decision. "I think I may have found a better suspect than my brother."

"Really?" He looked surprised and interested and stepped back in toward me. "Who? Do I know him? I assume it's a guy, right?"

"I don't really know gender yet." I wrung my hands and suddenly felt silly. "I know, how can I know who did it and not know their gender?" I swallowed. "You see I discovered that Blackmore Brothers Security that works all of the hotels and motels around Oiltop."

"Sure, I work for them sometimes," Lance said. "What does that have to do with Tim and Harold?"

"There was a security guard on duty when Harold was murdered."

"You think a security guard murdered Harold? Isn't that reaching? I mean, we're all vetted and bonded. It's not like Blackmore Brothers Security is a fly-by-night firm. Heck, even Chief Blaylock has been known to pick up an extra shift or two. . . ." He grew silent. "You think maybe the killer is someone in the police department?"

"It's all speculation at this point," I said. Whoever is framing my brother knows police procedure very well. They are such a part of the community that no one thinks twice about them at the crime scene or leaving packages of drugs in my garage." I took a step toward him. "Look, everyone knows Mrs. Dorsky sees everyone who comes and goes from the homestead. Whoever is framing my brother would have to be so familiar that the neighborhood watch wouldn't even note his coming and going."

"Or hers," he said and leaned against the glass counter.

"Or hers," I agreed. "Tasha told me that each security guard has an employee number that is scanned by the hotel when they arrive. I took the list Grandma Ruth gave me of the dates and rooms that Tim supposedly rented and called the hotels to see what security number was scanned that day. I was able to match an ID number with each time Tim was supposed to have rented a hotel room."

"Why would a security guard rent random rooms around town?"

"I'm not sure, but it may be that he was dealing drugs out of these rooms."

He narrowed his eyes and shook his head. "Why rent a room? If you're the security guard, you could deal drugs outside cameras' reach and no one would think twice. Who's going to catch you? You?"

"Oh, I hadn't thought of that." I frowned. He'd just punched a great big hole in my theory. Why *would* anyone rent random rooms if they could deal drugs from a car out in the open just out of cameras' reach?

"It doesn't track," he continued. "Just because it was the same security guard doesn't tie them to the room rentals or the murder. You're reaching, Toni."

I felt completely deflated. I might have a number I could turn into a name, but that was the end of my investigation. Without being able to tie the guard to the rooms or the murder I was basically at a dead end.

"Let me make a suggestion," Lance said seriously. "Why don't you worry about baking and dating and let the professionals figure out how to help your brother?"

"He's my brother," I said. "It's Christmas. I need to help clear him. You understand, don't you?"

"Sure, but seriously, leave it to the police. Okay?" This time it was Lance who patted my hand. "Thanks for the bear claws." He sent me a smile and walked out the door, leaving me feeling like a fool.

CHAPTER 29

"Two guys asked you out this morning?" Tasha sat in the bakery kitchen to keep me company while she waited for Kip's session with his paraprofessional to end. "Please tell me you said yes to at least one of them."

"Sam was the first to ask and I said yes." I was proud of my decision. "Then weirdly Lance Web stopped by and bought coffee and a bear claw. Then he asked me out."

"The Lance Webb who was in here the other day making fun of your gluten-free stuff?" Tasha asked. "That Lance Webb bought a bear claw and asked you out?"

"Yes," I said. "But I told him no."

"Good for you," she said. "You deserve better. What about Brad? Wasn't he interested?" She cuddled a warm cup of Christmas tea in her hands.

"Yes, he was interested." I stopped rolling out sugar cookie dough. "But he's sort of seeing my cousin Mindy."

"What do you mean, 'sort of seeing'?" Tasha straightened.

"Did that girl steal him from you, because I swear, if she did . . ."

"No, no," I reassured her. "I finally found out what brought Mindy into town. She's got an issue at her work. Brad's helping her figure out what's best for her."

"So he's not dating her?" Tasha cocked her head. Her lovely blonde hair fell to one side, cascading over the pale blue sweater she wore.

"See, that's where things get tricky. I thought they went on a date the other night, but Mindy told me about her problems right after that 'date.' I got the distinct feeling it was more of a working dinner than a date. That said, he's taking her to the Wichita Symphony tonight for their Christmas concert."

"Yeah, see, that doesn't sound like work to me."

I shrugged and turned back to my cookie dough. "I don't blame him. I told him I wasn't dating. How would he have known I would change my mind?"

"You're a woman," she said and sipped her tea. "It's your prerogative to change your mind at any time."

"I guess that's true." I cut out neat snowman and Christmas tree shapes. "It doesn't matter. I said yes to Sam. He wants to take me ice-skating."

"Sounds like fun," Tasha said. "Lots of opportunity to put your hands all over that gorgeous body of his."

"What? No . . ." I stared dreamily off into space. "I did warn him I have no experience and would probably fall."

"What'd he say to that?"

"He said he'd catch me." I smiled.

"Like I said, sounds like a perfect date. What are you going to wear? Do you have a wool skater dress you can wear with tights?"

"What? No. Do they make those for regular people?"

"What do you mean by 'regular'?" Tasha asked.

"Nonskaters," I answered and picked up two full sheets of cookies and stuck them in the top part of the oven then set the timer. "Forget it. I'm going to wear jeans and a comfy sweater. I need padding. Does Kip still have his knee, wrist, and elbow protectors from his inline-skating days?"

"You are not wearing knee pads." Tasha frowned at me. "You really are rusty at dating. When are you going?"

"The day after Christmas."

"Good, I'm off. I'll come over and see that you're dressed right. We can do your hair and makeup, too."

"Am I that bad?" I asked.

"Not that bad." She stood and gave me a small hug. "Trust me, you're going to be glad I came when you open the door and see the happiness on his face." She put her mug in the sink. "I've got to go pick up Kip. Are you still hosting Christmas Eve?"

"I'm still hosting," I said. "Grandma and I decided it was best to try to act as normal as possible. Trust me, that's tough for my family."

Tasha grinned. "Good, Kip has done nothing but talk about your Christmas Eve party. You know how he can fix-ate on things."

"Tell him it's going to be a great party."

"And Tim?"

"Tim will be there. I thought I was pretty close to figuring out who's behind this terrible crime."

"Good! Are you going to tell us?" She grabbed her puffy down coat from the hooks on the wall by the door.

"As I said, I thought I'd be happily solving the murder this morning, but when I told Lance, he explained that I've only proven a coincidence that the same security guy signed in every time Tim's name was used. I haven't proven motive or even put him at the scene."

Tasha winced. "That's a lot to prove." She buzzed a kiss on my cheek. "If anyone can solve this it's you." She patted my arm and wound her scarf around her neck. Last, she plopped a multicolored knit cap on her perfect hair. "See you Christmas Eve. Stay safe."

"I will," I said. "We can't jeopardize Kip's Christmas."

"Thanks, you're the best." Tasha pulled the back door open and left in a swirl of frozen air and blowing snow. I frowned at the snow on the floor and grabbed a mop to wipe it up. When did another storm start? I'd been working in the kitchen all day. It was dark out now and I still didn't feel entirely safe when I was alone in the bakery and it was dark.

I turned up the radio and bopped to the beat of The Best of the '80s and '90s. I shook my head at how my high school years were now "oldies"—sheesh.

As I was finishing up the last batch of sugar cookies, the door from the bakery pushed in startling me. I jerked, gasped, and squeezed the decorator bag of frosting a little too hard, squirting it out in a squiggly line down the front of the snowman cookie I was frosting.

"Hey, I waited out front, but you didn't come out, so I was just checking to see if you're okay back here," Officer Strickland said, standing in the door frame.

My heart raced from the scare he gave me. I reached up and turned down the radio. "You startled me. I thought the door was locked."

He stepped into the back. "You were blasting the oldies station."

I grabbed a frosting knife and scraped off the ruined snowman. "I saw the snowstorm and wanted to keep abreast of the weather." I put the knife in the jar of water I kept nearby and wiped my hands on the towel that hung on the ties of my apron. "How bad is it out there?"

"Pretty bad," he said and stepped in closer. "That's why I stopped by to see if you might need a ride home."

I glanced at the clock. It was nearly 10:00 P.M. How did it get to be so late? "Goodness, I had no idea it was so late.

I need to close up and clean up." I looked around and made a quick list in my head of what all had to be accomplished before I left. "It's going to take a bit of time. Thanks for the offer, but I can't ask you to stay while I clean up."

"I don't mind staying." He stepped in close and reached up to tuck a strand of hair behind my ear. "I'd rather see you safe."

Um. "Oh." There was that blush again. "Thanks, but I don't think that's necessary."

He got stubborn then, crossing his arms. "You haven't been out there. It's blowing pretty hard. There was a semi in the ditch just off the turnpike."

"I really have a lot to do yet and I can't ask you to stay."

"I've got nothing better to do." He walked around me and looked into my office. "I'll hang out and wait."

I chewed on my bottom lip. How did you get rid of unwanted male attention? It'd been years since I experienced it. Wearing my wedding ring and having Eric had had perks in times like these. "Well, okay," I said. "It's your time."

"Great." He flipped on the office light and went inside. "Is this where you do all your detective work?" He wiggled my mouse and brought the screen to life. There on the desktop of my computer screen was a file labeled SUSPECTS. "What's this?"

I practically threw myself in front of the screen, squeezing between him and the computer. "Nothing," I said. "Just my thoughts on the murder."

"What thoughts are those?" he asked.

"It's not important."

"That's not what you told Lance Webb."

"You talked to Lance?"

"He's a good friend," Officer Strickland said with a small smile.

"Yes, well, then you know that Lance told me coincidence does not make a killer." I smiled ruefully as he stepped back.

My office really was a small space and he was a big guy. "Although I'd argue that coincidence is all they have on Tim."

"It's not a slam-dunk case." He sat down in my desk chair and made himself at home. "I'll admit that. There was a meeting this afternoon. I must say Calvin Bright really likes your family. He gave a strong case for why your brother was not the best candidate."

"He did?"

"Yes." Officer Strickland nodded. "Unfortunately there's no other suspect at this time and the mayor and county DA are pushing to get this resolved. They don't like lingering murder cases."

Huh, Calvin was on our side. I wouldn't have known it from the way he acted. I turned and sent off a quick e-mail to Tasha that Officer Strickland was here and then locked my computer.

"Tell me about your security suspect list."

"It's not important." I walked out of the office to start clean up. "Lance had some really good reasons why it would be premature to do anything with it."

He rolled my desk chair out into the door frame between my office and the kitchen and leaned it as far back as it would rock. "I figured you were a smart woman."

I concentrated on packing up the cookies. "I'm really disappointed." I shook my head. "I thought I might really be on to something. Anyway, I thought I'd go see Marcus Blackmore and at least make him aware of what might be happening. He should be able to tell me who belongs to the number."

He shook his head. "You tell your crazy suspicions to Blackmore and he'll laugh you out of his office. Why put yourself through that? People in town already think you're a little nuts, Toni, and worse, they suspect your brother is a murdering drug dealer. No one's going to take you seriously unless you have hard proof. Where's your proof, Toni?"

"There are the videos at the hotels. Officer Bright pulled all the available video feeds. If he wasn't looking for security guys he wouldn't see them. He'd expect them, wouldn't he? Which is what this guy wants, right? All I need to do is get Calvin to really look at the video and if I have Marcus Blackmore confirm which man belongs to the number then they'll have to see that Tim is not involved."

He stood. "Even if you identify the guy, there's no motive, no proof he had anything to do with the murder."

"That's because they don't know who it is. Once we identify him, then they can do some serious checking into the security guy's background. I'm certain all the pieces will come together. It all hinges on the videos."

"If that's true, why didn't the videos exonerate your brother already?"

"That's just it. As far as I know, no one has seen the video yet. . . . Tasha gave the recording to you. . . ." I froze. "You work for Blackmore Brothers Security."

"I told you I did." He moved in close.

I scurried over to the counter and pulled a bread-cutting knife from the water jar. I held it out in front of me and slowly backed toward the door between the front of the bakery and the kitchen.

"Now, why do you have that knife?" he asked. "I'm an officer of the law. We protect and serve. Remember?"

"That security guard that matches Tim's supposed room dates is you, isn't it?"

He kept walking toward me slow and deliberate. "Like I said, coincidence." He threw out his hands in a gesture of innocence that I saw right through. "Give me that knife, Toni. Don't make me have to take it from you. I can." He nodded and kept coming toward me. "Then I can and will cuff you and arrest you for assault. You don't want that now, do you? It would ruin your reputation in town and your precious bakery would fail."

"Stay back!" I ordered. "I know how to defend myself."

"I'm sure you do." He grinned. "But I'm a cop—trained to take down resisting suspects."

I pushed the door open with my back, thankful it was on hinges that were simple push-pull with no latch. "I said stay back." The knife was in my right hand and I started to shake. I dug my free hand into the pockets of my apron. I usually kept my cell phone in my apron. I patted the pockets and a sense of horror ran through me.

"Looking for this?" he asked and picked my phone up off the counter where I'd placed it. "There's no one you can call. I'm a police officer. Remember?"

I eased out of the kitchen and into the front of the bakery. The best chance I had was to make it to the open front door.

"I wouldn't go any farther." His grin widened. "I locked the front door and turned your OPEN sign around."

I glanced helplessly at the door and saw not only was it locked and the sign turned but the snow outside blew so hard that no one would be out and about to see me even with the front of the bakery lit brightly from my lights.

"Why'd you do it?" I had to ask as I kept slowly backing away from him. Maybe I could make it to the ladies' room and lock myself in.

"Now, I told you I didn't do anything. In fact, what happened was you discovered your brother actually did it. You were so distraught that you slit your wrists."

I swallowed hard when his gaze moved predatorily to my wrists. He put his hand in his pocket and pulled out a hunting knife. He unfolded it.

"It seems my knife is sharper than yours."

I calculated how far I had to dash to the bathroom. It was still far away. If I dashed too quickly he would be on me. I took another step back.

There was a pounding on the front door that scared me so I screamed. The distraction was enough for Officer

Strickland to grab me. "Drop your knife," he whispered in my ear as his knife point cut through my clothes and nicked my skin. I did as I was told.

"You can't get away with this," I said. Isn't that what they said in every television show with a bad guy? It worked, didn't it?

He chuckled in my ear. "I already have."

The knock at the door grew louder and Officer Emry pressed his skinny face up against the front glass window of the bakery and waved his hands. "Hey, Strickland, open the door. Someone just ran into your squad car."

"Open the door," he said, his knife at my back, his free hand filled with my apron strings. "Keep your mouth shut or Emry will be the next to die."

"You can't kill everyone."

"I didn't kill Emry—you did."

I glanced at him.

"I'm an officer of the law. I caught you murdering Emry in cold blood. Then I took you down—you put up a fight. I had to stop you."

"Hey, Strickland." Officer Emry banged harder on the door. "It's cold out here. Let me in."

"Let him in."

I took a deep breath and unlocked the door. Officer Emry stood shivering. His police-issue coat covered in swirling snow. His cheeks were bright red and the tip of his skinny nose was blue. His Adam's apple bobbed as he pushed his way inside. "It's about time. It's like twenty below." He went straight to the still-warm coffeepot. "Storming like heck out there." He poured himself coffee. "So glad I saw your light on."

I didn't move from my position near the front door. Officer Strickland's knife poked me in the back. The sting of it reminded me to keep my mouth shut.

"What are you doing out this way?" Strickland asked.

His voice was deep and chilling near my ear. He poked me to take a step forward.

I stubbornly kept my position near the door. He shoved the knife deeper. I gasped at the pain of it and instinctively stepped forward.

Emry sipped his coffee. "Oh, right. Someone's hit your squad car," Emry said. "I noticed it as I drove by. Looks like you were sideswiped."

"What!" Strickland dug his fist into my apron strings as if squeezing me would fix things.

"I know, right?" Emry said. "There are skid marks and the driver's-side door is crushed in. Go check it out."

Strickland mustered something dark. "I haven't been in here that long."

"Must have happened right before I rounded the corner from Locust to Main. I didn't catch the car or I would have stopped them." He sipped more coffee and made a face. "This tastes burnt. You should make fresh."

"I'll get right on that." I stepped toward the coffeepot, fully intent on running out the back. But Strickland's fist in my apron held me back.

Officer Emry didn't even notice the tussle going on in front of him. He poured creamer into his cup. "Blaylock's going to be pissed. He doesn't have the budget to get a new car."

"I'll tell him you saw it and failed to get the make and model."

"Oh, oh, now, that's not . . . that's not right," Emry stuttered. His Adam's apple bobbed and his motions became jerky.

"Who do you think he's going to believe? Me or you?"

"Ms. Holmes will back me up, won't you?" His voice cracked and the question ended on a high pleading note.

"Sure. In fact, why don't you call the chief right now?"

Strickland poked me hard. This time I could feel blood running down my back in a warm stream. I gasped.

"Even better, why don't you go out and see if you can find the sideswiper," Strickland said. "They can't have gone that far."

"The snow's blowing too hard to follow any tracks." As if on cue a large snowplow blew by, throwing snow against the windows. We all turned at the sound.

As much as I didn't like Officer Emry, I really didn't want to see him killed and I certainly didn't want to be blamed for his murder. To be honest, there were people who might actually believe I did it. Not because I'm the murderous type, but because they all know how much Officer Emry's bumbling ways get on my nerves.

"I bet the car left paint on the side of the squad car," I said. "Why don't you go out and see if you can at least figure out what color the car was." I waved my hand toward the door.

"Good idea," Officer Emry said. "How much do I owe you for the bad coffee?"

"It's old so you don't owe me anything," I said as Strickland twisted his fist in my apron. How was it that Officer Emry didn't notice that Strickland stayed behind me the entire time? Or the fact that I hadn't moved more than two feet since I'd unlocked the door?

"Oh, now, I have to pay you something," he said. "I'm on duty and I don't want anyone to think I was taking bribes." His gaze was on Strickland as if afraid he'd tell Blaylock I'd given Emry coffee.

I rolled my eyes. "Shouldn't you go out and check out the paint color? I mean, the car that swiped the squad car might actually be close by."

"Why, are you trying to get rid of me?" He snickered at his own joke.

"Yes," I answered. Strickland pushed on the knife and I gasped. "I'm trying to get rid of everyone. It's twenty minutes past closing time," I said quickly. "You both should get going so I can lock up." I widened my eyes and moved them back and forth looking from him to the door and back, but Emry wasn't taking the hint.

"I've had enough of this," Strickland growled near my ear. He turned the lock in the front door of the bakery, bolting us inside.

"What? Why did you do that?" Emry's eyebrows veed.

"Run! Out the back, quick!" I shouted.

I should never have used the word *quick*. It made Emry freeze.

"What?"

Strickland brought the knife up to my neck, pulling me back against him. "Hands in the air or I will slice her throat." The knife was sharp against my skin. For a brief moment I wondered if he had the strength to actually slit my throat.

Instinctively I reached up to pull his arm away from me. The man was strong. I wasn't able to move his arm at all. Once I realized how stuck I was, I kept my gaze on Officer Emry. He reacted to the situation by dropping the coffee cup. It bounced against the floor tiles, spilling coffee everywhere and ending up rolling under a table.

Emry fumbled for his gun.

"I said hands up!" Strickland said and pressed harder against my neck. The pain of it made my eyes water.

Emry stopped and slowly put his hands in the air. I knew then that I was the only one who could save me now. I'd done it before. I could do it again. What was that acronym? SING?

I took a quick inventory. My hands and feet were free. Even if he stabbed me, the chances of his hitting an artery were lower than the chances of him slitting my throat if I stayed here. So I let go of him, fisted my left hand, covered it with my right, bent my elbow, and shoved it as hard as I could into his gut. The knife sliced my skin as he grunted and bent.

I ran. I had already plotted my means of escape. I moved

without thought, pushing past Officer Emry through the kitchen and out the back door. The cold wind tore at my bare skin and snow drilled into my eyes as I ran and ran. Terror fueled me as my black athletic shoes ate up the distance. I hit the end of the alley and went out into Central Street, tearing past Main.

I have no idea where I was headed. Suddenly the bright lights of a pickup truck blinded me as it turned in front of me. I paused long enough to shield my eyes. The pickup pulled close and rolled down the passenger-side window.

"Toni, get in!"

I grabbed the handle, conscious of how my cold hands had lost most of their grip. The door was opened from the inside and I leapt inside, slamming it shut. "Go, go!"

"Where am I going?" Sam's voice penetrated my panic. "Holy Moses, Toni, you're bleeding! What happened?" He unwound his scarf, folded it, and pressed it on my neck. "Hold it there and put pressure on it."

He must have seen how terrified I was because his words were forceful enough to reach through my panic. He locked the doors and made a U-turn in the middle of snowy Central Avenue. He stopped at the red light long enough to reach over and pull my seat belt into place. Then he turned the heat up high, blasting it at me.

"Drive, go!" My voice was rough. I didn't have to say it again; he slammed on the gas pedal and we fishtailed through the light and barreled down Central.

"I'm taking you to the emergency room."

His words barely penetrated my fear as my teeth chattered and my muscles shook uncontrollably. I think he cursed. Next thing I knew he'd tucked his coat around me. How he did this and kept driving, I have no idea. Personally I had my right foot pressed into the floorboard as if I could press the gas pedal and push us faster down the road.

He slowed just enough to bump up and over the snowbank

that blocked in the emergency room drive. The next thing I knew he'd slammed his driver's-side door closed, opened my side, unbuckled my seat belt, and gathered me into his arms. I closed my eyes and concentrated on the heavy thud of his heart.

"I have you, you're safe," he said over and over, and I believed him.

"What's this?" Shawna Daniels asked as Sam carried me to the back.

"She's bleeding and frozen." Sam put me on the patient bed. I grabbed his hand as he pulled back.

"Don't let go." Tears poured down my face.

"I'm right here." He patted my hand. His coat was replaced by a warming blanket. The scarf was gently pulled off.

Shawna addressed me looking into my eyes. "Follow my finger." She moved it side to side and up and down. "Good. We need to get your clothes off to see where else you're hurt. Okay?"

"Okay," I said through chattering teeth.

I watched as she shooed Sam out. I made a protesting sound and they both assured me he was just outside the curtain. The soft pink curtain with tiny rosebuds on it was pulled closed and the two women carefully but efficiently undressed me and tsked at the shallow stab wounds on my back.

"What happened?" Shawna asked. "You've got several wounds in your back. I'm going to clean them out and then put in a few stitches. They aren't dangerously deep, but I imagine they are painful."

I nodded and let the tears flow.

"Okay, it's okay. You're safe now." They put in an IV and warm fluid slowly trickled into my veins. They had me hug my knees as they worked silently on my back. Then they carefully pressed me back. Lying on the cleaned wounds stung.

"I know," Shawna said at my gasp. "But we need to get stitches in this cut on your neck. There is a painkiller in your IV. You should start to feel warm and sleepy. I'm going to numb your neck and then get you cleaned and stitched up. Okay?"

"Okay," I said and closed my eyes. "It was Officer Strickland."

"What?"

"Officer Strickland tried to kill me." My voice wobbled and tears squeezed from my closed eyes. "I managed to get away, but Officer Emry—" I opened my eyes and pushed to sit up in a rush.

Both women pressed me back. "Shhh," Shawna said. "It's okay."

I closed my eyes. "He's in danger," I said. "Officer Emry he was there. Strickland told me he would kill us both and pin the murders on me."

"Shh," Shawna said. "He can't do that now. You got away."

I turned my face away and she gently pressed me back straight.

"You have to hold still while I work. Okay?"

I have no idea what was in the IV, but I woke up and Sam was holding my hand. The nurses were nowhere to be seen. "Hi."

"Well, hello there," Sam said. "How are you feeling?"

"Thirsty," I said, my voice hoarse.

"Shawna said you would be. Here, have some ice chips." He fed me a spoon of crushed ice from a paper cup.

I closed my eyes as the cool ice soothed my throat.

"Chief Blaylock and Calvin Bright are here. They want to talk with you. Do you feel up to it?"

"Officer Emry?"

"He's fine. Whatever you did gave him enough time to draw his gun." Sam's dark gaze warmed me. "He may seem bumbling, but in a pinch he comes through."

"He got Strickland?"

"Yes, he did," Sam said and patted my hand. "You're safe."

"Oh, thank goodness." I closed my eyes.

"Hey," he said and patted my hand. "They need your story. Okay?"

"Yes."

"Then there's a crowd outside waiting to see you," Sam said. "Shawna gave me special permission to be with you." He leaned down close to my face and whispered. "I told her we were dating." Then he planted a kiss on my forehead. "I'm going to get Blaylock now. Okay?"

"Okay."

The interview was short as they already had Officer Emry's report. Strickland was currently in the county jail on charges of kidnapping and battery. He was not talking and had asked for a lawyer. This time it wasn't Brad who had to run to the rescue.

My wounds were photographed and carefully cataloged by a female crime scene specialist. My story taken over and over until my head throbbed. Shawna chased everyone out of the curtained section of the emergency room.

"Your family's here to take you home. Are you okay with going home? I can keep you overnight for observation if you need to rest."

I smiled at her. "Thanks, but it would be good to be home."

"The CSI took your clothes, so Brad had your cousin Mindy bring some clothes from home. Sam Greenbaum barely left your side." She smiled as she checked my bandages and took out the IV. "You have a good man there."

"I know," I said.

Mindy came in and helped me dress. She kept saying, "Oh, honey." Over and over. She had a better view of my wounds than I did. All I knew was that I was on some pretty strong painkillers and suspected that I would wake up in the morning feeling as if I'd been hit by a truck.

I was ushered into a wheelchair and taken out to the waiting area. My family and friends were there—Grandma Ruth, Bill, Tasha, Kip, Tim, Brad, Mindy, and Sam.

"The sisters and Rich wanted to be here," Tim said and took my hand. "But the storm closed the roads and airport."

"It's okay." I shrugged. "It's only a few stitches this time."

"Twenty stitches in your neck," Tasha told me. "They promise that you won't be able to tell once it heals."

I reached up to feel the bandages that were wrapped around my entire neck. "He wanted to cut my throat."

"He did," Tim said with anger in his tone. "The bastard barely missed your artery."

"Let's go home," Grandma said. I noticed that she'd left her scooter at home and instead used a cane and Bill's arm to walk out with me.

The sky was gray, but it was clearly daytime. The ER drive had been plowed.

"How long was I in there?" I asked Mindy as Tim brought the car around. It'd been pitch-black out when I'd rushed out of the bakery.

"Twelve hours," Mindy said.

"Wait—the bakery . . ."

"Meghan said not to worry; she has everything covered," Sam said and helped me from the wheelchair into Tim's car. "Doctor's orders are for you to rest for the next two days. Then it's Christmas, so you need to forget about work for now. It will keep."

I blew out a long breath as he tucked a blanket around me and buckled me into the seat. He planted a kiss on my lips and closed my door.

Tim drove. Mindy sat in the front passenger seat. Tasha sat in the back with me, Kip riding beside her. "You gave us quite a scare."

"Are you okay, Auntie Toni?" Kip asked as he ran a Matchbox car along his thigh and over his knee.

"Yes, I'm fine," I said.

"She needs to rest." Tasha patted my hand. "But she's smart, and remember, she and Mommy know how to defend ourselves."

"Like in Tae Kwon Do," Kip said. "You said I could learn self-defense when school starts again."

"Yes, I did," Tasha said. "And I meant it." She patted Kip's head and he pushed away from her.

"You're free, Tim, right?" I asked. "After this they have to be able to prove Officer Strickland was the one framing you. He must have killed Harold."

"I'm free." Tim glanced in the rearview mirror and smiled at me. "Strickland's going down. Lance Webb came forward. He's going to testify that Strickland was blackmailing him and Harold into dealing drugs. Harold wanted out and Strickland made an example out of him. I'm sure once they look into Strickland's finances they'll have evidence to back Webb's claim. If not, they have him on assault and attempted murder."

"What does *assault* mean?" Kip asked.

"It means he hurt someone on purpose," Tasha said.

"Like when I get mad and hit you?"

"Worse," she said. "Much worse."

"Okay." Kip went back to playing with his car.

We were all very aware of the little man in the car and the conversation grew quiet. When we arrived at the house, Kip asked if he could go play in his old room. We all agreed.

I was bundled up into my own bed. It felt good to sink into fresh sheets and warm blankets.

Mindy stayed downstairs to make everyone breakfast. Tim took my hand and kissed my cheek. "Thanks, sis, for watching out for me."

"Grandma made me," I teased.

Tim looked up at Grandma Ruth and Bill. "Thanks, Grandma."

"My pleasure," Grandma said.

"We'll talk later." Tim patted my hand and slipped out the door.

Grandma Ruth hobbled over on Bill's arm and kissed me. "That's my girl. I knew you could do it."

"It was your clue that got me started," I said. "I traced all the dates that Tim allegedly rented rooms and discovered the same security guard had worked all those nights. I was about to give the information to Calvin when Officer Strickland figured out I knew too much."

"Well, I knew you could do it." Grandma straightened and patted my shoulder. "You take after your Grandma."

Grandma Ruth and Bill left. Brad stood near the door, his arms crossed over his chest as Sam took my hand and settled into the chair next to the bed.

"You started dating again," Brad said. He nodded toward Sam. "Treat her right or I'll see you don't work in Oiltop again."

Sam grinned and brought my hand up to his mouth, placing a soft kiss on my fingers. "Don't worry. I know a good thing when I see it."

Brad nodded. "See you at Christmas."

Tasha pulled a chair up close and brushed the hair out of my eyes. "Officer Strickland used our hotels to deal drugs. The thought of that makes me sick."

"He used his position as security guard to hide what they were doing." I shook my head. "Then he used Tim's name to hide the rooms he was renting."

"Calvin said Tim's wasn't the only identity Strickland used," Tasha said. "He got suspicious at the drugs found in the garage. Calvin's been here daily. He was pretty certain he would know if there was anything illegal going on. But he was afraid that whoever was framing Tim would try to involve Kip and me. That's why he had us move out. He wanted us out of the line of fire."

"I'm glad. For a while I thought it was because he thought we were drug dealers."

"No," Tasha said and shook her head. "When Strickland insisted on picking up all the video and getting it to processing, Calvin got suspicious. When he checked on it he discovered that the video had never made it."

"That's what got him," I said. "He arrogantly figured no one would miss a few discs."

"Exactly," Tasha said.

Sam's thumb brushed the top of my hand with slow, comforting strokes.

"Lance Webb said Harold was the one who originally used Tim's name to rent the rooms. Harold was mad at Tim and thought it was funny. Besides, people would see Harold and Tim together so much that they often mistook one for the other. But Harold and Lance decided they'd had enough and wanted out. Harold called Strickland in that night to tell him he was done. According to Webb, Strickland killed Harold and told Webb that if he said anything, he'd be the one to go to jail. After all, who would believe a drug dealer over a cop? Webb said Strickland used his knife, shoving Harold into the shower. He gave Webb a warning then went home, cleaned up, and came back in time to see you enter the open room."

"He left the Red Tile and made a show of being seen in Walmart so others would remember him and alibi him."

"But the timeline didn't work out," Tasha said. "Calvin says he's going to be in jail for the rest of his life. Thanks to you."

"Was the knife he used on me the same one he used on Harold?" I asked. The idea gave me the creeps.

"They're running tests on it, but it fits the wound marks."

"If he weren't in custody, I'd beat the tar out of him," Sam said low, his grip on my hand tightening.

I patted his hand. "He's scum, and not worth your effort."

"You need to rest now," Tasha said and stood. "Tomorrow's Christmas Eve. We'll see you for dinner."

"Bye."

Sam held my hand and frowned as he eyed my bandages.

"I'm so glad you found me," I said. "I had no idea where I was going."

"You were heading home," he said. "Makes sense, considering. . . ."

I closed my eyes, suddenly tired. "Are you coming over for Christmas?"

"Christmas Day, if that's okay. Grandmother has a big party on Christmas Eve."

"Okay," I said and closed my eyes.

"Merry Christmas, Toni." He kissed me.

"Merry Christmas," I said and drifted off to sleep.

CHAPTER 30

Christmas Eve the family started to arrive early. Tim and Mindy roasted a goose and a turkey, set up the buffet, and filled the house with Christmas music.

I was still a little groggy from the pain pills, but I refused to stay in bed. So I was bundled up and back into the blue parlor, where I could look out the window and see people arrive. Joan and her clan came first, then Rosa and her family. Richard and his brood came later in the afternoon as the sun set in the gray sky. Luckily the storm had stayed away and the roads were clear. Eleanor Skyped us all from her place in San Francisco.

Tasha and Kip and Calvin Bright showed up just after Richard. I smiled when Calvin and Tim shook hands. "I was doing my job," Calvin said.

"I know." Tim nodded and things seemed to be settled between them.

Grandma Ruth arrived with Bill and her cane, having left her scooter at her apartment. "Toni, kiddo." Grandma hobbled over and gave me a smacking kiss on my forehead. Then she sat down with a huff, her knees wide. Today she wore a Christmas sweater, a green-and-red butterfly skirt, and her ever-present athletic shoes. "How are you feeling?"

"I'm good, Grandma," I said and touched the bandage around my neck. "I hardly feel a thing."

"That's my girl. An investigator has to make some sacrifices when she's tracking down the truth."

"I guess that's true," I said with a nod. "Good thing I'm not an investigator."

"Not yet," Grandma said and then looked up at Bill. "I could go for some of those appetizers I know Rosa brought." He shuffled off to bring her a plate. "Don't forget the eggnog."

Bill waved his hand in answer. Grandma was pretty predictable in her demands. Bill had a good memory, so he usually anticipated her needs.

"We brought you this," Lucy said as she handed me an envelope.

"What is it?" I asked as she herded her family to taking off their coats and hanging them in the coat closet.

"Open it," Rosa said.

So I did. Inside was a lovely Christmas card that said holidays are for celebrating friends and family. Then inside was a check. "What's this?" I picked up the check and stared at the sum of money. "Lucy?"

"That's the balance from the online orders we filled," Lucy said as she walked in, tugging her green sweater down over her jeans.

"You filled orders?"

"Yes, silly. You had a full list and we couldn't see letting all those people miss out on Christmas."

"So Meghan and Lucy and the girls filled them for you," Grandma said. "I was there to supervise, of course. Quality control and all that."

We all laughed. With Grandma Ruth we all knew what "quality control" meant.

"Thank you," I said. "This is the best Christmas."

"It's our first Christmas without Mom," Eleanor said with tears in her eyes. "We know she would have wanted us to help see you succeed."

"This will go a long way toward paying the bills. Thank you, everyone." I hugged as many people who would get up and give me a hug. "I'm afraid I didn't have time to Christmas shop."

"Really?" my niece Kelly said. "You must be confused. Everyone has a present from you under the tree."

"They do?" I sent her a look of confusion. "Really?"

"Really," my nephew Kent said. "I counted them."

"We'll open presents after church," Grandma Ruth said. "It's Jesus's birthday, not yours."

"Oh, Grandma. . . ."

"You heard her," Rosa said. "Go set the table. It's time to eat."

The twins slumped off to do as they were told.

"I don't understand," I said. "I don't remember getting presents for everyone."

"A little bird took care of it," Grandma said and patted my knee. "A little bird with a good Internet connection and a tablet computer."

"Thanks, Grandma," I said and leaned back, suddenly tired but happy.

"That's what family is for, kiddo," Grandma Ruth said. "We help and support each other."

"I'd almost forgotten that part," I said. "Thanks for reminding me." I closed my eyes and listened to the sounds of family fill the house. The kids laughed and shouted and ran through the parlor. Aubrey barked and chased after them while adults ignored it all and talked about what was important in their lives.

For a moment I thought I heard my mom laugh in the kitchen. I imagined her there with her Christmas apron on, sneaking treats to the kids. The smells of roast turkey, yeast breads, pies, and cookies filled the air. In the den was the sound of a football game on the television.

The check would make the money I had saved to keep the bakery open go far. I'd come so far in a few months. I'd not only opened my bakery, but I'd solved three crimes and in the process I'd renewed bonds with my family. In two days I had a date with a man who made me smile whenever I thought of him.

Maybe, just maybe, I was finally settling into the life of my dreams.

BAKER'S TREAT RECIPES

Gluten-Free Chicken Salad Puffs

ORIGINAL RECIPE MAKES 8 PUFFS

1 cup water
½ cup butter
⅛ teaspoon salt
1 cup tapioca flour
4 eggs
¼ cup red onion, chopped
1 stalk celery, chopped
1 tablespoon raisins
2 teaspoons Dijon mustard
⅓ cup mayonnaise
¼ cup plain yogurt
½ teaspoon salt
¼ teaspoon dill

Preheat an oven to 400 degrees F (200 degrees C). Grease a baking sheet.

Combine the water and butter with ⅛ teaspoon salt in a saucepan. Bring to a boil over medium-high heat. Once boiling, reduce heat to medium, and pour in the flour all at once. Stir vigorously until the mixture forms a semitranslucent ball. Remove from the heat and allow to cool for 10 minutes.

Mix in the eggs into the dough, one at a time, adding the next egg only after the first has been completely incorporated. Drop the dough onto the prepared baking sheet by the heaping tablespoon.

Bake in the preheated oven until puffed and golden brown, 30 to 35 minutes. The puffs should be hollow on the inside, and just browned on the bottom. Remove from the oven, and cool to room temperature on a wire rack.

To prepare the filling, stir together the onion, celery, raisins, mustard, mayonnaise, yogurt, ½ teaspoon salt, and dill in a bowl until combined. Fold in the chopped chicken meat until evenly combined. Cut the tops from the puffs and spoon the chicken filling inside. Replace the tops before serving.

Gluten-Free Mascarpone Strawberry Cupcakes (Easy)

1 package gluten-free white cake mix
2 egg whites
1 cup water
½ cup strawberries (can use frozen if thawed)
8 ounces mascarpone cheese
2½ cups powdered sugar
¼ cup butter (melted)

Preheat oven to 350 degrees F (175 degrees C).

Line 12 muffin cups with liners.

Stir cake mix, water, mascarpone cheese, butter, and egg whites in a bowl until well combined.

Pour cake mixture into prepared muffin cups.

Bake in preheated oven until lightly browned, about 20 minutes.

Place strawberries in a food processor or blender; puree until smooth.

Stir pureed strawberries and powdered sugar together in a bowl.

Spoon strawberry mixture on top of cupcakes.

Gluten-Free Puff Pastry

2 cups gluten-free all-purpose flour (or a mix of gluten-free flours to your taste—I like 1 part tapioca, 1 part almond flour, 1 part potato starch)

¾ teaspoon salt

4 tablespoons cold butter

⅓ to ½ cup ice water

FOR BUTTER PACKET:

4 tablespoons all-purpose gluten-free flour

16 tablespoons cold unsalted butter

In a large bowl, place the 2 cups flour and salt, and whisk to combine well. Chop the 4 tablespoons cold butter into large chunks, and place them into the bowl of dry ingredients. Gently stir the butter in the flour, to cover the chunks of butter with flour. With well-floured hands, press each chunk of butter flat between your thumb and forefinger. Create a well in the dry ingredients, and add ⅓ cup of ice water to the center. With a wooden spoon, stir the mixture to combine. Add more ice water one tablespoon at a time until the dough stays together when pressed. Turn the dough out onto a piece of plastic wrap, cover, and press together into a ball. Place in the refrigerator to chill until firm, about 1 hour.

While the dough is chilling, make the butter packet. Dust a sheet of parchment paper with 2 tablespoons of gluten-free flour. Place the two sticks of butter, side by side and touching one another, in the center of the flour. Sprinkle the butter with the remaining 2 tablespoons gluten-free flour. Cover with another sheet of parchment paper and pound the butter with the rolling pin to begin to flatten it and to press the two sticks of butter together. Remove the top sheet of parchment, fold the butter in half, and cover once more. Pound again until flat, and repeat the process until you have a butter packet that is about 5 inches square. Place the butter packet in the refrigerator until beginning to firm (5 minutes).

Remove the chilled dough from the refrigerator and place it on a lightly floured piece of parchment paper. Sprinkle with more gluten-free flour and cover with another sheet of parchment. Press and roll the dough until it is about a 9-inch round. Remove the top sheet of parchment, and place the chilled butter packet in the center of the round of dough. Lightly score the perimeter of the butter packet and set just the butter packet aside. Dust the top of the dough once more with gluten-free flour, and roll out the dough from the 4 scoring marks and out, away from the center of the dough, to create 4 flaps. Dust with more gluten-free flour as necessary to prevent the rolling pin from sticking to the dough. (Hint: I cover with parchment paper and roll to prevent sticking. Place the butter packet back in the center of the dough, and fold the 4 flaps onto the butter like you would the bottom of a cardboard box. Press the dough around the butter packet to seal it in.

Replace the top parchment paper, and press and roll the dough away from you into a long rectangle that is about ½ inch thick. Starting at a short side, fold the rectangle into thirds. Turn the dough so an open end of the dough is facing you, and roll it, covered in parchment and dusted again with gluten-free flour, into another long rectangle, the same size and shape. Fold in the same manner, once again, starting at a short side and folding into thirds. You have just completed the first "turn." With a floured knuckle, make one single impression on the dough, to represent the completion of one turn. Cover the dough with plastic wrap and place in the refrigerator until firm, about 30 minutes.

Once the dough is firm, remove it from the refrigerator, flour the outside and place between two sheets of parchment paper. Once again, with an open end of the folded dough facing you, roll away from you and into a long rectangle about ½ inch thick. Fold once more, and mark the dough twice with your knuckle, to represent two completed turns. Refrigerate until firm, and repeat the process of rolling, folding, marking, and chilling for a total of 5 or 6 turns. Separate into 4 sheets wrapped tightly in plastic wrap. Can be frozen for later use.

Gluten-Free Lemon Tartlets

1 sheet of puff pastry
1 tablespoon gluten-free flour for dusting (can dust with powdered sugar for extra sweetness)
1 egg, beaten
⅓ cup lemon curd
12 fresh blackberries
1 tablespoon powdered sugar (or superfine baker's sugar)

Preheat oven to 400 degrees F (200 degrees C). Line a baking sheet with parchment paper or a silicone baking mat.

Roll out puff pastry to ¼-inch thickness on a work surface dusted with gluten-free flour. Using a 1½- to 2-inch round cookie or biscuit cutter, cut out 12 round pieces. Place pastry rounds on the prepared baking sheet. Using a slightly smaller round cookie or biscuit cutter, cut out inner circles in each pastry round, leaving them in place. Brush each pastry round with beaten egg.

Bake in the preheated oven until browned and puffed, 13 to 15 minutes. Allow to cool completely before filling.

Cut around the small inner circle of each pastry round and gently push it down. Fill each tartlet with lemon curd and top with a blackberry. Dust with powdered sugar.

French Macarons

3 egg whites
6 tablespoons superfine sugar
1 cup almond flour
1½ teaspoons finely ground almonds
1⅓ cups powdered sugar (sifted)
2 tablespoons dark cocoa

Preheat oven to 320 degrees F (160 degrees C). Line baking sheets with parchment paper.

Whisk egg whites in a clean metal mixing bowl until thick, about 5 minutes; whisk the superfine sugar into the egg whites until stiff peaks form about 5 to 8 more minutes. Place a sieve over the bowl containing egg whites and sieve almond flour, ground almonds, powdered sugar, and cocoa into the egg white mixture. Gently fold, retaining as much air as possible.

Spoon the meringue into a piping bag fitted with a ⅜-inch tip. Pipe 1-inch disks of meringue onto the prepared baking sheets, leaving about 2 inches between cookies.

Let the cookies stand at room temperature for about 15 minutes to form a thin skin. Pick up the baking sheets and let drop from several inches above the work surface to adhere cookies to the baking sheets.

Bake in the preheated oven until tops are dry, about 15 minutes; let cool completely on the baking sheets before peeling off the parchment paper.

Gluten-Free Cherry Chocolate Shortbread Cookies

1 cup butter
½ cup sugar
½ teaspoon almond extract
1 cup almond flour
1 cup tapioca flour
¼ cup cornstarch
½ cup dried cherries, finely chopped
1 ounce bittersweet chocolate, finely chopped
1 tablespoon sugar

DRIZZLE:
2 ounces bittersweet chocolate, chopped
1 teaspoon butter

Mix butter, ½ cup sugar, and almond extract thoroughly using an electric mixer. Gradually blend in flours and cornstarch. Add cherries and chocolate.

Form into 1-inch balls and place on ungreased baking sheets. Pour 1 tablespoon sugar on a small plate; dip bottom of drinking glass in sugar and gently press down on each cookie to flatten.

Bake in a preheated 300 degrees F oven for 20 to 30 minutes, or until bottoms begin to brown.

Cool 5 minutes; remove to a wire rack to cool completely.

For drizzle: Place 2 ounces chocolate and butter in a small resealable freezer bag. Microwave on HIGH for about 30 seconds, until chocolate melts. Snip off corner and drizzle over cookies.